The Claws of the Gryphon

Peter Turnbull was born in Rotherham, Yorkshire, in 1950. He was educated at local schools and at Richmond College of Further Education, Sheffield, before going to Cambridge Technical College, where he gained a London University External Degree. He later attended Cardiff University for a Diploma in Social Work. He has had a variety of jobs, including steelworker and crematorium attendant, but for the past ten years he has been a social worker, working in Sheffield, London, Glasgow, and – under an exchange programme – Brooklyn, New York. He lives in Glasgow.

Peter Turnbull is the author of four acclaimed Crime Club novels: *Deep and Crisp and Even* (1981); *Dead Knock* (1982); *Fair Friday* (1983); and *Big Money* (1984).

Available in Fontana by the same author

Big Money
Fair Friday

PETER TURNBULL

The Claws of the Gryphon

FONTANA/Collins

First published by William Collins Sons & Co. Ltd 1986
First issued in Fontana Paperbacks 1988

Made and printed in Great Britain by
William Collins Sons & Co. Ltd, Glasgow

Chapter One

Dusk: December 15, 1944. Karl Schweitzer flicked the Zippo lighter and took the first drag of the Chesterfield deep into his lungs. He plunged his hands back into the pockets of his field tunic and shivered as he looked about him. In the fading light the low sky hung like a dark grey blanket. The ground was deeply rutted, chewed up by tanks and half-tracks, and in the bottom of the ruts the puddles had turned to ice, while the rest of the soil had frozen into a sharply corrugated clearing in the forest. The forest, the forest. Beyond the clearing was the forest, square mile upon square mile of dense pine and spruce. Mainly pine. Schweitzer glanced sideways at Hoff, the big man, overweight, who sat gripping the steering-wheel with a look of fear in his eyes. Schweitzer didn't know Hoff and feared for him. Hoff and Schweitzer kept their carbines standing butt down on the floor of the Willys.

In the rear, Genscher sat lengthways across the vehicle, cradling his weapon in his arms. He wore a woollen balaclava underneath his helmet and kept his hands in fur-lined gauntlets he'd taken from some guy during a brawl in a bar. Schweitzer didn't worry too much about Genscher; he could recognize a killer instinct. Stiffly, he turned and looked along the lines of jeeps. There were sixty at least, maybe more, three men to a jeep. They were going into action that night, they'd be in action throughout the next day, and the day after that. Maybe even the day after that.

Schweitzer heard the engines of the other vehicles start up and tapped Hoff on the shoulder, then made a winding motion of his hand. Hoff pressed the starter and gunned the engine. In the rear Genscher stirred and pushed his helmet back.

'Relax,' growled Schweitzer.

The Waffen SS Sturmbannführer began to send the jeeps off in batches. Three jeeps every two minutes, bouncing and lurching over the frozen soil, their exhausts cloudy in the crisp, rarefied air.

'This is some way to spend Christmas.' Hoff chewed on an old cigar stub. He took his foot off the accelerator and the engine idled.

'Dry up.' Schweitzer spat on the ground. 'Give it some gas, will you? We don't want to foul up because of a cold engine and remember to keep speaking English. Anyway it ain't Christmas yet, not till December twenty-four it ain't Christmas.'

Hoff put the hammer down and the engine screamed.

'Ease off.' Schweitzer glared at Hoff.

'You said . . .'

'I don't care what I said. Ease off!' Schweitzer took a deep drag on his cigarette. Hoff waited a few seconds and then eased off. When the engine had stopped screaming Schweitzer said, 'Don't push it, big man.' He tossed the remainder of the cigarette on to the ground.

A half-track growled across the clearing, a white star painted on the side, two rows of soldiers sitting in the rear. When it had passed, the Sturmbannführer indicated Schweitzer's jeep and beckoned it on. Schweitzer pointed forward with a single precise jab of his fist. Hoff let out the clutch and the jeep rode over the clearing behind the half-track. Hoff followed the half-track down the badly churned forest trail until they met a metalled road. The half-track turned right, northwards. Hoff turned left.

Movement was slow. The roads in the Ardennes region followed the deep river valleys which ran in a north-west/south-east direction. Hoff followed the road in the south-easterly direction and then took a bridge over a ravine, whereupon the road seemed to double back on itself in a north-westerly direction. After driving for fifty miles, they had made approximately twelve miles to the south-east. The forest on either side of the road was thick, the night dark, the jeep's slit headlights gave dimly and then, about midnight, fog began to form, forcing Hoff to slow to a

6

ten-mile-per-hour crawl. Inside the jeep the three men shivered uncontrollably. None spoke, none even attempted to speak. Hoff drove through the night and by dawn, at 7.30, the fog was still thick and showing no sign of dispersing. Hoff leaned forward involuntarily, his eyes attempting to penetrate the murk.

Half an hour after daybreak they heard a shout from somewhere ahead. Schweitzer slapped the dashboard of the jeep and Hoff stopped the vehicle. In the rear Genscher gripped his carbine.

'Stay cool,' hissed Schweitzer. 'Kill the motor.'

Hoff switched off the ignition and the motor died. Schweitzer leaned out of the jeep. It was cold, still and quiet, and the fog was getting even thicker, visibility down to ten metres, he guessed. Feet! Christ, feet, feet, feet. Down to thirty feet.

'Who's there?' the voice called again. It was a young voice. Nervous, the voice of someone who was cold, tired and scared half way to hell.

'American,' said Hoff quietly.

Schweitzer nodded. 'Our guys, remember. Remember that, Hoff. Remember that, Genscher.'

'Yeah, yeah,' said Hoff. Genscher didn't say anything.

Schweitzer called out, 'Friend.'

There was a pause. The voice in the fog said, 'Oh yeah?'

'Yeah,' Schweitzer yelled.

'Apple pie,' said the voice.

'Go screw yourself,' shouted Schweitzer.

There was another pause. It was longer than the first, lasting for perhaps two or three minutes and eventually broken when the voice called out, 'OK. Come on, real slow.'

Schweitzer nodded to Hoff, who pressed the starter and let in the clutch. 'Think before you speak,' hissed Schweitzer. 'These guys are nervous, they'll be trigger-happy.' The Willys crawled forward, inch by inch, through the fog. Eventually Hoff pulled up when he saw the smudgy outline of a US army truck, a six-ton 6×6, he thought. Schweitzer stepped out of the jeep and eased the safety-catch off his carbine. Instantly he heard safety-catches being taken off all around him, at least fifteen, he guessed, as he automatically crouched by the front wheel of the jeep. Beside him, he saw Hoff step out of the vehicle, quite silently for such a large man, and crouch by the opposite wheel. From the rear of the vehicle he heard a scuffling noise as Genscher flattened himself as best he could. Finally it was Schweitzer who spoke. 'All right, who's out there?'

'OK, OK, I guess we're all a little edgy.' It was a soft-spoken voice, cooler, calmer, more collected than the voice which had challenged them.

Schweitzer turned to his left, the direction from which the voice seemed to come. He saw a figure emerge from the gloom and stood. 'Lieutenant,' he said. 'Say, we're real glad to see you, we've been driving around in this crap all night.'

'All night?' The officer approached Schweitzer.

'All night, since 1800 hours yesterday, sir.'

Schweitzer noted with amusement that the officer was wearing a tie. A necktie with battledress! He noted the blue and yellow divisional patch on the officer's tunic.

'We're with the Ninth.'

'The Ninth!'

'Yes, sir.'

'You're up north of Aachen.'

'Sure are, sir.'

'Well, Sergeant, you're at least fifty miles south of your position.'

'Jesus.'

'Is right,' said the officer. 'Down this road is St Vith. You'd better turn north from there.'

'Whose territory is this then, sir?' Schweitzer looked at the lieutenant. He was young and seemed competent. He'd got off the mark quicker than Schweitzer, but that was war, the giver of opportunity. It was not long after leaving America that Schweitzer had found himself in uniform, but he had been older than this officer now seemed. The age at which someone first put on a uniform had always seemed important to him; it was a measure of commitment, of worth, of experience. The earlier in uniform, the better the soldier.

'We're in the 106th Infantry Division, Sergeant. Part of the First Army.'

'The First! We sure have wandered south.'

'Like I said. Run into any krauts?'

'No, sir.'

'See any signs?'

'Hey, Lieutenant, in this crap we could have passed within six feet of the whole German Army and not seen nothing.'

'I guess so.'

Schweitzer noticed other figures looming out of the mist, four, five, six. He eased the safety-catch back on and slung his carbine on his shoulder. He saw Hoff doing the same.

'You sure you didn't see any krauts?'

'Sir, I'm sure, I'm sure.'

'Seems strange, Sergeant, you came down from the Ninth to here, which means you ran the whole length of the front line, and where exactly the front line is Christ only knows, and you saw nothing?'

'Sir, excuse me –' Schweitzer began to stamp his feet against the cold – 'but that information I don't like to know. And we saw no Germans.'

In the mist someone laughed. The lieutenant smiled. 'No, I guess not,' he said. 'I'm just trying to get a picture of what's up front.'

'I'll tell you what's up front, sir.' Schweitzer reached for his cigarettes and casually offered one to the lieutenant. 'There's fog and there's trees and there's fog and there's trees.'

'So long as it stays like that.' The lieutenant leaned forward while Schweitzer held up his lighter, shielding the flame with his other hand.

'Sure hope so, sir.' Schweitzer lit his own cigarette.

'Nice and quiet. What do you have here, Lieutenant? You a forward post, picket duty?'

'That's us, Sergeant. In this section there's nobody further east than us, until you get to the krauts. I have twenty guys, a six-wheeler and a jeep.' The lieutenant slipped his helmet from his head and Schweitzer saw the grooves that the straps inside

9

the helmet had made in the man's thick, waxy black hair. He also noticed the scorch marks on the front of the officer's leggings, which could only have been caused by his standing too close to field stoves.

'Well, I guess I'll need to make contact with my Division, sir.' Schweitzer turned towards the Willys. 'I'll drive on and ask the guys at St Vith to report our position over the wire.'

'I guess that would be OK, Sergeant.'

'Be seeing you, sir.' Schweitzer tapped the brim of his helmet and swung himself into the jeep. Hoff joined him.

'Yeah,' the lieutenant said and started to shiver. 'Christ, it's colder than Hitler's heart.'

'Sure is, sir,' Schweitzer said and then turned to Hoff. 'OK, let's snap ass.'

'Sergeant!' The lieutenant approached the jeep and, for the first time, looked hard at Schweitzer. Schweitzer held his stare.

'Yes, sir,' said Schweitzer.

'What did you say your name was?'

'I didn't, sir,' replied Schweitzer. 'But it's Fergusson. Julius R. Fergusson, from Chicago, Illinois.'

The lieutenant stepped backwards, 'OK, Fergusson. Good luck.' He waved the jeep on, Hoff let in the clutch and the vehicle moved off with a sudden jolt forward.

Hoff nosed steadily through the freezing fog, inching forward across the Eifel region with its narrow roads, deep sheer gorges and thickly wooded hills. They reached St Vith and drove on unchallenged. By midday they were in Bastogne and the going had become easier as the hills and forests gave way to gently undulating farm land. Shortly after leaving Bastogne they saw the road sign that they had been looking for. Like all the road signs in the region it was metal, black letters on a white background and just two or three feet above the ground. Hoff slowed and stopped by the sign, peering at it in the fog. It read: Paris 160 km.

*

The 106th Infantry Division of Eighth US Army Corps had been in the field for just four days on December 16. Fresh out from the States, it was a newly formed division and it went up the line with each man still wearing his necktie. For Lieutenant David Conner of the 106th, the day he blooded his guns had started normally enough. They had been in position on the eastern edge of the 106th sector for two days. It was quiet and wet and very cold. During the day the temperature nudged a few degrees above freezing; during the night it fell sharply and the men off duty huddled in their blankets in the rear of the truck.

At about 0800 hours a jeep had approached their position. They'd heard it in good time to rouse the off-duty men and to take up defensive positions. Conner had told McGinley to challenge the vehicle. McGinley was nervous, but he'd handled it all right. The vehicle came on, slowly, and all around him Conner could feel the other guys also growing nervous, but Christ, they had a right. The German front line was less than five miles away to the east and anything coming from that direction was certain to make any soldier edgy. This time they had nothing to worry about, the vehicle emerged from the mist and showed itself to be a jeep with three GIs, one a sergeant, a good-looking blond guy called Fergusson. They were part of the Ninth, had got lost in the fog, and had been driving about all night. In the morning they'd reached the American lines and intended to swing north at St Vith and rejoin their unit. When the jeep had gone, Conner ordered the field stoves to be warmed up and the K-rations broken out. He was on his second coffee and a D-bar of chocolate when all hell broke loose.

There was a woosh-woosh-woosh sound caused by something flying over their heads, low but obscured by the fog. Conner and his unit stood dumbfounded. The rumble of heavy artillery was heard away to the east, followed by the sucking sound of shells passing overhead before exploding a long way behind them. Somebody said, 'Christ, we're in the middle of a war,' and Conner became aware of young, frightened faces looking anxiously at him. He hesitated, swallowed the coffee that was already in his mouth, choked, then yelled, 'Cover!' The GIs dropped their canteens and ran for the rocks on either side of the road. Conner grabbed McGinley and told him to fire up the six-wheeler. Then he ran to the X-42 set, which hung in a canvas sack over the rear of the jeep. The operator had already contacted 106th headquarters.

'What the hell's going on?' screamed a voice over the radio.

'Christ knows!' yelled Conner, forgetting himself.

'Report, report!'

'Artillery and rocket barrage, sir,' said Conner, beginning to collect himself. 'Coming from the direction of the enemy. Falling behind us.'

'Who are you?'

'Conner, sir. Position red twelve.'

'Any ground troops yet, tanks?'

Yet? Yet? 'No, sir,' Conner replied as a sudden chill struck him.

'OK. Hold your position, Conner, but get ready to pull out, the whole front's on fire.'

Conner ran from the jeep to his forward position and crouched next to his sergeant, Nixon, who was a twenty-four-year-old veteran of the Normandy landings. Conner made to speak, but Nixon held up his hand and said, 'Shaddup – sir!' So Conner shut up and listened. At first he could hear only the rumble of artillery and the sound of the flying shells, but then, slowly, very slowly, he began to discern a rattling, squeaking sound, accompanied by the grumble of petrol engines. Faint, but getting louder.

'Armour,' said Conner, peering into the fog and seeing all of thirty feet in front of him.

'Not just any armour, sir.' Nixon spat on the ground. 'Them's Tigers. I hear Tigers.'

'Tigers.' Conner turned to him. 'They're big, ain't they?'

'Biggest damn tank in the world, sir. We're about to have the fear of God put into us. Believe me, I've been this way before.'

'Jesus, I believe you. How many? Can you tell?'

'Three, maybe four.'

12

'Coming this way?'

'Right along this road, sir. Ain't nowhere else for them to go.'

'Don't they know they're supposed to be losing this war?'

'You go tell it to them, sir. Right now it looks like they're coming out for round two.'

Conner turned and began to move backwards. Nixon grabbed his arm.

'I was going to report, Sergeant. Let me go!'

'Look at this, sir,' said Nixon, unconcerned by Conner's indignation. His voice was calm, but there was a definite chill to it. Conner slid back to Nixon's side, flattened himself against the rock and peered over the top. The fog seemed to be clearing a little, but he had spent so long living in a gloom that his eyes took a second or two to focus. When they did, he saw a sight that he never wanted to see again.

Again he was able to see the road ahead of his position. It was a narrow grey road which snaked away through the trees. Coming along the road at that moment, broadside on to him and partially hidden by the trees, were Tiger tanks. Five of them. In the forest itself, not using the road, coming steadily towards his position, were hundreds of soldiers, a seemingly unstoppable flood, pouring out of the mist into the sudden hole in the fog, all wearing the unmistakable mottled battledress and cape of the Waffen SS, the nearest group being about a quarter of a mile away.

'We've gotta snapshit out of here, sir,' hissed Nixon. 'We've got the whole German Army coming this way.'

Conner turned and indicated to the nearest GI. 'Go tell McGinley to get the truck over the brow of the hill, tell him to keep the engine turning over.' The soldier scrambled away. Then Conner yelled, 'Bring that BAR here!'

Two GIs ran forward, one carrying the machine-gun, the second carrying extra magazines as well as his own carbine. About him Conner saw the other men of his command nestling behind boulders, all easing the safety-catches from their rifles.

'You're not going to take a stand here, Lieutenant?' Nixon was incredulous. 'We do not have a dog in hell's chance.'

'We're going to take a few out and then withdraw. And we have to do it now before their armour clears the trees.'

Conner unslung his carbine from his shoulder, beside him Nixon swore softly, then turned and rested the sights of his carbine square on the chest of a particularly large stormtrooper who was coming on like an automaton. Conner turned and yelled, 'Enemy to the front, prepare to fire. Fire!' Small-arms fire clattered around him and the air became heavy with cordite. He expended the magazine of his carbine in the general direction of the advancing Germans. Beside him Nixon fired slowly, carefully, methodically, and the machine-gun traversed grimly. Conner saw one or two Germans fall, but most seemed to dive for cover. He was pleased that his machine-gun continued to fire, chewing up the forest floor.

'Prepare to withdraw,' Conner yelled, pushing another magazine into his carbine. He ordered Nixon to the rear to cover the withdrawal. Nixon slid from the rock and began to wave the men back towards the brow of the hill. Then the Germans began to return fire. It fell like rain in the narrow confines of the gorge, ricocheting off the rock. Two men fell heavily, a third rolled clutching his guts, screaming. Conner watched in horror as Nixon made it half way to the brow of the hill, fell, scrambled to his feet and fell again.

Conner and those men still alive began to inch back along the side of the road, jumping, crouching, crawling from rock to rock. He glanced behind him; the floor of the forest about four hundred yards distant seemed to be sprouting small vicious jets of orange flame. Occasionally a stormtrooper would stand, dash forward and then dive for cover. Over to the left he saw the leading Tiger begin to exploit a gap in the trees. It halted and swung its turret round towards Conner's position. There was a large bright red flash from the barrel and Conner just had time to yell 'Cover!' and throw himself to the ground before the shell impacted somewhere on the rock-face above him. He felt the tremor of the explosion, the rush of air about him and the deafening resonance inside his helmet. Someone a long way away was screaming. He saw a man whose face and chest were scarlet; the man seemed to be falling in slow motion. Conner staggered to the jeep and reached for the microphone on the radio transmitter.

'Red twelve, red twelve,' he heard himself say.

'Receiving. Report! Report!'

'I'm pulling out,' said Conner pressing down the 'call' button. 'What's left is pulling out. Sergeant, six, seven guys are down. We're coming in.'

'Report! Damn you. Report! Report!'

'What is there to report, for Christ's sake? The whole German Army is coming down on us. Tanks, the lot. All hell's broken loose.'

Conner let the receiver fall. There was a second explosion and again he felt the rush of air and the echo inside his helmet. But this time he saw the ground fall away from him, he saw the jeep from a peculiar angle, he saw one of his men with both arms blown away. Conner couldn't hear anything, but he knew the man was laughing hysterically, and beyond the man he saw the forest floor dancing with small vicious flames.

It was the stream of icy fluid trickling over his scalp and inside his helmet which brought him round. Slowly he regained consciousness, his body ached, his skull screamed with a sharp penetrating pain. He was lying head down on the inclining rock-face at the side of some road, with one arm twisted up behind his back. It was dark, raining heavily, with the occasional fleck of snow. He moved his head slowly and looked around him, saw a narrow road, a vehicle on its side, some bodies in battledress. He didn't know where he was; he closed his eyes. The stabbing pain inside his skull seemed to ease. There was a horrible, haunting sense of unreality about what he was seeing, what he was feeling, yet somehow he knew it wasn't a dream.

He thought back; home in a crowded brownstone in Brooklyn, near to Flatbush Avenue; the closeness of his family, himself, four brothers, all in the war now; the hunting trips with their father in Pennsylvania. He suddenly remembered the little things, like the scratching noise made by the cockroaches in the night, the chill of winter, the muggy summers, his mother's cooking; he remembered his mother's cooking. He remembered quitting school so he'd be in the war before it was too late, and he remembered the training camp in upper New York State. Then the journey to England on a liner called the *Queen Mary*, the one with three funnels, sharing the same bunk with two other guys in eight-hour shifts; eight hours asleep, sixteen hours kicking round the deck, throwing up over the side and losing money in crap games. The camp in Southern England, the flight to Belgium, the billet in the Hôtel Léopold in Liège. His unit, the 106th, his first command, all as green as grass, except the sergeant, who'd come ashore at Omaha. His first mission, a six-wheeler, a jeep, twenty guys and the sergeant on picket duty. All they had to do was sit tight for three days on the quietest sector of the front. A donkey job. A dead cat could've handled it. Then the fog clearing and the entire German Army barrelling down on them. Jesus H. Christ. That Tiger swinging around, the second shell . . .

He moved carefully, but his body screamed in protest. It hurt even to think. Gradually he was able to fight the pain and pull his arm from where it was pinned behind him. His watch showed two o'clock. He felt his chin, there was about one day's growth. He reckoned it was 2.00 a.m. on the night after the battle; eighteen hours after he had been blown off his feet.

He slowly turned and began to inch down the rock-face, head first, for six feet until he reached the road surface. Painfully he stood, and groaned as the pain in his head increased. He sank backwards against the rock and placed both hands at the side of his head in an attempt to ease the throbbing, penetrating torment. Cautiously he took his hands away and began to walk with weakened legs, staggering like a drunk. It was a dark, cold night and at first he was unable to make out any detail. Eventually he made out the wreckage of his jeep, crushed by a tank, and a few feet beyond the jeep he saw two bodies, both GIs. There was no movement and no activity, save for his own, but far away to the west he saw the flash of artillery and heard the rumble of the barrage.

Conner moved down the road and as his eyes became used to the gloom he was able to make out more bodies. He counted ten in all, including Sergeant Nixon, who seemed to have been hit in the legs and then in the back. He made his way slowly to the brow of the hill; there was no sign of the six-wheeler, which meant that ten guys had got away. Maybe.

He took his rubber poncho from his pack and put it on as protection against the rain and snow, which by now was more snow than rain. He clipped the detachable hood to the collar and began to walk back down the road to where his men lay. Mustering what reserves of strength he had, he embarked on the prolonged and exhausting task of wrapping the dead in their ponchos and taking one dog-tag from around the neck of each man. The second dog-tag he placed in the mouth of the soldier, with the chain hanging out, and forced the jaws shut. It was a slow and difficult task, not made easier by the fact that the soldiers had been dead for eighteen hours and had lain all that time in near-zero temperature; rigor mortis had set in, but Conner stuck to his task, following the manual, and, after two hours each man was wrapped in his own poncho, each man had a dog-tag in his mouth, and Conner had ten dog-tags in the pocket of his tunic. He had dragged the bodies from where they had fallen and left them in a line by the side of the road, where they would remain until collected by the Graves Registration Unit, or until they were buried by sympathetic villagers.

He took K-rations from three bodies and as many D-bars of chocolate as he could find, and started to walk, westwards, towards the sound of the gunfire. He felt dangerously weakened and nauseous, occasionally he entered into a strange trancelike state which he recognized as the after-effects of concussion. He knew he needed to rest, to lie down, but by now the rain had given way totally to snow, which fell thickly, and he also knew that if he lay down in snow he would never get up again. So he continued to place one foot in front of the other and to talk to himself, singing to himself, reciting poetry, doing anything that

17

would keep him awake. Occasionally he would hear something rustling in the forest and once he heard a wolf howl.

At about 4.00 a.m. he heard the sound of motor vehicles behind him, moving slowly through the snow and the fog. He turned and saw, with relief, that the footprints he had left in the snow were being rapidly obliterated by the falling flakes. He stepped off the road and scrambled up the embankment and crouched in the trees. Eventually the German convoy rumbled past. Two motorcyclists in rubberized greatcoats led the way, then a Volkswagen scout car, then the trucks, Conner counted twenty-five. They were an odd assortment of vehicles, mainly German M.A.N., but also in the convoy were three General Motors, and two chunky British Albions. Each vehicle had a tarpaulin covering the rear, and so Conner could not see what they carried. But there was no doubt that the trucks were full, they moved slowly and their engines strained under the weight.

When the convoy had passed he climbed back down to the road. Dawn came at 0730; it was dull grey and did not bring with it a noticeable rise in temperature. One hour after dawn Conner saw a small stone hut standing back from the road. It wasn't the ideal place to rest up, with Nazi troops passing within a few hundred feet, but there seemed no alternative. He approached the hut cautiously, his feet sinking deeply into the snow. The hut contained only the remnants of a bed and a table. Tiles were missing from the roof and snow fell gently on to the stone floor. The door opened outwards, held by only one hinge. Conner took off his poncho and laid it on the table. He sat on the old bed and forced himself to stay awake just long enough to eat a bar of chocolate.

Hoff drove through Libramant, Sedan and Rheims. In the morning of December 17, just as Conner was cautiously approaching the roadside hut, the jeep came upon a roadblock manned by two military policemen just south of Soissons. It was a small roadblock, more of a checkpoint, with a single Willys jeep parked across the southbound lane. Hoff slowed as one of the MPs raised his hand. The second MP looked on, grim-faced, thumbs hooked into his belt.

Schweitzer leaned out as the jeep slowed to a halt. 'What gives?' he said, and then glanced about him: nothing but fields and some farmhouse away off. No other traffic.

'Where are you going, Mac?' The MP rested his forearm on the roof of the jeep and peered inside.

'Paris,' said Schweitzer. 'We're going to Paris.'

'Says who?'

'We says,' said Schweitzer, whose hand was inching towards his carbine.

'You got orders?'

'We got leave.'

'Well, tough luck. Maybe you didn't hear, mister, but all leave's been cancelled.'

'Whadya mean – all leave's been cancelled? We got three-day passes.'

'You had three-day passes.' The MP's voice hardened. 'Get this heap turned around and get back to your outfit. Uncle needs you.'

'For what?'

'For fighting the Germans, musclehead.'

'Go easy,' Schweitzer snarled.

'You go easy, meatloaf. Let me see your pass. I ain't seen a three-day pass since I came to Europe. So what did you do, shorten the war by six months?'

'You could say that,' said Schweitzer.

'So let me see the pass.'

Schweitzer slipped his hand inside his tunic and took out a sheet of paper. The MP snatched it and read it.

'You guys are with the Ninth . . . What the hell you going to Paris for? It'll take you four days . . . Hey, this pass isn't good for another two days . . .'

But by this time the muzzle of Schweitzer's carbine was only inches from the MP's stomach and Schweitzer's finger was caressing the trigger. The carbine leapt in Schweitzer's grasp, the MP doubled over and was catapulted backwards. Hoff stepped out of the jeep and levelled his carbine at the second MP, who had just time to raise his hands and say, 'Please . . .'

Schweitzer snatched the forged pass from the still trembling hand of the MP and then clubbed the man with the butt of his carbine. Quickly the corpses of the two MPs were dragged off the road and pushed into a waterlogged ditch. Their jeep was driven on to the verge as if parked. Hoff, shaken, let in the clutch with a jolt and kept the accelerator pressed to the floor. They had reached the outskirts of Paris by midday.

SCHWEITZER

By the time Schweitzer was twenty-five he hated the English, the Jews and the Communists, and he reckoned he'd already killed two of the latter. He lived alone in a trailer at the bend of the river, just across the railroad trestle from JJ's bar.

Karl Schweitzer wasn't Karl Schweitzer until he went to Germany in 1937. Before that he was Carl Fergusson. He had started life as an unwanted extra mouth in an Irish-German family of fifteen who lived in two rooms in the Bronx, and his belly always used to stick out until he was six years old, by which time he began to realize an extra supply of food by snatching it from the street stalls.

The first thing Schweitzer remembered was his family huddled around the stove one winter and the grandmother telling the story she was always telling, of the year the potatoes failed. The old woman had grimy wrinkled skin and silver hair. 'I'm old now,' she said, and Schweitzer watched her mouth move in the glow from the oil lamp as she told how she was a young woman when the potatoes failed. 'And the English, you know the English, you know what they did? They let us starve.'

Some dark nights she'd tell the story of the grain being shipped out of Dublin and Cork and Belfast, bound for England, being seen leaving Ireland by starving Irish folk and starving Irish children, who grew a fine soft hair all over their bodies when their ribs began to show. And it was the British landlords who were shipping the grain out because they needed the money to keep up their grand houses which they had built all over Ireland.

And some dark nights she'd tell the story of the landlord who had a crop of good potatoes, potatoes that hadn't got the blight, and do you know what he did, this fine man, this English gentleman, do you know what he did? He got all the starving men from the villages round about and he got overseers and he got donkeys and carts and he said to the starving men, 'I will give you one field of potatoes to pick for yourselves. But first you must spend the day picking the crop from my other fields and putting the good tatties in the carts, and if an overseer sees a man taking a tattie for himself, that man will be dismissed and will not be allowed to pick the last field.' They worked all day and at the end of the day, when the estate was harvested except for the last field and it was not a big field, the Englishman on his chestnut mare said, 'Go and pick for yourselves,' and a hundred men fell upon this field, clawing the ground for food. Some were killed in the fighting and their bodies left to rot, because the others were too weak to carry them to the churchyard for burial.

The old woman died when Schweitzer was eight years old. By then he hated the English, not because of the tales the old woman had told him, but because of the way she had told them. She hated so much that her hatred was infectious.

When Schweitzer was old enough to know who were the Irish and who were the Germans, and who were the Poles and the Lithuanians and the Hungarians and the Russians, and when he was old enough to be taken down to the Municipal Library and shown in the atlas where all those peoples came from, except the Jews who don't come from no place, his father told him how he came to be fixed up with the name Fergusson.

'It took me a long time to figure out. All I did was say "I forgot",' said the man. 'I came over with a little English, enough maybe to say "God Bless America" and I came a long time ago, I'm a lot older than your mother, and these guys at Ellis Island, the immigration officials, they are shouting at me questions and questions and I end up saying, "*Ich habe vergessen*," so they say "OK, Fergusson, on you go." I figure they must have been asking me my name right about then. So this is how I became

Gottlieb Fergusson of New York, married to Mary Murphy. But here, this is where my home is, it is a region called Bavaria, where there are rivers and lakes and woods and castles in the mountains. I think this is where you too belong and I think your name is Schweitzer, say it, Schweitzer. Yes, that's it, and I think maybe you should go back there because this is not the land of plenty.'

And when Schweitzer was a little older, not a man but no longer a boy, he saw for the first time the way his father stooped as he walked, because of the work he did in Israel Bloom's leather shop. Then he noticed how his father began to bring his work home because money was getting tight, and how he'd work in the night by the stove until he fell asleep with the leather on his lap and the needle in his fingers. In 1937 Schweitzer heard his father crying because his employer was raising the hours and cutting the wage. So that night he went out with a baseball bat and put it over the head of the fat Jew who ran the pawnshop. He didn't know whether he'd killed the guy or not, but he wasn't too bothered because by then he wasn't fond of Jews or Englishmen, and he wasn't enamoured enough with the US of A to be concerned about the rules. The fat man's wallet contained fifty dollars. Five dollars he left inside the wallet and the wallet he left inside the jacket of a drunken Negro who was lying in an alley close by the felled Jew. Schweitzer also made the drunk a gift of the baseball bat. Thirty dollars he took home and gave to his mother: it would be enough to get the Fergusson mouths through spring and into summer. Fifteen dollars he kept for himself. It wasn't a fortune, about as much as a man could get after a week or two of push and shovel, but it bought time. Schweitzer stole a car and headed west, ending up in a small town near Sacramento just as the sheriff was recruiting Special Deputies because the nogoodsonofabitch Communists were marching from the farm labour camp to the mayor's house with a petition.

The beer-gutted, cigar-butt-chewing sheriff, who hadn't shaved for a couple of days, looked at the tall blond youth and smiled. 'What's your name, son?'

Schweitzer said, 'Fergusson.'

'Ever been in trouble with the law, boy?'

'No, sir.'

'That's good enough, raise your right hand.'

Schweitzer became a Special Deputy of the Leaver County Sheriff's Office, with a bronze badge and a Winchester 44 repeating rifle, and he shot two men in ragged dusty denim overalls in the bread riot outside the mayor's house. The local newspaper reported the incident on the inside page under the headline LAW AND ORDER STANDS FIRM IN LEAVER COUNTY.

Schweitzer saw that there were basically two kinds of American: the landowners and businessmen whom he called 'sir', and the regular guys whom he called 'mister' but who he expected to address him as 'sir'. The rest were bums rolling in with their old heaps piled high with furniture, usually with Oklahoma plates. If they had kids and if they called him 'suh', he'd tell them there was a camp just down the road where they could stay. They'd say, 'Thank you, suh, thank you kindly,' and drove on. The camp was fifty-three miles 'just down the road', but they cleared the county so Schweitzer was happy and the men he called 'sir' were happy. There was another type of bum who had a cold look in the eyes and didn't call him anything. If they were strip-searched, preferably by the roadside, Schweitzer would often discover pamphlets put out by Labour organizers and Communist groups. These guys could easily be provoked into assaulting a Special Deputy, which would get them one to five in the state pen.

Schweitzer rented a trailer near the bend of the river and after work he'd read up on the news from Germany. He was impressed by this guy Hitler, who seemed to be the only guy going in the right direction, after Jews and Communists, and maybe even the English. One evening Schweitzer strolled across the railroad trestle to JJ's and during the second jug of beer he shared with 'Bull' McLeod he said he was quitting.

'Just like that,' said the sheriff. 'You ain't been here but eighteen months and there's no work no place. So where do you figure you're going, Fergusson?'

'Germany,' he said. 'And you can call me Schweitzer.'

In Bavaria, Schweitzer lodged with a relative and worked on a road gang, all the time perfecting his German. In 1938 he joined the National Socialist Party, and, in 1939, by successfully masking his Irish blood, he passed the selection procedure, entered the Schutz Staffel, and swore the *Sippeneid*:

> I swear to thee, Adolf Hitler,
> As Führer and Chancellor of
> The German Reich,
> Loyalty and bravery.
> I vow to thee and to the
> Superiors whom thou shalt appoint,
> Obedience unto death.
> So help me God.

On September 9, 1939, the anniversary of the Munich putsch, Schweitzer was permitted to wear the uniform, less collar patches. On January 30, the anniversary of the seizure of power by the National Socialists in 1933, Cadet Schweitzer was issued with a provisional passbook. On April 20, 1940, Hitler's birthday, Schweitzer was given collar patches and a permanent passbook.

Schweitzer thrived in the SS, which drew its numbers, both officers and other ranks, from the working people and the lower middle class. The SS had none of the social divide which characterized the Wehrmacht. It was also an organization which gave opportunity to the young, so that the Standartenführer in charge of Schweitzer's training regiment was just thirty years old and had been a baker in former times. The SS was the military expression of National Socialism, throwing the older order aside, taking Germany to greater and greater fortune. Schweitzer found a sense of direction and purpose in the SS. He did not falter when called upon to take part in the machine-gunning of seventy men from the Norfolk Regiment who surrendered to his unit in France in 1940. Neither did he flinch when he formed part of the firing squad which executed a Sturmbannführer who had defiled the honour of the SS by molesting a French girl.

In April 1944, Sturmbannführer Karl Schweitzer of the Das Reich Panzer Division entrained with his division. They were leaving the Eastern Front and going to the South of France to rest, repair, re-equip and hold themselves in readiness in case the American and British armies should attack the southern French coast. As dawn broke on June 8, forty-eight hours after the Allied armies landed in Normandy, the Das Reich division began to drive north. The journey was intended to take three days, but the maquis held them up at every turn. On June 10, two days after leaving Toulouse, days of sniper attack, ambush, landmines and roadblocks, Schweitzer formed part of a 250-man Panzer Grenadier Force which drove into the village of Oradour-sur-Glane. They arrived at the village at 2.15 p.m. and left shortly after 6.00 p.m. In the intervening four hours the SS Panzer Grenadiers murdered the entire population and fired each building. Schweitzer himself commanded the squad of raw Alsatian recruits who herded the women and children into the village church before setting the building on fire, machine-gunning those who tried to escape the flames. Towards the close of the afternoon one such Alsatian looked questioningly at Schweitzer.

'It is nothing,' said Schweitzer. 'Compared to what we did in Russia, it is nothing.'

But the maquis had done their work. The Das Reich Division was delayed by ten precious, invaluable days and reached the battle zone too late to prevent the Allied armies gaining a foothold. It was ultimately decimated in the Falaise Gap.

In December 1944 Karl Schweitzer huddled over a 'Hindenburg light' stove and wrapped his *Zeltbahn* about him. Outside was his command, a scratch company made up of men taken from the Navy, old men, boys hardly taller than their rifles, Hungarians, Czechs, Spaniards and a group of firemen from Hamburg who always kept together and said they had nothing to go home for.

Schweitzer and his men were in the mountains of northern Italy, and in the mist-filled, rain-soaked valley below them were the British, pushing, probing, with men and ammunition to spare.

Schweitzer turned the buff-coloured envelope over and over in his hands and took out the paper and read it again for perhaps the twentieth time, smiling as richly as he had smiled when he had first read it that morning. A posting to Friedenthal, under the command of Standartenführer Skorzeny – the legendary Skorzeny who had masterminded the snatching of Mussolini from the Allies. It had come like manna from heaven.

Chapter Two

The man and the woman walked by the side of Kleiner Wannsee. In the summer the small beach on Berlin's lake was a mass of basking bodies; now, in the bitter December of 1944, it was deserted, and the small grains of sand picked up by the wind were sent stinging into the walkers' faces. The man was old, well over sixty, and he said, 'You must go.'

'Now?' asked the woman. Younger, much younger, and, in the old man's eyes, quite beautiful.

'Yes,' he said, enjoying her company, maddened at the prospect of their parting. 'The route is prepared. We can do no more here. The war is over.'

'What will you do?'

'Me? I am a good Communist. It will be well for me when the Russians arrive. If not, then it is no matter. I am too old to care. But I think it will be well.'

'You think the Russians will get here first?' She slipped her arm around the man's waist and gave him a brief hug. 'Most people think the Allies will beat them to it. Look at the damage they have done.'

The man looked at the jagged shapes on the dim skyline. Rubble that had once been fine buildings. 'Don't ask me to look around me. I am a Berliner, I love my city, don't ask me to look at what the terror bombing has done.'

'I'm sorry,' said the woman. 'But people are saying that the Allies hate the Russians and the Russians hate the Allies, so why else should the Allies bomb Berlin if not to help them get here first? They must be racing, the Allies and the Russians.'

'I hope you are right,' said the man, preferring to look down at the ground rather than up at the destruction, the occasional still smouldering fire in the rafters of a building which sometimes sent a shower of sparks into the evening sky. 'It will not be good for Berlin if the Russians arrive first. It will not be so bad for me, but I think the Berliners will suffer.'

'So we are going?'

'You are going.'

'To the West.'

'Yes, of course, by the route I showed you, to the house I took you too. You must stay there until the Allied advance has passed, then you must give yourself up. You may have to tell your story a thousand times before they will believe you, but in the end it will be well for you, I think.'

'How do I go?'

'You still have that pass?'

'The one Heinrich gave me? Yes, I have it safe. It helps me get around Berlin. The Gestapo do not argue with it.'

'Good, use it. Go soon, as soon as you can get away. The Russians are only three hundred miles off and they have not moved for months now, they can only be building their forces for their final advance. We do not have much time. Do not attempt to contact me. I too will be making my plans.'

'Shall we see each other after the war?'

'Perhaps,' he said. 'Perhaps. Who knows?'

They walked together until they came to the subway station where they parted. He walked on and Petra Oelkers took the subway to the Obersalzburg Platz.

It was a prestigious address, only two rooms, but it stood less than a hundred metres from the Chancellery. Yet just six months previously she had been in Rotterdam, observing German troop movements and transmitting information to London each night. By day she worked in a shipping office; the evenings she spent with Heinrich Leuger, whom she had initially seen as a useful source of information but whom she had come to realize was a sensitive and cultured man. He was utterly unlike his SS comrades whom he despised and hated. He sought escape in her company and also in drink. One day he said, 'I have been posted to Germany. If you would like to come, I can arrange it.' Then he added, 'I shall be working in the Chancellery itself.'

She entered the apartment building and walked up two flights of stairs. Heinrich was in the flat when she arrived. She advanced and kissed him. As she stepped back she noticed how tired he looked, how worn. 'I didn't think you would be here.'

'I have to return,' he replied. 'There is a signal coming in from Paris.'

'From Paris?'

'Yes, we have not retreated fully.'

'But Paris,' she persisted. 'That has fallen to the Americans.'

'You may be surprised.' He smiled again. 'But I have to return to the Chancellery to await the signal. I asked permission to leave for two hours, though, in order to attend to personal details.'

Petra smiled and slipped out of her coat, approached him and allowed him to undo the buttons of her blouse, gasping as his flesh touched hers.

'Where have you been?'

It was a sudden question. It frightened her by its suddenness. She ran her fingers through his hair before answering. 'I went for a walk and I ran into a friend. We walked by the lake and talked about the war. He thinks the Russians will arrive in Berlin before the Allies.'

'He?' But he did not interrupt his caress.

She smiled. 'Don't be jealous, Heinrich. I've told you about him, the old man, a friend of our family.'

'Is he not in uniform? God, they are putting everybody in uniform.'

'He is an invalid. He was gassed in the last war. He is a hero and excused duty.'

'Until they catch up with him. When that happens he won't be the first one-legged, shell-shocked war hero to be put on fire-fighting duties. If he's really lucky he could be sent to the

Russian front. Now that would be a death for a war hero, freezing to death on the Steppes.'

'You're bitter, Heinrich.'

'Angry.'

'Still?'

'Yes. Just as I said last night, but it's too late now. Now there is only one way out of Hitler's great new order.'

'Don't talk like that.'

'But it's true, Petra. I was an idealist in 1939.' He paused. 'No, I wasn't, I was an opportunist who thought he was an idealist. With my connections I would have been commissioned into the Wehrmacht, instead I joined the National Socialists and became an officer in the SS. See, don't I thrill you in my black uniform?' Heinrich Leuger removed his hand slowly from inside her blouse and sat in the chair by the fire, which had not been lit since the beginning of November. 'He's mad,' he said, shaking his head.

'Heinrich, don't say things like that.'

'You don't think he's mad, darling?' He looked at her. 'Are you a fanatical Nazi still?'

'No, no.' She knelt on the floor before him and put her hands on his knees. 'But if you're heard speaking like that, Heinrich, they'll take you away.'

'What does it matter? When the Allies discover the camps in the east, all Germany will suffer, especially the men and women of the SS. Do you know that men queued to join the SS, to wear this uniform? Do you know that Germany raised SS divisions in every occupied country? Such was the attraction of this uniform, such was the fanatical hatred of Jews and Communists.' He patted his tunic with its Reichsführer SS flash. 'To many this uniform was the ultimate. Women would go with you if you were an SS man; in bars airmen and sailors and the Wehrmacht would give you their seats. Now we shall have to burn our uniforms when the Allies arrive.'

'So the Allies will get here first. That's a relief.'

'I think so, if only because we attacked in the west this morning.' Her shocked silence did not surprise him. He smiled at her and nodded. 'Yes, that's what I said. I told you he was mad. He's committed all our western forces in a mad dash for the sea.'

'But why?'

'He wants to set the Americans and the British at each other's throats. He, the Führer, Herr Hitler, Chancellor of Greater Germany . . .'

'Heinrich!'

'All right.' He paused. 'He attacked in the Ardennes, of all places, against a weak sector in the American front. He hopes to reach Antwerp, which is the only port the Allies have available to them. Basically, the British are north of Antwerp and the Americans are to the south. If we can capture the port the Allies will be cut off from their supplies, at least temporarily, and they will be divided on the ground. Hitler hopes this will divide them politically. Then he wants to negotiate a separate peace, first with the British, then with the Americans. When he has done that he can switch all his forces to the east. He will not negotiate with the Russians and the Russians will not negotiate with him.'

'I can see a certain logic there, Heinrich,' she said. 'The Russians have not moved for months, we can't fight on both fronts forever . . . why not attack in the west?'

'It's lunacy.' He laid his hands on her shoulders. 'We no longer have the resources to attack and consolidate ground. We have only the resources for a few weeks' fighting, and to go through the Ardennes in winter is madness.'

'Guderian went through the Ardennes in 1940.'

'That was Guderian in the spring. This is Hitler in the winter, and with difficult supply routes. He's throwing us to the wolves.'

All she could say was, 'Heinrich.'

'Tomorrow the Germans will read about our magnificent advance, our latest victory, the papers will applaud Hitler. My God, if the people could see him now, the snivelling wretch!'

'Heinrich! You must be careful how you talk. If you talk like that in the Chancellery . . .'

'I'll just be saying what everyone is thinking. Oh God, our poor people, our poor Germans, all they remember is the demi-god on the plinth, taking the salute from thousands of stormtroopers. He has not appeared in public now for months, and no wonder; he's shrunk, he's about half his old size, and he wraps himself in a greatcoat that's too big; he shakes uncontrollably, he sleeps at odd times, he talks to himself, he eats only with the domestic servants in the Chancellery, and he takes his wretched dog with him everywhere. Petra, I have seen more capable men in asylums, and this is the Führer, the man who is leading Germany.'

'What can be done?' she said softly, quietly. 'I had no idea, no one has said this about him before.'

'I have talked too much already, but by heaven, we all need someone to talk to. No, nothing can be done. Von Stauffenberg tried, failed, and made things worse. All the Wehrmacht officers now want SS aides-de-camp to demonstrate their loyalty, so the only thing Von Stauffenberg's bomb did, apart from singeing the Führer's eyebrows, has been to strengthen Hitler's grip. No one dare oppose him now.'

She rested her head on his knee and ran her hand up the inside of his leg. 'Do you think the Allies know he's mad?'

'I doubt it, not unless they have a spy in the Chancellery. Mind you, the attack in the Ardennes is hardly the inspired work of a military genius.' He took hold of her hand. 'No.'

'No?'

'I must return.'

'Your message from Paris? Of course.'

'Tonight, perhaps.'

'Yes, Heinrich,' she said. 'Yes, yes.'

Hoff drove steadily down the Avenue Elysée Reclus de Paris towards the centre of the small township of St Denis in the northern environs of Paris. He followed the sign to Le Bourget Airport, relieved that the jeep did not seem to be attracting attention. In the district of La Courneuve he stopped the vehicle by the kerb. It was a high kerb, trees lined the road, denuded now, but Hoff had time to reflect how attractive it might be in spring and summer. He took a map from his tunic and consulted it. Beside him he could sense Schweitzer's growing impatience. Laboriously Hoff ran his index finger over the maze of streets, then grunted and started the engine. He drove off the main road and into the side streets and eventually pulled up in the narrow Rue St Germain. At the end of the road was the Route de Flandre along which passed convoys of trucks laden with troops and equipment.

'Some big fight up north,' said Hoff, leaning forward on the steering-wheel, peering through the grimy, mud-splattered windscreen.

'The biggest,' replied Schweitzer. 'I heard it's an attack on the whole front. We're going to push the Allies back to the sea. Divisions have been brought from the east to strengthen the attack.'

'Leaving the back door open for the Soviets,' said Genscher sourly from the rear of the jeep. 'You sure this is the right street?'

'Sure I'm sure,' said Hoff. 'I checked it on the map. This is it.'

Schweitzer lit a cigarette.

'Gimme a smoke, Schweitzer,' said Genscher.

Schweitzer tossed the pack behind him without looking over his shoulder. Genscher caught the pack in one hand and expertly tapped out a cigarette from beneath the label at the top of the packet. He lit it with his own Zippo.

A black Citroën which seemed to have got caught up in the traffic turned off the Route de Flandre and drove towards the jeep. The driver was a woman, but she did not look at the men in the jeep, despite Hoff's wave.

'Don't over-act,' said Schweitzer.

'Who's over-acting?' But he stopped waving.

Before Schweitzer had smoked half his cigarette, the black Citroën again detached itself from the convoy, which rumbled incessantly northwards, and again drove slowly down the street.

'She's driving round and round the block,' said Hoff.

'They don't have blocks in Paris,' growled Schweitzer. 'It ain't like home.'

'Home,' echoed Genscher resignedly.

This time the Citroën slowed to a halt beside the jeep. The driver was a handsome woman in her forties with auburn hair. She lowered the car window and looked up at Hoff.

'Excuse me, GI,' she said haltingly in heavy accented English, and as though she had been rehearsing the line. 'I am looking for an outfit they call the Winged Lions.'

'Could they be known as the Gryphons?' said Hoff.

'Perhaps,' said the woman.

Hoff saw her tighten her grip on the steering wheel. Schweitzer leaned across Hoff and said, 'And I guess they're looking for a guide to the nest of the bald eagle.'

The woman looked coldly at Schweitzer, then nodded. In German she said, 'Follow me.'

Hoff swung the jeep around and followed the Citroën through the narrow back streets of northern Paris. Eventually the car stopped in front of an open lock-up garage beneath a house in a street of drab terraces. She stepped out of the car and indicated to Hoff to drive the jeep into the lock-up. It was 4.30 p.m., just becoming dark, rain becoming sleet. The woman left her car and shut the double wooden doors of the lock-up behind the jeep. She then entered the garage through a smaller door set within the right-hand door and lighted a gaslight as the three men leapt from the jeep.

'Follow me,' she said again. She spoke harshly, turned and started up a wooden stairway at the side of the garage. It led to a small room above, which contained a table, two chairs and a stove. The men entered the room and stood in a line in front of the table, at the side of which stood the woman. They looked at the woman standing to one side; she had a commanding air and a thin, severe mouth.

'Heil!' she said, suddenly throwing the salute of the National Socialists.

'Heil!' the three men responded in unison, clicking their heels.

'So,' said the woman. 'Schweitzer?'

Schweitzer clicked his heels and bowed his head.

'Genscher?'

35

Genscher identified himself.

'And so you must be Hoff?'

Hoff also bowed his head.

'And I am Klara Heidler.'

Each man stiffened slightly. The woman nodded with evident satisfaction as she said, 'You will regard any order coming from me as coming from the Führer himself.' She paused, allowing a silence to extract the maximum effect of her words. Then she continued, crisply, precisely. 'You will not leave the building. In the next room you will find sleeping quarters. There is food, more will be brought to you as needed. You will remain in your American uniforms and you will address each other in English, using the American names which you have been given. Which are?'

Schweitzer said, 'Fergusson.'

Genscher said, 'Davey.'

Hoff said, 'Pearson.'

'Very good.' Again the woman looked at each man in turn before continuing. 'How was your journey? Without incident, I hope.'

'No, Fräulein,' said Schweitzer.

'No?'

'We killed two military policemen.'

'There was no other way?'

'No, Fräulein.'

Another short silence, and then Klara Heidler said, 'Did anybody see you?'

'No.'

'Good. Other than that, you passed through the American lines without incident?'

'Yes.'

She began to pace up and down in what space the small room afforded. The three men remained at attention. 'I do not yet know when you will have to do what is required of you. But it must be soon. It must be part of the offensive that is driving the Allies back to the sea. Did you see our troops in action?'

'No,' said Schweitzer. 'We heard gunfire, before that we came across a group of nervous children in American army uniforms, but we did not witness any of the fighting.'

'Nor should you have done, driving ahead of our forces as you did. We have electrified Paris. The Allies are nervous, they had thought the Reich to be on its last legs, but it is different now we are advancing again, magnificently. Soon the Allies will be like a chicken without a head. Have you seen a chicken with no head?'

'Once,' said Schweitzer.

'An amusing sight, is it not?'

'Indeed.' Schweitzer nodded stiffly.

'Soon this big fat chicken which now squats on Paris will be without a head. And you, you three together, will wield the axe. Meanwhile stay here. It is quite safe. You will not be disturbed.'

Klara Heidler left the small lock-up and pulled up the collar of her coat against the rain. She got into her car and drove through the city to her apartment in the southern quarter of Gentilly, close to the Cité Universitaire. It was a slow and difficult journey, the small number of civilian-owned vehicles being compelled to yield to the military traffic which congested the roads. A military policeman in a white helmet and white puttees indicated to her to pull in to the kerb while a convoy of army lorries rumbled past, northwards. She sat in the car and shivered, occasionally moving the windscreen-wiper lever from side to side to clear the windscreen, and she thought about the moment it had all started, the forty-eight hours which were as fresh in her mind now as they were when it happened, when in June of that year, just seven months previously, she had been taken away by the Gestapo to the dreaded 72 Avenue Foch.

Klara Heidler had just commenced afternoon class at the Kindergarten when the black Mercedes saloon pulled up outside the building. At first she thought little of the car's arrival; a routine check, perhaps? A parent might have denounced a member of the staff as a Jew or an anti-collaborationist. Such a strange thing to do now that the Allied armies were already on French soil.

Certainly she had little to fear, for she had joined the Parti Populaire Français soon after arriving in Paris and had subscribed to and written for *Au Pilori*. Both activities she now made little of, for the maquis by this time were coming out of the woodwork and threatening death to *collabos*. The writing was on the wall, quite literally.

But that day the Gestapo had come for her. She recalled the hushed, horrified silence as the door of the classroom was pushed open and two men in civilian clothes stood there, just looking at her. Calmly she picked up her bag and walked out of the room, following the men down the staircase to where the car waited in the courtyard. In the car she sat on the rear seat, flanked by the two men. As the driver took the car speedily through Paris she glanced out of the window: the trees, the *vélo-taxis*, the austere summer clothes of the Parisians on the sidewalk, the German troops. She was sure she would never see the city again.

The men in the car did not speak. This she could understand, recognizing it as the time-honoured method of inducing fear and anxiety. What she was less able to understand was the way in which she was being treated by the Gestapo. When they arrived at the Gestapo headquarters, she was escorted into the building by the two men, one walking ahead opening doors for her, the other walking a respectful distance behind. When she was shown into a room it was not the damp cellar she had feared, but a comfortable, spacious suite, with tall windows and long velvet curtains. Four leather armchairs were arranged round a glass and bronze coffee table. In three of the chairs were middle-aged men whom Klara Heidler took to be high-ranking officers of the Geheime Staats Polizei. They stood smartly as she entered. One officer smiled at her and beckoned to the vacant chair, walking round the table to hold it back for her as she sat down. Another well-built man smiled at her. The smile did not fit easily on his face; she sensed he was a cruel man. The three men sat down. The door of the suite was closed with a gentle click.

'Mademoiselle Heidler,' began the cruel man. 'I presume you call yourself Mademoiselle?'

'Yes,' she answered softly.

'Not Fräulein?'

'I have been so long in Paris,' she replied.

'I see.' He seemed to accept the explanation.

'You seem to know about me?' she said.

'A little. Forgive us for the way we brought you here. It was a subterfuge, the reason for which you will soon understand. We have been making some enquiries about you and we feel we have the right woman.'

'And so fortunate that you have always been living in Paris,' said a second officer.

'Not always,' she replied.

'We'll come to that,' said the first man, the cruel man. 'It is first necessary we ask you some questions about yourself, Mademoiselle Heidler.'

'Of course.' She was slowly recovering her confidence, but was not able to trust these men. All these gracious surroundings, this courtesy, might be part of an elaborate trick.

'You were born in August 1901, I understand.'

'Yes. August the fourteenth.'

'Where?' The third man spoke for the first time. He was more aggressive than the others.

'Braunau am Inn.'

The first officer looked puzzled.

'It is a small village in Austria,' she explained. 'I am Austrian by birth.'

'Where is it?' asked the second man.

'In the district of Waldviertel. Near the German border.'

'Describe it!' the third officer snapped.

'It is a small village.'

'In the middle of fields?'

'No. In the mountains. There is woodland and hill pasture.'

'Your father was a carpenter?'

'He was a farmer,' she said firmly, but beginning to become agitated. 'We were a poor family, like most in the village. I was born in peasant holding number 153 in the village of Braunau am Inn in the district of Waldviertel in Austria.'

'And then?' The third officer again, pressing her hard.

'We farmed and cut wood for the winter. When my father died, my mother and I left the village. She took a post in service in Vienna.'

'You never returned to Braunau am Inn?'

'No.'

'And then?'

'I grew up in Vienna, living at the top of a big house. It was very cold in the wintertime. We had no heating in our room and my mother and I lived together in that small room for ten years.' Then she added with satisfaction, 'It was owned by a Jew. I denounced him in 1940, when my mother wrote and told me he was pretending to be Aryan.'

The second officer nodded approvingly.

'After that?' The first officer again, being kind, but still she thought him more suited to sadism.

'I won a scholarship.'

'To the university?'

'To a college attached to the university. I trained as a kinder-garten teacher.'

'When did you arrive in Paris?'

'In 1941.'

'You were then forty years old.'

'Yes.'

'Why did you come to Paris?'

'As you said, I was forty years of age. I had not lived outside Austria. A post was advertised for a teacher with a foreign language. I had taught myself French from records.' She made a circular motion in a horizontal plane with her finger. 'German is my first language. So I applied and got the post.'

'I gather you joined those Parisians who were sympathetic to the Reich?'

She nodded. 'I was an early member of the Parti Populaire Français. I am still a member. I wrote articles for *Au Pilori*, I helped in a small way, a minor clerical role, in the raising of the Charlemagne Division. A fine body of French boys willing to fight on the Eastern Front in the SS.'

'A good division too, I heard,' said the second man. 'Any problems we had in occupied countries soon vanished after we invaded Russia. We were able to raise SS divisions in Holland, Belgium and Norway. Our crusade against Communism inspired people.'

'We understand you denounced Jews and Freemasons,' the first man said, bringing the interrogation back on course.

'I felt it was my duty.'

The second man took a letter from a folder which lay on the coffee table. He read it. '. . . *I have the honour to draw your attention, for whatever purpose it may serve, to the fact that an apartment at 37 Avenue Verdier, belonging to the Jew Ratner, contains very fine furniture indeed . . . yours for the Reich, Klara Heidler.*' He took a second sheet of paper and read from that. '*I have the honour to bring to your attention the fact that Monsieur Hernan, husband of Madame Hernan, headteacher at Areveil Académie, is a member of a Masonic Lodge. Heil Hitler. Klara Heidler.*' He replaced the letters in the folder.

'You have done your homework, sir,' she said.

'You seem to have been a loyal subject of the Reich,' said the first officer. 'The Hernans were . . .'

'My headteacher when I taught at the Académie.'

'I see. They were deported?'

'Oh yes, on July 16, 1942, in *La Grande Râfle*, as it was called. We requisitioned fifty buses to take all the Jews and Freemasons and Communists and Trade Unionists from five districts. In eight days we arrested 15,000.'

'We?'

'I had the honour to play my usual minor clerical role. Mainly the operation was performed by the Gestapistes Français.'

'With a little assistance from the Geheime Staats Polizei, I think,' added the second officer.

'Of course,' she conceded. 'Nevertheless, all went to Auschwitz.'

'You seem to have played many minor clerical rôles.'

'I like to be useful in the evenings,' she replied. 'It enables me to live my life on two levels, a teacher by day, a political by night.'

'Quite so,' said the first man. 'It is in connection with your second level that we feel that you may be of assistance to us.'

'How?' Klara Heidler was puzzled. 'There must be others equally suited to your needs.'

'But few so well placed as yourself,' smiled the second officer.

'You see, you are accepted by our enemies as part of the community of a conquered nation, soon to be liberated from the Reich,' said the first man. 'Please don't be shocked, we accept that soon we must leave Paris. It has been a good posting.'

'Some know me as a *collabo*. There are death threats made against *collabos*,' she said. 'I cannot guarantee my safety after the Germans have gone.'

'Do not worry. We are taking steps to assure your sympathetic welcome back to your community,' the first man said.

The third was more explicit. 'We are at present searching your flat. Unfortunately some of your possessions will be destroyed.'

'You will be handsomely compensated,' added the second quickly.

'It is necessary to make you seem a victim of the Reich. We would like you to tear your dress a little before we return you.'

'Which will be the day after tomorrow,' said the third officer. 'We wish to give the impression that you have been detained and interrogated for two days, hardly the treatment we would give to a – er – *collabo*. This is because we wish to invite you to be of service to the Reich.' He reached forward and took a silver cigarette case from the table, opened the case and offered her a cigarette. They were expensive Turkish cigarettes . . . Never, not since the Occupation . . . She snatched one quickly and instantly regretted her obvious excitement.

'Madame,' said the first officer, who also leaned forward, extending a cigarette lighter towards her, 'such commodities will become commonplace for you.'

Klara Heidler raised her eyebrows, caught the tip of the cigarette on the flame and reclined again in her chair. She thought back over her life, her peasant childhood, the years as the daughter of a servant, her prosaic existence as a teacher, a life spiced in later years with the spiteful pleasure of successfully denouncing a Jew or a Communist or a member of a Masonic

Lodge. She knew that a proposition was to be put to her, and she knew that, whatever it was, she would accept.

'You must know, as indeed you have indicated,' said the first officer, 'that the war is, for the moment, not going well for the Reich. The Allies are pushing out from their bridgeheads and pressing southwards.'

'Paris,' said the second man, cutting into the flow of his brother officer, 'is too far south for us to defend while making a strategic withdrawal to the north. Soon, within the next few weeks, German forces will leave Paris. But we do not wish to leave completely.'

'We would like to leave behind,' said the third officer, 'someone who is loyal to the Reich, someone who could and I am sure will be of use to our future, prior to our eventual return.'

'A spy?' she said. 'You wish me to spy on the Allies.'

'No, we will not ask you to spy. We ask, Mademoiselle . . .'

She held up her hand. 'Please call me Fräulein.'

The three men smiled warmly.

'Fräulein,' echoed the second man with evident pleasure. 'We wish you to provide a point of contact for us in Paris after the Allies have arrived, as they surely will. We wish you to secure premises we can use to hide personnel we may wish to infiltrate through enemy lines, for whatever purpose may be deemed appropriate. Can we ask now if you accept, prior to telling you what you will receive in terms of remuneration?'

'So we can be sure that your motivation is not the money,' added the first officer.

'The English,' she said, 'have an expression: over a barrel. I think you have me over a barrel. I can only accept, but I hasten to add that I do so willingly. There will of course be proper security?'

'This whole operation will be conducted in the strictest secrecy. All documents relating to it will be coded, all messages will be sent by overland courier, safer than by air.'

'And so to remuneration,' the first officer said, smiling. 'We have opened a numbered account in a bank in Geneva.' He handed her an envelope. 'In this envelope are details of the account which you must present when withdrawing from it. In

43

that account there are three and a half million Swiss francs. In addition, you will receive ten thousand French francs to assist you in your duties here.'

Klara Heidler was speechless.

'You will have to spend the next two nights here in our guest quarters,' said the third officer, 'but be assured of our hospitality.'

'You are after all an honoured guest,' the second officer added.

'Meanwhile we shall make a systematic search of your flat, as is our normal procedure, so be prepared to expect a mess on your return. I'm sorry, but it's necessary for us to establish your bona fides, as it were.'

'Of course.'

'While searching your flat we will conceal a radio transmitter and receiver. And also the coding machine, the operation of which you will be taught before you return.'

'The use of the coding machine is very important,' added the third officer sternly. 'The codes change every day. If you do not change the code at midnight each day, you will be out of synchronization with the rest of the German armed forces. We shall not be able to understand your signals, you will not be able to decode ours.'

'How did you locate me?' she asked.

'We visited the offices of the PPF on the rue de Rivoli,' explained the first officer. 'Your name was readily available.'

That evening the three men entertained her at the Moulin de la Galette, the Germans-only nightclub in Paris. She slept that night in a comfortable bed between silk sheets. In the early hours she heard a man screaming from somewhere deep in the building. She was unconcerned by the sound.

When she returned to her flat in Gentilly, she avoided her neighbours' pressing questions by feigning tiredness and resisted offers of help to clean up her flat. She found the radio transmitter neatly concealed in a cupboard; next to it was the coding machine, looking not unlike a typewriter. She commenced daily transmissions, changing the code at midnight.

GENSCHER

The first man that Genscher had killed had been big and fat and Genscher remembered the way the folds of flesh under the man's chin wobbled and shook as he choked on his own blood. Genscher remembered how he had dropped the knife and vomited and, feeling faint, had clung to the drapes to stop himself from falling. Then his strength returned and he slid out of the window on to the verandah roof just as the fat man's wife began to shout his name. He slid down the pole and ran across the garden to the road, leaping the fence as the fat man's wife began to scream. He ran down the road as the pistol began to crack. Most of the bullets had gone wide, but one had nearly hit him; he remembered the sound as it passed, as though someone standing above him had drawn breath between clenched teeth. That was also the first time that he had been shot at.

Now, the men were not big, they were thin and drawn and wasted with the cold. They didn't protest in death like the fat man had protested, but fell almost gracefully, probably thankfully, and lay still in the snow. And now, when the bullets came towards him, they all came close, sometimes he heard them, but, when they passed very closely, all he remembered was an odd, near-psychic sensation of his life being saved.

He pulled his greatcoat about him and glanced at his watch: 0900, it would soon be dawn. He heard a scuffling in the snow above him and then the bulk of the SS Truppenführer slid into the foxhole.

'It will soon be dawn, Herr Untersturmführer,' he said through chattering teeth.

Genscher nodded. 'I know. How are the men?'

'Tired. Hungry. Cold.'

'How is Pohl?'

'He died in the night.'

'Pass around his clothing for the others. Take his food and distribute it.'

The Truppenführer grunted and nodded. Genscher guessed it was all the man could do in the seeping, insidious cold which cut like a steel blade, robbing men of the will to live. He recognized it was not the time to complain that protocol was not being observed. Discipline was the important issue, and discipline was intact. The men were wondering when the Untersturmführer was anticipating rejoining the German lines, said the Truppenführer. Untersturmführer Genscher looked at the man. His eyes were pleading with him, but they also showed a blind faith in rank and authority. What could he say: 'Today, tomorrow, the next day, the day after that? Never?' Instead he asked, 'How much food do we have left?' And the Truppenführer said, 'Enough for one day.'

'Then we shall make it to our lines today, because if we don't we shall die today.'

The Truppenführer said, 'Yes, sir,' and scrambled out of the foxhole and into the teeth of the wind which moaned across the steppe.

His men were following him. Still. Genscher, the small officer who had led them too far east, probing too deeply into the Soviet positions, so that now they were trapped. For five days they had been trapped, and his men still followed him, as the *Wanderkessel* slowly inched its way westwards.

Genscher opened his rations and warmed the food a little by placing it between his glove and the palm of his hand. Yet, when he came to eat it, the food still chilled his stomach. Half an hour later, when the dawn was still grey and was only gradually and grudgingly giving way to a daytime sky, Genscher led a small column of unshaven men in white camouflage smocks away from their foxholes. They walked on, each man slowly lifting one foot in front of the other, while about them stretched a white expanse, broken only by an occasional stand of trees, a burned-down farmhouse and a knocked-out eastward-facing tank which seemed to have been part of the great advance of 1941. The twenty-three men were the only things to move in the landscape, save for a periodic whirlwind of snow particles whipped up by two merging streams of air which would dance for a few hundred yards before collapsing.

Sometimes, Genscher recalled, it could be as cold as this in Wisconsin. Going out to cut wood and just taking your gloves off for a couple of seconds, you'd get frostbitten. Christ, the hours his parents worked just to keep those 360 acres of bottom land going, and they might have been grubbing away still if the Depression hadn't come, and if the sheriff and the special deputies hadn't shot the Genschers out of their farm one night.

But there were also good times. The summer and the fall, pulling dogfish and trout from the creek, the schoolhouse, one room only, where he learnt English, just enough to read the official notices that came, and just enough to stumble through the letter from the landlord's lawyer. Genscher remembered too how he sat on the high-backed sofa on winter nights in front of the fire while his old grandmother told the story of how they came to Wisconsin from Holstein. 'The whole village waved us off,' said the old woman, who had refused even to attempt to learn English, 'and we got to Hamburg and had to be inspected by the medical man. Then we got a ship to England. All the men went to the bows in what the captain called the 'bull pen' and the women and children were in the back of the ship, where everyone was seasick, so very bad. You were alive then and are lucky to have been so young that you do not remember it. We crossed England by canal barge and in Liverpool we got a large ship bound for New York. We saw a black man on the station platform and we were scared. Then we got a train to Wisconsin and raised a mortgage for this land and began to farm. That is how we came to America.'

The story never changed, but it had occasional embellishments, like trying to eat their first banana without peeling it, and if the old woman was feeling particularly homesick, the hardships of the journey would be recalled. How they had to bribe their way at every turn, particularly when going across England; the bargees' palms were always outstretched; how they were kept waiting for three days at Ellis Island. How the immigration official slapped Pa because he thought he was being lippy. In the evenings, as the Genscher children listened to the old woman, they always sat on the high-backed sofa to prevent the draught sucking them into the fire.

'Herr Untersturmführer!' The man behind him spoke slowly, the cold slowed everything, even human speech, but there was an unmistakable urgency in the voice. Genscher turned and saw the man pointing to his left. Genscher looked in the direction indicated and saw two figures emerging from a denuded stand of trees five hundred metres away. The two men approached Genscher's patrol, moving slowly in snow.

'Just two?' Genscher asked the Truppenführer.

'I think so.'

'Not German?' Genscher gripped his MP38. His men unslung their Mausers.

'No, sir,' the Truppenführer replied, staring keenly at the figures. 'Partisans or Red Infantry.'

'Let them come on, prepare to fire.' Genscher raised his voice. His men slowly raised their rifles.

They opened fire at a range of one hundred metres. Both men fell immediately and lay still. Genscher knew, by the way they had fallen, that most of the twenty-three rounds had missed their mark. The cold was telling on his men. On a warmer day each bullet would have found its target and the two men would have been flung backwards by the impact. Instead they had fallen as if life had been gently snuffed out of them.

The two men were Mongols, small men with narrow eyes. They had inferior uniforms, and where their flesh was exposed it was covered in cold sores. They were unarmed. Genscher had seen how the Russians had used their Mongolian troops, sending large numbers of them running ahead of the tanks to explode the mines. These two were probably deserters, they might even have been trying to surrender to Genscher: a wasted gesture, since neither side took prisoners on the Russian front in 1944. Genscher became aware of his men looking at him in that hungry, pleading way that he had noticed earlier, then they looked at the dead men. Genscher said 'Yes. But keep the smoke to a minimum.' Half an hour later he and his men discovered that roast human flesh does indeed taste as sweet as pork.

The landlord had been like a pig. Genscher had read the letter to his father and had watched as the man rose from the table and took his pipe from the shelf over the fire. 'I think he wants us out, by golly,' said the man, stooping to light a taper from the flames. 'They can't do that, this is America, by golly. Tomorrow I go and see this man.' The next day Franz Genscher left his house before dawn and returned after midnight. He collapsed into his chair. 'I walk forty miles,' he had said in a weak voice. 'Twenty miles into town just to be told we ain't got no home.'

'No home?' Genscher's mother had always spoken in a wailing tone.

'He's going to – what's that word on the mortgage?'

'Foreclose, Pa,' Genscher had said. 'Foreclose.'

'That's it. That's the word, that's what he's going to do, by golly. I know times are hard, but if he throws us out, how can we farm to pay him the money? I'm an honest man, I will pay what I owe, but I can't pay if I can't work. I'm not leaving, no, by golly. Here we came and here we stay. We couldn't go now anyhow, there's no work in the city, instead there's breadlines three miles long. Farming is all I know.'

'What shall we do, Franz?' The woman wrung her wrists.

'Heinz.' Genscher always would remember the way the older man turned to him. 'Tomorrow you must go to Sugar Creek and look up the Jaekters, they know us from the old country. Give him a note from me, and maybe they will help us.'

'It's a four-day journey,' Genscher had said, but not intending a complaint. He clarified himself. 'Have we enough time?'

'I think so. But it's a journey for a young man. So you go instead of me.'

'They won't have any money, Franz,' the woman had wailed, continuing to wring her wrists. 'Nobody has any money. You know what I saw in the village store the other day? I saw the Grebler kids eatin' raw flour, even when the storekeeper was rainin' blows with the broom handle they didn't let go of the sack, not till he began hitten' them about the head. Everybody has problems like us, ain't nobody going to be able to help us.'

But the man had said, 'I want you to go, son, to do this for us. It's not charity we're seekin', we'll pay it back and then some.'

'Sure, Pa,' said Genscher because he wanted to, because he remembered the winters when the man was up before dawn and had been working on the farm for anything up to two hours before the Genscher kids were due at the schoolhouse. 'I'll leave at first light.'

He had left when the sun was coming up over the hills. He had walked away without turning back, kicking up little clouds of dust with his heels. The man in Sugar Creek had said, 'Franz Genscher? I know that name, he is of Holstein, I think. He sent you to ask me for money. He is a desperate man, you should be at home with him, son. Tell him I would lend him a few dollars if I could, but I can't. I can give you a meal, son, and a few cents for the road. That's all I can give you.'

When he returned home, the Genscher place was riddled with bullet holes. Gunter Neilson from up the valley was leaning on the fence pulling on a briar, just as though he was leaning on the low bough near the creek watching the trout jump for flies in the summer evenings.

'I've been waiting for you,' he said as Genscher approached.

Genscher looked at him.

'He wouldn't come out, old Genscher, just wouldn't move. He should've come out when the Sheriff arrived, but the Sheriff ought not to have done what he did.'

Genscher sat down on a boulder next to the old fence. 'What happened, Gunter?'

'Sheriff O'Malley returned with deputies and called your pa to come on out with his belongings on account of an eviction order, which had been signed by the judge and which O'Malley was obliged to enforce. Sort of words like that.' Gunter spat on the ground and pulled on his pipe before continuing. 'Your pa had a shotgun, threatened to shoot anybody who came near. Then he fired over the deputies' heads. He didn't stand a chance. Sheriff's deputies had Thompsons and Winchester 44s. They just poured in everything they had.'

'Ma? Grandma?'

'In there too.'

'The kids?'

'At my place. Your pa put them in the woodshed after O'Malley had called the first time. I reckon he made a stand for all of us, your pa did. Could well be my mortgage next.'

'O'Malley, you said?'

'Now don't get sore with O'Malley. He went home sicker'n any man I saw. No, it was the landlord killed your pa, foreclosing like he did. Make you feel any better, two deputies were killed in the battle.'

'Pa shot them?'

Neilson shook his head. 'Killed in the crossfire would be my guess, surrounding the house on three sides like they did.'

Genscher sat silently, expressionless.

'Night's coming on, son. You're welcome to spend it at my place, but we can't keep you but the one night. Your brother and sister are going to the orphanage tomorrow, less you can care for them.'

Genscher had shaken his head slowly before saying, 'You care to walk on ahead, Gunter? I want to get a couple of things from the house.'

By the time Genscher joined Gunter Neilson a mile further down the road, the Genscher house was ablaze, so was the barn, so was the woodshed. The animals were liberated.

'Guess there's a few cows down there if anybody in the valley wants to go get them,' said Genscher as he rejoined Gunter Neilson.

'Guess they'll be found homes,' grunted Neilson, who then added, 'I guess I'd have done the same. Guess anybody would.'

They took the clothing from the dead men and divided the articles among them. Genscher declined the offer of a shirt and directed it to a slightly built soldier who wrapped it around his neck. The arms of the second Mongolian were hacked off with entrenching tools and wrapped in the man's tunic. They would provide a meal for the next day, and possibly the day after that. Genscher looked at the sky; there was perhaps an hour of daylight left, one hour before the temperature dropped to 50° below zero, when men must dig holes to crouch in, to escape the wind. He ordered the fire to be extinguished and a hissing of ice on flame punctuated the incessant drone of the wind. He began to walk westwards, his men falling into line behind him. They walked slowly, as everybody did on the Eastern Front in winter. Men moved slowly, machines moved slowly, giving battles and skirmishes alike an eerie, dreamlike quality. They walked for an hour and came upon the remains of a slit trench just as the light was fading. The corpses of German soldiers lay about the trench, frozen in contorted positions, eyes open and jaws grinning, their weapons lying about them. Around the trench were shellholes, the frozen earth thrown up the sides like brown petals. Barbed wire had been blown apart and lay in disarray, a wooden hut had collapsed on one side, exposing the interior. Genscher and his men crossed the old German line without comment.

Genscher had left the Neilson place early the next morning. He spent the day walking into town and was able to thumb a lift for the last five miles from a farmer with a pick-up. 'Going into town to sell it,' he had told Genscher. 'This is the last thing I got worth sellin'. Ain't got but nothing else. Hopin' for maybe twenty, twenty-five dollars.'

'She's worth more.' Genscher glanced out of the window at the rugged landscape.

'She's worth twice, maybe three times that.' The older farmer spat on the floor of the cab. It seemed to Genscher to be a habit the man had got into and he did it without thinking. 'Trouble is, everything's being sold and nobody's buying. You heard the latest?'

Genscher shook his head.

'Relief money's run out. Ain't no more relief.' And he spat again on the floor of the cab.

In the town of Reeder Springs, Genscher had asked a cop for Lafayette Avenue. The cop had looked sideways at Genscher.

'What do you want with Lafayette Avenue, boy?' he asked after an over-long pause. 'Wrong side of the tracks for you.'

'I figured I'd ask for work,' said Genscher. 'Gardening maybe, or cleaning autos.'

The cop sneered. 'Just keep outa my jail, country boy, for today anyhow, 'cos that's all the time you'll need to find there's no work here. And when you find that out, just start walking. There's not enough work for the town boys; hicks like you just make it even more hard to come by.'

'So where's Lafayette Avenue and the Post Office?'

'That way. Both that way.'

Genscher located the landlord's house. The number on the gate checked with the number in the telephone directory in the Post Office. It was a large white house with a verandah running the length of the house and down one side. He walked on and spent the rest of the day sitting by a creek beyond the town limits. After night had fallen he returned to Reeder Springs and stood in the shadows outside the house. The lawns neatly tended, the white Packard in the driveway; it was like another world. Eventually he saw the man who he felt must be the landlord, fat, fifties and bald, dressed in a white shirt and a white jacket, as white as his auto. He stood in the front upstairs room and tugged the drapes shut. A few moments later the light was switched off.

Genscher waited for half an hour and then inched forward. Then he hesitated and waited for another half-hour before crossing the lawn, climbing on to the verandah roof. On the roof he crouched low and crawled towards the landlord's window. The window was open and Genscher could hear the fat man snoring. He took the knife from inside his shirt and parted the drapes. He wanted the landlord, just the landlord, but if his wife was there he'd kill her too. He'd have to. He stepped into the bedroom and stealthily crept across the carpet. The landlord was alone in bed. Genscher placed the knife on the man's throat and drew the blade sharply across the larynx. The man woke, his eyes peered up at Genscher, but he couldn't talk because he was drowning in his own blood. Genscher had said, 'That's Franz Genscher's mortgage all paid up.' It was then that the man's double chin began to wobble.

Genscher ordered his men to dig foxholes on the far side of the old slit trench. The sky was darkening, the surface of the snow, after thawing slightly during the day, was beginning to harden again and Genscher knew that in another hour the ice would be too hard for the entrenching tools to penetrate. He would explore the old German position next morning. There might be some reference which would help him determine his position, and the old wooden hut could be broken up for wood to make the fire they would need to roast the arms they had hacked from the body of the Mongolian.

In the night he wanted to sleep, but the temperature seemed lower than ever and he felt that if he slept, if they slept, they would not wake. He listened to the wind howling across the landscape, making the old wooden hut creak and twist and convulse.

Genscher struggled out of his foxhole and groaned as the wind sliced through his clothing. He crawled from foxhole to foxhole, urging each man out and ordering them to crawl to the old trench. Most obeyed, forcing their bodies to move, shaking off the numbing, lethal sleep. Some did not move, either because they could not or because sleep had already taken them. In all, fifteen men crawled from their foxholes and slid into the abandoned trench, which offered less protection from the wind, but afforded more room to move. Genscher went from man to man, pushing, prodding each man into action, until finally all fifteen men were doing push-ups, or running on the spot, or clapping their hands above their heads. He made them exercise for ten minutes, then forced them to sing for ten minutes, then they exercised again for ten minutes. In this way they survived until the wintry sun reappeared, the wind dropped slightly, and the temperature rose a few life-saving degrees. They left the trench and sought their comrades in the foxholes. All had died in their sleep, one cradling the arms of the dead Mongolian to his chest. These they wrenched from him, and took wood from the hut to make a fire in the bottom of the trench.

Pretty soon the area around the landlord's residence had been filled with shouts and screams and police sirens. The cops had brought dogs, maybe two, but Genscher was a farm boy; he knew dogs. He knew that dogs can smell fear and he knew fugitives always laid a good scent by running scared. So he stayed cool and ran at a steady pace from shadow to shadow towards the rail tracks in the centre of Reeder Springs, reckoning that the dogs were perhaps half a mile behind. There was time, there was still time. Genscher also knew that the dogs were not smelling the ground, no creature on earth leaves a scent on the ground. Dogs may appear to be smelling a trail along the ground, but they're not, they're smelling the air. That's where you leave your scent, in the air. That's why Genscher had once watched a bloodhound trail a man for one hundred feet along a creek. If you're being chased by dogs, don't go near water, it does nothing but slow you up, yes sir! Genscher knew what he was looking for and he was content to travel at a good steady pace until he found it. At a point where the houses gave way to a line of stores, Genscher saw a parking lot set back a little from the road. It had a smooth, hard surface, nothing to trip on, and still had one or two autos parked, probably there for the night. He ran on to the parking lot and then ran twice round the perimeter. Then he turned and ran twice round the perimeter in the other direction. Then he ran diagonally across the area, twice, just for good measure. Genscher walked off the flat ground, very calmly, very steadily, and made his way to the tracks. With any luck, the dogs would run every which way when they got to the parking lot and would end up baying at the moon in their confusion. He reached the tracks and followed them out of town and sat and waited, certain that he'd shaken the dogs.

Early in the morning, about an hour before dawn, Genscher saw the light of a train coming on slow. It was a long freight train pulled by two steam locomotives, made up of box cars and flat cars. Eventually he saw an open box car. He ran alongside it, placed his elbows on the floor of the car and tried to lever himself up. He was about to give up when a pair of hands appeared from the gloom and hauled him into the car. He lay panting on the floor of the box car and, as his eyes grew accustomed to the dark, he made out the outlines of hungry faces. Eventually one asked, 'Got any money, son?'

'No,' panted Genscher.

'Any grub?'

'No,' he said gasping for breath. 'Ain't got nothing.'

'Just thought I'd ask,' said the voice.

Genscher levered himself into a sitting position and began to draw slow, deep breaths. 'Where's this train heading?' he was finally able to ask.

'Chicago,' said another voice. 'They all end up in Chicago sooner or later.'

'Suits me,' said Genscher.

'It won't when you get there,' said the voice in a manner which suggested the owner liked to have the last word.

So Genscher let him have it.

In Chicago he lived in the back of an old Ford pick-up with a canvas roof and a piece of tin for a door. His neighbour who lived in a lean-to made of cardboard, told him the last occupant had died of scarlet fever, but that was last winter so it should be OK, son. They were on the edge of the municipal garbage dump with others who lived in old cars and oil drums. It was a small Hooverville as such places went, fifteen families and the occasional loner, about a hundred people all told. Genscher got a job in the stockyards at ten cents an hour, twelve hours a day, six days a week. He stuck it for five days. He stuck it until he saw men going round the floor of the meat-packing plant taking bits of meat from the mesh over the drains to make sausages for the poor in the ghettoes. He stuck it until he saw the carcases of the drought cattle being shipped in from Oklahoma and the good meat being cut from the rest to make up food for the soup kitchens.

By then he was a member of the American Nazi Party and ran with the Street Wolves, all blond Aryans who wore swastika armbands. One night after a raid in which they burned out a Jewish-owned shop, one member of the gang said Chicago was tame, said people like the Street Wolves were in power back home in Germany. So he was going home. Genscher said, 'Can you fix it for me to go too? There's no future for me in the US.'

When he arrived, Germany was mobilizing her forces. Genscher joined the Wehrmacht primarily as a quick and convenient way of obtaining clothing, food and accommodation. He served in France in 1940 and then volunteered for the Parachute Division of the Luftwaffe. In May 1941 he dropped on Crete. In September of that year, with his unit, he was stationed in a small village near the eastern tip of the island. A grenade thrown from a vineyard into a passing scout car killed one paratrooper and wounded a second. In retribution, Genscher's unit took every male in the village, from 16 to 60, tied them to lamp-posts and shot them. They stood guard over the corpses and when the village dogs chewed at the decaying flesh the Germans shot them too. Only when the bodies had remained in the open for two weeks and were in an advanced state of decay did they allow the womenfolk to bury their men.

Just before Christmas, Genscher was recalled to Berlin where, because of his command of English, he was commissioned and began to enjoy a comfortable war as a staff officer. Then in the closing months of 1943 Genscher heard that new postings were imminent. It did not surprise him, having watched the recruiting standards drop until men barely fit for military service were conscripted. The most he could hope for was a posting to the Western Front, but when his posting did come through he was to report to the 4th SS Panzer Corps at Lvov. The first thing he saw on his arrival was a group of soldiers who had stripped themselves and were daubing their flesh with motor grease, being particular liberal when applying grease to their heads and hands. It was still only November.

At midday, Genscher and the fourteen men who remained mounted a crest. Then there was an ear-piercing screech, as if a huge silk sheet was being torn. Genscher and his men dived for cover.

One man said, 'That's an MG42.'

Another said, 'It's the most beautiful sound I ever heard.'

Genscher held up his Mauser machine-pistol, butt first, until the firing stopped.

'You are indeed a fortunate man, Oberleutnant,' said the Oberst, offering Genscher a tin mug half full of ersatz coffee. 'Very fortunate.'

Genscher took the mug gladly and drank greedily. It was warm inside the Oberst's command post and he felt his body getting less numb.

'We were lucky to get back,' he conceded. 'The first engagement disorientated us. I went too far east before realizing my mistake, and our losses were heavy, due mainly to the cold.'

'You have to write your report immediately.'

'Immediately . . .?'

'Immediately.'

'But, sir, it is usual to rest, I have not slept . . .'

'Immediately. You are a lucky man, Genscher, because here is an order for you to return to Germany. You are to report to the command of Standartenführer Skorzeny at Friedenthal. You have heard of Skorzeny, Il Duce's liberator? Here, read it yourself.' The Oberst thrust a piece of paper into Genscher's free hand. 'You are to be on the first available transport, which leaves from the airfield in an hour, which means you leave here in half an hour, which means you have just time to prepare your report.'

'Herr Oberst . . .' Genscher was barely able to conceal his pleasure.

'There has always been something about you, Genscher. I have always thought you led a charmed existence. Over a year on this front and not so much as a scratch, and now this just before their big push begins. Curse you, Genscher.'

Chapter Three

Spencer Floyd, Captain, of the US Military Police, slowed his jeep as he approached the cluster of vehicles on the narrow road, pressing the brake harder than necessary. All hell was breaking open in the north, the krauts were pushing out, the US was pulling back, and now this, a couple of guys murdered. That was all the sergeant had said when he called over the radio. 'Murdered, sir,' said the crackly voice. 'I think you'd better come at once, sir.' So Floyd had come at once, driving north out of Paris, his journey taking nearly two hours because the roads were full of military convoys. But at least this stretch of road was quiet. He halted the jeep. The sergeant approached and saluted. Behind the sergeant there were four or five MPs, an army ambulance, two Willys jeeps, and two stretchers lying side by side at the side of the road. The stretchers were covered with white sheets.

'Report, Sergeant,' said Floyd, looking down at the stretchers.

'Murdered, sir,' replied the sergeant, one hand on his night stick, the thumb of the other hooked in his belt.

'I said report.' Floyd looked at the man. 'Not conduct a one-man court martial.'

'Yes, sir. Shot, sir. Privates Baxter and Tsentes. A Company.'

'That's better. Your men?'

'Yes, sir.'

'Shot when?'

'Maybe 1300 today, sir. As near as we can pinpoint it.'

'Witnesses?'

'One, sir.'

'You have a witness?' Floyd turned again to the sergeant, this time with interest and enthusiasm.

'A civilian, sir. He lives in that house over there, sir.'

About half a mile from the road there was a grey, solid, rambling farmhouse. It seemed to be squatting on the rich brown soil of the field, one of a number of fields which were interlaced with ditches along which grew stumpy trees. At this distance the trees were black silhouettes against a darkening sky. It occurred to Floyd that he was looking at a pastoral scene which probably hadn't changed in over a hundred years. Yet here on the road, at his feet, was the reality of war in the mid-twentieth century.

'And they said the last war was the war to end all wars,' he said.

'Excuse me, sir?'

'Nothing, Sergeant. How did you come to be notified of the incident?'

'Their relief found them, sir.'

'Not the witness?'

'No, sir. The relief found the deserted jeep and then came on their bodies pushed into the ditch. Baxter was shot in the belly at close range, there are burn marks on his tunic near the entry and the bullet didn't hang around inside him. He was clubbed as well. Just to make sure, I guess. The other was shot in the chest, not at such close range, but close enough for the round to come out the other side as well.'

'How did you find the witness?'

'I went to the house, sir. It's the only building for miles. I figured I had nothing to lose.'

'And?'

'Nothing,' said the sergeant.

'What's that?'

'The witness I was speaking of is some kid who left his shit in the field when he saw the shootin', high-tailed it into the house and has been shaking in a corner not talking to anybody ever since. I talked with the old guy who also lives in the house, he's got a bit of English, reckons he might be able to get the kid to speak. Asked me to leave and come back later. Tells me the kid's scared of uniforms.'

'How old is the kid?'

'Ten, twelve – what's the difference? His eyes are older. He's got a thousand-year stare, like some battle-smart veterans I've seen.'

'Jesus,' said Floyd. 'What's this war doing to people?'

The entrance to the farmyard was through a wicker gate fastened to the gatepost with leather hinges. Floyd and the sergeant walked up to the door and tapped on it. Eventually it was opened by the hunched figure of an old man with long grey hair and a grey beard.

'Captain Floyd,' said Floyd. 'US Military Police.' The old man looked at Floyd and the sergeant and then began to walk backwards into the dim interior of the house, beckoning the two men to follow him.

The floor of the house seemed to Floyd to be earthen and covered with flagstones. He noticed a wide fireplace with an iron grill on the wall opposite the door. A small wood fire crackled in the hearth, giving little light and little heat. The only other source of light came from a hurricane lamp which hung from one of the roof beams. As his eyes became accustomed to the gloom, Floyd saw a small boy cowering in a corner and whimpering.

'It's OK, son,' said Floyd soothingly, but he made no attempt to approach the boy.

'He has no English,' said the old man.

'Has he said what he saw happen on the road?' Floyd asked.

'A little,' nodded the man, stroking his beard. 'I will ask him. Excuse.' Then he added, 'I learn English from the war when there were Tommies billeted with us. You know Tommies? You have seen Tipperary?'

'No,' said Floyd, shaking his head.

The old man grunted and then spoke gently to the boy in soothing tones. The boy did not respond, so the old man began to encourage him with gentle prompting. Still the boy did not respond and the man turned to Floyd. 'During the Occupation some boys fixed a Boche patrol good just using shotguns. It was when the Boche were retreating this summer, going back to Germany, but they stopped for reprisals, all across the country-side here. The boy's father, my son, was shot outside the house.'

'I see,' said Floyd.

The old man turned again to the boy and this time the boy began to speak in a high-pitched, nervous voice. The old man listened and then turned to the two military policemen. 'He says he saw an American jeep stop at the military police jeep. The policemen and the soldiers in the jeep talked. Then the soldiers shot the policemen and pushed their bodies in the ditch. That is all he saw.'

'Could you ask him how many soldiers were in the jeep?' The man turned and spoke to the boy who held up three fingers. Floyd asked, 'Could he describe the soldiers?'

'Sir,' said the man, 'to him soldiers are all alike . . .'

'Ask him, please,' pressed Floyd.

Again the old man spoke to his grandson, who replied nervously. Then the old man said, 'The one who fired first was like a Boche.'

'What does he mean?' asked Floyd. 'The way they acted or something?'

'Sir,' said the man, 'he says he looked like a Boche, tall with blond hair.'

'So do a great many of our guys,' snarled the sergeant.

'How come he saw their hair?' asked Floyd. 'Didn't they have helmets, or caps?'

Strangely, the boy seemed to understand Floyd because he made the motion of a man taking off his helmet and wiping his brow with his forearm.

'Which way did they drive off?' Floyd asked. 'Southwards, I suppose?'

'Yes, sir,' replied the old man. 'The boy already said that.'

'Deserters.' The sergeant spat the words. 'The army's fallin' apart.'

'Looks like it,' said Floyd, turning to go, preparing to thank the old man. 'Better get a detail ready to turn Pigalle upside down. If they're in Paris they'll be in Pig Alley.'

This time it was the cold which woke him, gripping him as though his very clothes were ice. He pulled himself up from where he lay on the old bed, forcing himself to move, swinging his arms, stamping his feet, driving the numbness from his body. He glanced outside. The snow lay thickly and evenly; the fog still hung, reducing visibility, Conner estimated, to little more than thirty feet. He heard the drone of a solitary aircraft flying overhead, but could not determine its direction. He broke open a pack of K-rations which he ate cold, forcing the tasteless gruel down his gullet. Then he rested, conserving what strength and warmth he had because he knew that come nightfall he must be on the road again.

That day darkness came to the Eifel at about 1630. Conner ate a bar of chocolate, picked up his carbine and left the hut. He followed the road westwards. In the distance he occasionally heard the clatter of smallarms fire and in the further distance he could hear the rumble of artillery. He was isolated, he was cold, he felt very small, very vulnerable; he was more frightened than at any time in his life, including the day the German Army came out of the mist. Then he had had tanks and men with guns to fear; now, walking on this lonely road in the middle of the forest, his imagination was taking hold of his fear, teasing his nerve-endings with a feather.

At about 0200 he came upon a crossroads. First, while still some hundred yards distant, he heard noises, then, closing stealthily through the night and the fog, he eventually began to make out figures moving, stamping their feet and flapping their arms in the cold. He inched forward. The figures were definitely military personnel with two vehicles, and one vehicle was definitely a half-track, an American half-track. The other was smaller and parked beyond the first, a Willys maybe? Conner began to smile, he felt a surge of relief pass through his chilled body. Yet he hesitated; he'd read up on fatigue in battle, he knew there was the possibility he was willing himself to see American troops. He also knew that men will see whatever they want to see. His own father had been killed in broad daylight by another hunter who was convinced he was shooting white-tailed deer. Nevertheless that half-track was a half-track, and those guys could mean safety, warm food, orientation, news of whatever it was that was going on around him. But he knew he had to resist the impulse to rush forward, hail a greeting, because the only thing he might get in return was a burst from a Thompson across his chest. Conner continued to inch forward, straining his eyes against the darkness and the mist, desperate to get some indication of nationality. Then a star shell burst in the air close by, the figures crouched low, and in the light reflected on the snow Conner saw the rounded helmets and olive green battledress and a white star on the side of the vehicle, which was beyond doubt a half-track and not a Panzer.

Conner stepped into the middle of the road holding his carbine by his side, 'Hey, you guys,' he hailed as the star shell faded.

The GIs at the half-track turned, one yelled, '*Achtung!*' Conner froze, then he saw bright flashes come from the direction of the vehicle and heard bullets suck the air above him. He threw himself forward and rolled to the side of the road. He crawled into the scrub and inched backwards into the pines. He saw two GIs walk up the road, dark figures in the night. He eased the safety-catch off his weapon and raised the barrel until the sights rested on the head of the nearest GI. The two soldiers stopped when they were close enough to Conner for him to see their breath hanging in the air. They were also close enough for Conner to make out the unmistakable US Army battledress. He was tempted to move forward, he reckoned they might just have been jumpy, a little tired, a little trigger-happy. Getting shot at by your own side is nothing new. The only thing that made Conner hesitate was that kraut word, and now, looking at the figures in their familiar uniforms, he doubted whether he'd heard right. He was tired, maybe he'd imagined it. He knew krauts used that word, but this was the first time he'd heard it; he held back. He didn't know how likely it was you could have imagined hearing something you never heard before. The two figures took a few more steps, then halted again.

'Hey, we're sorry,' one of them yelled into the night, the second traversing his weapon as if expecting an enemy. 'Listen, don't get sore, anyone can make a mistake.'

Conner studied the second man. There was something about the way he was holding his carbine; his posture was stiff and rigid. Maybe it was just the guy, but for some reason Conner could not imagine that guy with his chin strap hanging loose and a mouth full of gum.

'We got coffee.'

Conner flattened himself into the snow. Now they were tempting him, trying to lure him out. Any regular GI would tell him to go ahead and freeze his balls off, but there's coffee if he wants it. Not these guys. Soon there'd be hot chow and booze down at the half-track, and if that didn't work they could maybe lay on some women. Conner kept his eye on the two men and felt his finger itching as it caressed the trigger. The two figures stood silently for a few minutes, just listening. Eventually they began to walk back towards the crossroads. Conner watched them go until they had melted into the night. He didn't know who they were, but they sure as hell didn't move like any GI he'd ever seen. He lay in the snow and felt the impulse to move but resisted it, remembering what his father had once told him about developing the patience of an Indian. So Conner assumed the patience of an Indian and lay in the freezing snow, wondering what the hell the old man knew about Indians, growing up in Brooklyn like he did, even though he had been a mean hunter. Him and his father, Sean O'Conner.

Conner decided to wait for half an hour. He guessed the time, not daring to move to look at his watch. It was a cold, still night and even now that his eyes were well accustomed to the gloom, he could see little. When he reckoned that the half-hour was up he decided to wait for an additional five minutes, just to be on the safe side, just to observe the Indian spirit. At that moment something moved on the far side of the road, a few feet further down towards the crossroads from where Conner lay. It was a round object which slowly became a man and then became a GI. He walked slowly down the road towards the half-track. A chill ran the length of Conner's spine, the skin on his forehead tightened. There had been three men; one had stayed behind to outwait him.

He let the third guy get out of sight and then began to inch backwards into the woods, cringing as each brittle branch snapped as he brushed against them. He stood and turned and, moving in a crouching run, worked his way deeper into the forest, up the slope, forcing an arc to his left as he did so. He stopped briefly as the thin air chilled his lungs. He tugged the glove from his left hand and clenched it between his teeth in an attempt to warm the air as he inhaled, and then pressed forward, creeping as he approached the crossroads.

Conner came out of the forest on to a ledge overlooking the crossroads. He was about twenty feet above the half-track and he could make out seven guys clearly. There was an air of calm about them. Beyond the half-track was a Willys jeep. An eighth man sat in the driver's seat of the jeep smoking a cigarette, the tip glowing in the dark. Conner sank down, lay on his belly, and edged to the lip of the promontory. Suddenly he stiffened. There were lights in the distance, slit headlights of a vehicle, bouncing around in the dark, coming down the road towards the cross-roads. The guys around the half-track noticed the oncoming vehicle, grabbed their carbines and went for positions at the side of the road or underneath the shelter of the vehicles. One guy clambered into the cab of the half-track and swung the 20mm cannon towards the lights. Conner bit down on the glove. His entire body was shaking with cold and fear.

The lights drew close and Conner saw that they belonged to a jeep. There were two guys in the jeep. It slowed to a stop and the guy in the front passenger seat raised himself up above the top of the windshield and waved to the soldiers by the half-track. 'Hey, you guys,' Conner heard him shout, 'are we glad to see you.'

'Oh yeah?' A man emerged from the trees at the side of the

road, grinning at the two men in the jeep. 'Where are you guys from?'

The driver of the jeep said something which was unintelligible to Conner. Then he heard the driver of the jeep ask, 'What the hell's going on, krauts everywhere?'

'Beats us,' replied the man who had stepped out of the shadows. 'Anybody behind you?'

'Only krauts,' laughed the driver. 'Is that coffee I smell?'

'Sure is,' replied the GI on the road. 'Step down, buddy.'

So the two guys stepped out of the jeep; it was about as far as they got. Two shots rang out clearly in the night air, both GIs crumpled and lay still. Conner looked on in utter disbelief as the other soldiers came out of cover and dragged the bodies off the road. He twisted to one side and brought his carbine up to his shoulder. There were eight guys down there, he didn't know who they were, but sure as hell they were not GIs. He rested his carbine over the lip of the promontory and reckoned he could take out two, maybe three, before they returned fire. Then what? Then he'd have to get the hell out. He turned and looked behind him. The wood was thick and rose steeply up a rocky slope which was partially covered in snow and ice. He would only have to go up the slope about fifty feet before he'd be in the firing line of the 20mm which would be traversing from left to right firing a hundred and twenty rounds a minute, each round containing one pound of trinitro-cellulose, and generally making a mess of everything. While that was happening there'd be maybe four or five guys scrambling up from the road. Conner took his finger from the trigger and withdrew his carbine.

Below him two men climbed into a jeep and drove off in a southerly direction. The rest of the men mounted the half-track. The engine roared into life and it lurched forward and drove away following the jeep. Two dead men lay at the side of the road; their jeep stood motionless in the middle of the crossroads.

Stealthily Conner climbed down to the road and approached the two corpses. They were both young men and, judging by the stubble on their chins and their grimy battledress, Conner guessed that they had been in the field and separated from their

68

unit for some days. He snatched the dog-tags from the neck of each man, slipping one of each man's dog-tags into his pocket. He then knelt and, for the second time in two days, forced open the mouths of the dead men and placed the second dog-tag inside. He laid each man out and crossed the arms over the chest before wrapping each corpse in its rubber poncho. He glanced at their jeep, was tempted to drive it, then thought that he would be safer on foot and began to walk away southwards, following the half-track. He glanced at the signpost as he passed. He was going towards a place called Bastogne.

In the shelter in Berlin nobody spoke, but they clung to each other with fear as the noise above them rose to an indescribable crescendo and remained like that for hour after hour. The building shook, jumped, settled and jumped again, people's knees bounced off the floor as each shockwave passed through the basement. People sat with their heads bowed, their chins pressed close to their chests, silent, all silent, even the children, as the shelter swayed as though it was made of rubber and the concrete floor undulated like waves on an ocean. At the back of everyone's mind were the stories that had come from Hamburg and Cologne, where the terror bombers had caused a firestorm, and where people in the shelters had first suffocated, then baked, until their body chemistry disintegrated and all that was found in the shelters was a grey, soft ash.

Suddenly the bombing stopped. As always, there was no gradual reduction in the intensity of the bombardment, nothing to indicate to the people in the basements and the shelters that the worst was over. The awful noise continued unabated until it stopped, very suddenly. The people in the shelter raised their heads slowly and smiled at each other, some laughed hysterically, others cried. Gradually conversation developed. It was 4.00 a.m., they knew that above them the city would be burning and they could not expect the all clear until well after dawn. In the corner somebody began to sing. Again Petra Oelkers noticed how the bombing was reinforcing the spirit of the German people, just as four years previously the blitz had reinforced the spirit of the British. Benjamin Service had told her that in the letters he had sent her. Letters she had loved receiving, letters to which she had not been permitted to reply.

When the all clear came the people stood, stiffly, and began to file up the stairs into the cold grey December day, the sun smudged by a layer of dust and grit which hung over the city, causing a perpetual brown twilight. The dust and grit was something that the Berliners had learned to live with; it got on food, inside clothing and was harsh against the skin, it stung eyes and clung to the back of throats. That morning the dust was especially thick. Petra coughed deeply, half closing her eyes, and looked about her; the dust gave the impression that she was looking at an old sepia photograph of Berlin, a moving sepia print of devastated buildings, hunched figures pushing hand-barrows leaving the city to camp in the fields before the Americans came later that day, before the RAF came again the next night. It was a sepia print of a city still on fire, at least three buildings on each street were raging infernos and were being left to burn themselves out. There was a body of a terror bomber who had fallen by parachute. His flying jacket and fur-lined boots had been looted, and so had his survival rations, most valued of all because they contained sugar and chocolate. It was unclear how he'd died, whether in the air, or on the ground at the hands of hate-crazed fire-fighters.

On the other side of the street, through the brown-red stinging haze, Petra saw a group of people sifting through rubble; they were either looking for bodies or coal, probably coal, she thought; it was far more precious. She walked through the streets; everywhere Berliners were being friendly, talkative, compassionate to one another, helping the shocked and the dazed. She passed the hospital, a queue was forming of the injured, the walking wounded, who would receive medical care, fifty marks, and a good meal before being sent on their way. If they were homeless, then the Nazi party would provide accommodation, even if it was only a tent in a field, with food from a mobile canteen. Again she saw the signs which lately had begun to proliferate in the city; the one put up by the civilian police in five languages because of the number of foreign workers, warning that anybody found looting would be shot, and a second put up by the Nazis and in German only which read, 'They may break our homes, but our hearts, never!'

When she reached the flat Heinrich was already there, slumped on the sofa, one of his boots half tugged off, his black uniform grimy and soiled. He was half asleep when Petra entered the flat.

'I was worried about you,' he said. 'I wasn't sure you'd survive. It was a bad night. The worst we have had for some time.'

'I was in a shelter,' she replied, going into the kitchen. Then she called, 'Heinrich, there's no gas, the gas main must have been fractured.'

'I know, I tried to light it when I came in. We shall just have to have beer and bread for breakfast.'

She turned from the kitchen and sat in the armchair. 'That's the effect of the bombing,' she said. 'It's not the destruction of the buildings, it's the loss of sleep. You cannot work if you can't sleep. That's why Germany's economy is failing. Where did you spend the night, in the Chancellery?'

'Underneath it.' He forced a smile. 'With the Führer and his staff. But things are going well for Germany.'

'Heinrich,' she said disapprovingly.

'I mean it,' he said with heavy sarcasm. 'The attack is going well. The American resistance is weak and unco-ordinated. We have some logistic problems, but . . .' He waved his hand as if to dismiss them. 'The Führer is pleased, his Gryphon troops are doing well, and the claws of the Gryphon have reached Paris.'

'Paris?' She glanced up curiously. 'Has the front reached Paris? I thought you said we were pushing out towards Antwerp.'

'Not all the German forces. Just a little part of them.'

'Oh.'

'But having been told, you must now forget I told you.'

'Of course, Heinrich,' she said.

'He's mad, quite mad.' He shook his head. 'He thinks he's back in 1940, the deranged old fool.'

'Heinrich,' she gasped. 'Don't speak like that.'

'I have to, here is my home, I have to talk the truth, here where it's safe. I can't do it in the Chancellery, nobody can, we must all pretend to worship the Führer, when even a blind man can see he is leading us to destruction. I am ashamed of my uniform, Petra.'

'The German uniform?'

'This.' He looked down at his uniform with distaste. 'The SS. The Reichsführer SS, personal bodyguard to the Führer. I should have joined the Wehrmacht, I would not be ashamed of my uniform then. The difference, you see, Petra, is that one is a soldier of Germany, the other is a soldier of Hitler's.'

'Yes,' she nodded. 'I can see that. But I'm not sure what I can say. Just don't, please don't talk like that in the Chancellery or you and probably I will be dispatched into the night and the fog. People are disappearing even now when the war is surely over.'

'Yes, I will be careful. I want us to survive. I want us both to survive.'

She left the room to cut bread and pour wartime 'light' beer. She glanced out of the window: the brown city was still burning. In the next room Heinrich had wound up the gramophone and was playing one of the Brandenburg Concertos. The sound quality was poor because of the grit on the surface of the record.

Benjamin Service sat in the third-class smoker of the 4.10 to Bletchley. The train consisted of just three carriages of the Great Eastern Railway Company pulled by a blackened tank engine. The coaches shuddered and jerked as the driving wheels of the engine slipped on the wet rails before settling into a smooth if sluggish acceleration. Service watched the grey brick terrace houses of Cambridge slip steadily by as the rain spattered against the window. There was a leak in the carriage and the rainwater formed a pool in the groove at the bottom of the window-frame, close by Service's elbow. He was alone in the compartment and when the train was clear of Cambridge he opened the copy of *The Times* which he had bought at the news-stand, where there was a propaganda poster which had always amused him. It read, 'You can't spell Victory with an absentee.' He had found it a pleasant afternoon in the city. He had strolled along the Backs in the drizzle and found it not an uncomfortable experience; quite tranquil, in fact.

He had called in at the Eagle for a nostalgic pint of the strong Abbot Ale, but had decided against a second because the pub was full of drunken, jostling RAF boys who were painting the names of their squadrons on the tabletops and the ceiling. He had visited his college, taken tea with his tutor, and replied, 'Filling in forms, sir,' when the venerable old gentleman enquired as to the nature of his war service. He called at Caius College and saw with satisfaction that the saplings which had been planted to replace the original trees in Tree Court were now a good three feet high. He had been saddened to hear that the original trees had been felled at the outbreak of war because they represented an obstacle to fire-fighting appliances. The sight reminded him of the trees around the cricket ground at home.

He found himself thinking yet again of the girl he would have married had it not been for the war, had she not gone to Canada. He always seemed to think of her quite suddenly, usually in quiet moments when he wasn't worried or preoccupied. And again, in keeping with the pattern that had established itself, when he thought of her he thought of his village as it had been before the war.

He had grown up in Bishop's Upton but he never really saw the village until that day in the summer when his boyhood melted into adolescence, the day he followed the old droving road from Salisbury with a knapsack and a map. He passed through an expanse of broad-leaved woodland and emerged atop a gentle hillock with the village spread below him.

From this new vantage point he saw that the village formed a cluster around the church with its square tower from which flew the flag of St George. He noticed the main road, a narrow pasty stream which ran gently and sensitively through the village without seeming to disturb the tranquil nestling of one cottage against its neighbour. The cottages and houses were painted in pastel shades or built of the local off-white stone; they were either thatched or red-tiled. Each had a garden which in summer was green, interspersed here and there with colourful borders. On the further edge of the village there were one or two isolated houses; beyond these were richly tilled fields, green meadows and acres of ripening wheat. Beyond that again was the same patchwork of green and gold, the darker greens of the coppices, and silvery streams glinting in the sun, and on the skyline was the steeple of the church in the next village. The image of his village and the Dorsetshire countryside imprinted itself indelibly on his retina that day.

It was always following the recollection of the image of his home that he thought of the day he had first brought Petra Oelkers down from London in his old Morris with its torn canvas hood which to his intense annoyance, flapped continually. He taught mathematics, she taught German, and they had met at a meeting of the branch Labour Party in Toynbee Hall in the east end of London, where they had chosen to work. That had been in the spring of 1939. He remembered details of their journey, the cloudburst and the rain coming through the tear in the roof; then getting trapped behind the Debbages in their steam caravan, a green engine with brass pistons and wheels, a long white roof and a full funnel, which pulled a harvester, a thresher and a bailer; he had spent some time explaining to her the nature of the equipment. He remembered how they followed it for miles until the road straightened sufficiently to allow him to overtake. Even then he had had to run the offside wheels up on to the grass verge. Sam Debbage blew the whistle as they passed, Benjamin pressed the horn and waved a shirtsleeved arm from the open window.

During the journey, in her phrasing, which he always found endearing, she told him of the misfortune that had befallen her parents.

'My father, he didn't say anything when my mother and I told him about us,' she had said. 'We are not sure how much he is understanding. My mother thinks he believes he is still in

Germany. Sometimes –' she had swept her blonde hair back with a graceful sweep of her arm '– sometimes she finds him sitting in his chair, he has wheeled himself to the garden gate and he is shouting in German at the passers-by. My mother is worried for him but it is now more difficult these days because there are people who won't help because Father is a German. Even hired help is difficult to get.'

'Really?'

'Oh yes, really. There are so many people out of work in Oxford and Mother is offering one guinea for mornings only and she gets the worst people applying for the position, lazy women who won't care for the house or for Father. I think I'll have to spend more time with her.'

'You'll leave London?' He still recalled the jolt at the thought of her moving to Oxford.

'I don't know, Benjamin. I have a good job. It would be difficult to get a similar post in Oxford. The competition would be so fierce.'

It was at that point that they entered Bishop's Upton. He remembered how she sat forward in the seat, glancing from left to right at the cottages, down the smaller winding streets which led off the main road, at the square in front of the church, the half-timbered pubs. 'So English, this is what I have always thought an English village to be like. There are similar villages around Oxford but none so – so – just right.'

'I like it very much.' He recalled his pleasure at being home again, and looked at the familiar buildings: Hanniman's the butcher, Stan Royce the grocer, the George Hotel, and further up the steep incline, the Green Man.

He remembered too how his father had greeted them, standing at the door of his house just beyond the village, a portly man in plus fours radiating warmth and hospitality, and his sudden shock at first hearing Petra's German accent. It was late summer of 1939, after all, and the Germans were already The Germans.

His mother too had been uneasy but Benjamin had thought her nervousness, like Petra's, came from an anxiety to make a good first impression. The atmosphere was eased when he took her for a walk round the village. She walked comfortably, he remembered, in a fashionable dress with squared shoulders and short sleeves, in a delicate shade of blue. They walked to the square, and then down a lane beside the church; beyond the stile at the end of the lane was the cricket pitch. The cricket pitch was surrounded by trees and he asked her if she noticed anything about them.

'They all seem young trees.'

'Yes,' he replied in a manner which suggested there was more to notice.

Beyond the pitch, in the next field, a herd of shorthorns was being brought in for milking. Their lowing rolled across the meadow.

'They are of many species,' she said, looking across the pitch. 'You know, I do not think I can see two trees of the same species.'

'I say, well done,' he said, 'well done indeed.'

She glanced at him, quietly awaiting an explanation.

'For years,' he said, 'our family have brought visitors to this spot and asked the question I asked you, and you are the first to come up with the right answer. You're very observant.'

'I am?'

'Indeed, yes. Dad and I planted those trees. All of them. Well, he did really, I was about three at the time and I followed him round the ground dropping the acorn or whatever into the hole he had dug.'

'Really?' She watched a swallow arch and curve, catching insects, in the warm, early evening air.

'Yes.' He told her, how at the beginning of one summer, twenty years previously, in 1919, the village doctor was scoring during a cricket match when he decided that the ground needed trees around the perimeter. He spent the next few weeks collecting seeds or saplings of as many different types of tree as he could. One Saturday afternoon, while another match was being played, he walked the perimeter planting the trees at different intervals. 'All of them grew, the oak from just an acorn, not a sapling, in the village they're known as the Doctor's Trees and have been mentioned in guide books.'

On the way home they stopped at the Green Man. It was beginning to fill with men who carried with them the smell of the fields and of freshly tilled soil. Behind the long bar, under a black beam, was an engraved mirror which advertised Badger Beer, brewed by Hall and Woodhouse since 1777. Benjamin had a pint of old and mild and Petra had orange squash. He paid for the drinks with four farthings.

The next morning he sat in the kitchen. He heard Mrs Johns and Petra talking. He remembered the exchange.

Mrs Johns: His Majesty's in the kitchen.

Petra: His Majesty?

Mrs Johns: Benjamin.

He remembered Mrs Johns entering the kitchen grasping the wooden knob which was set in the door at shoulder height and continuing; 'Only he doesn't like being called Master Benjamin, so I call him "Your Majesty", don't I, Benjamin?'

He had stood and smiled at both women. He was dressed in baggy brown trousers, brown and white co-respondent shoes, and a white shirt. He poured Petra a cup of tea from the brown earthenware teapot with a chipped spout.

'That's Mrs Johns,' he told her when they were alone in the kitchen. 'She does for us.'

'Does?'

'It's an expression. It means she cleans for us, does the house-work. She's small but she fills the whole house like a molecule fills a large space just by sheer movement. Always darting about.'

Petra said she wished her mother could find somebody like Mrs Johns to help her. It was so difficult because of Father. Benjamin did not know what to say.

When the war was three weeks old they visited Oxford. The roads were full of army lorries and columns of soldiers. She said little on the journey but sat stroking the diamond ring on the third finger of her left hand, the ring he had bought her. They had telephoned the news to their families and intended to visit Bishop's Upton a fortnight after calling on Petra's parents.

'It's difficult,' Mrs Oelkers had said, after the congratulations, the kissing, the opening of the bottle that had been long kept for some special occasion. Benjamin could see her now, wringing her hands, the rays of the sun streaming through the window, picking out flecks of dust in the air, glinting in the grey hairs around her head and highlighting the lines on her brow. 'He knows what's happening and he'll wheel himself to the front gate and swear at the passers-by in German.'

She paused and seemed to gaze into the middle distance.

'He was such a clever, sensitive man. A good scholar and a good teacher. After we came here he only taught at the Grammar School for two years before he had a massive stroke. The boys from the school called in ones and twos to pay their respects and the people in the area have been good, but Wilhelm's state has left him aggressive and uninhibited and now people avoid us.'

Petra crossed the room and put her arm round her mother's shoulders.

'The war doesn't help. It seems to count for little that Wilhelm opposed the Nazis and we eventually had to flee Germany. Thank God, because I was English, we were able to settle here.'

That afternoon Petra and Benjamin took Wilhelm Oelkers out in Benjamin's car. They took the road from Oxford towards Boars Hill and stopped where they could look out over the fields at the sun playing on the spires of the colleges two miles distant. They remained there for some time, Wilhelm Oelkers leaning against the car, staring across the fields, occasionally making indecipherable murmuring sounds.

Mrs Oelkers remained at home, resting, listening to a Brahms concert broadcast on Midland Regional.

Three days later, in the early evening, Petra had called at Benjamin's bed-sitter near Russell Square. He was sitting at a table working on the model of a sailing ship, drawing black cotton from the spars to the deck.

'I'm leaving,' she told him. 'I'm leaving London.'

He said nothing, being unable to speak.

'I have to. I'm going soon. Maybe even tomorrow.'

Then he managed, 'Why?' and indicated one of the deep leather armchairs next to the gasfire.

'I can't stay here. I want to go back to my flat, pack up, pay the bill.'

'Why, why?'

'You ask for why? Because they have Father interned, that is for why. God, how could they?'

Benjamin was genuinely stunned. 'What happened . . .?'

'They came and dragged him away in his wheelchair to a concentration camp on the Isle of Man, a sick old man, just because he is German. Mother is distraught. She has sent to me a telegram.'

Benjamin remembered the way she handed him a crumpled sheet of paper. He read it in the fading light.

'And the way the messenger looked at me, like I was dirt. I think already the GPO is reporting me to the police, who will be checking my status. I will show them my birth certificate to show that I was born in London, that my mother is English. Will you tell them at the school that I had to leave? I shall send my resignation from Oxford.'

'Of course.'

'I intended to resign anyway to do something for the war.'

'I'll walk you back to your flat.'

They walked slowly through the streets of Bloomsbury. Occasionally, as the line of building was interrupted by a side street, they glimpsed silver barrage balloons swaying above the city. Their feet tap-tap-tapped in step and he noticed goose pimples on her arms.

'Summer's come to an end,' he said.

She nodded.

Outside her lodgings, owned by an old Lithuanian who did not permit visitors, they stopped and faced each other. Neither could find anything to say. Beside them was a post-box which had been painted a dull yellow with a paint which would change colour in the event of a gas attack.

'I shall write to you at your Oxford address,' Benjamin said awkwardly.

She twisted her ring. 'Yes, oh yes.'

That had been the last time he saw her. More than five years ago.

The 4.10 from Cambridge to Bletchley rocked steadily, his body swayed gently with the motion of the carriage, and he relished the sounds of the train; the click-click, clack-clack, and the meaty chugging. He paid no attention to the small, closely printed adverts that formed the front page of *The Times*, but turned instead to the third page for the headlines and the war news. The war news, Service realized, was always strictly censored and at least forty-eight hours old and indeed in this very edition P & O Lines were only now reporting losses of shipping due to enemy action three and four years earlier. The main focus of the war news on December 17 was the war in Greece as British paratroopers fought with ELAS guerrillas, the German retreat from the Balkans, and the Japanese withdrawals in the Far East. Yet Service knew that something big was brewing in Europe. The cyphers that had been intercepted and decoded at Bletchley Park indicated a big build-up of German reserves on the western front in the Eifel region, and a deliberate switching of units from the Balkans and the Russian front. Yesterday, when Service was on duty, the intercepted cyphers revealed the Germans reporting large-scale advances by SS troops and the previously unheard-of King Tiger tanks against the US First Army. All that was reported in *The Times* was 'small-scale German counter-attacks'.

He glanced out of the window as the train passed steadily through the damp, rolling fields of the Cambridgeshire/Bedford-shire border and found it hard to imagine that at that moment, less than two hundred miles away in Belgium, what was, by all account, an immense battle was entering its opening stages. He plunged his hand into his coat pocket and took out the packet of cigarettes he had managed to buy at the platform kiosk on Cambridge station. They were a new brand, Fifth Avenue, advertised as 'American Style'. He found them to be pleasant, but a little sweet and insubstantial. The taste did not suit him as much as Craven A, his favoured brand.

As the smoke rose only to be suddenly whisked away by a draught, he thought back over the last few days and remembered clearly the excitement and apprehension at Bletchley Park when a series of cyphers was intercepted which when decoded, revealed themselves to be orders from the highest German military authority. Division upon Division of troops, tanks and artillery were to be moved up to the western front under cover of darkness, with no vehicle permitted the use of headlights. The team at Bletchley Park hadn't been slow to realize the implication of these cyphers and had put copies of them, duly decoded, on to the standard 7 inch by 9 inch sheet, given them the Ultra classification, and dispatched them to Downing Street. It was intelligence of the highest grade which was also transmitted immediately to SHAEF in Paris. Now, seven days later, the German unit commanders were sending jubilant cyphers back to Von Rundstedt's HQ. Service stubbed the cigarette out in the slim ashtray which was bolted to the coachwork just beneath the window. He was depressed and angry. The Yanks had been given one week's warning of a German attack in force, and they seemed to have ignored it. 'A waste,' he said softly. 'All those lives.'

Later, the train began to slow in a series of jolts. Service looked at his watch: it was 6.15 p.m. He stood and buttoned his coat as the train hissed and squealed to a halt at Bletchley station. He opened the door of the carriage before the train had stopped and stepped on to the platform, running for the first few steps before slowing to a brisk walk towards the ticket-barrier. He gripped his gas mask to stop it swinging while searching with his other hand for his ticket. He found it in his coat pocket and, holding it between thumb and forefinger, pulled up his collar against the wind and the rain. He was one of four people to alight and was the last to pass through the ticket-barrier as the minute hand of the large clock behind the ticket-collector fell heavily on the quarter hour.

A taxi with a single slit headlight turned into the station

81

approach. There were a few solitary lights at Bletchley, courtesy of the recently introduced 'Dim-Out' regulations, which replaced the total Blackout, but were still only applicable to towns more than five miles from the coast. The ticket-collector, a small man with glasses, took Service's ticket and chirped, 'Cheer up, mate, you're not dead till you're buried.' Service grinned and walked out of the station and hailed the taxi to take him to Bletchley Park.

'Knew you was a boffin, guv,' said the driver, tripping the meter. 'No use pretending we don't know something's going on in the old house. We just don't ask what.' The exhaust exploded as the taxi drove off. The driver waited for Service's reply, his head half turned and one eye on the road. Service smiled inwardly, but wouldn't be drawn. It was not, he conceded, a bad attempt to get information. Eventually the driver gave up and turned both eyes towards the road, guiding the ancient Austin Ten towards the outskirts of Bletchley. Minutes later he stopped the taxi outside a gatehouse at the end of a winding concrete drive. Service alighted and paid the fare and the taxi turned and drove back towards the station, whining in first gear and backfiring occasionally. As he approached the gatehouse a sergeant of the Intelligence Corps stepped out.

''Evening sir,' said the sergeant with an icy pedantry. Service stopped and put his bag down. He slid his hand inside his coat and took out his identity papers. He handed them to the sergeant who studied them with his flashlight and then returned them. 'Very good, sir. Carry on, please.' Service walked up the driveway, his shoe heels tapping on the smooth concrete. To his left he saw the shimmer of the lake's surface and the ripples being created by the gently falling rain. Despite the cloud, the huge magnolia tree by the lakeside stood out in silhouette. He rounded the bend of the driveway and saw the house, a large, squat Victorian building with gargoyles at either side of the door. Beyond the house he could make out the harsh, angular shape of one of the concrete buildings, the one containing Huts 3, 6 and 8. Hut 8 was the naval hut and was just down the corridor from where he worked in Hut 6. Curious types, the naval types;

they never talked about their work, were never seen to have dealings with anybody but themselves, just sat in there receiving, decoding and sending, beavering away. A secret within a secret. Service walked past the front of the house with its taped-up windows, beyond the stand of Scots pine, and on to the narrow footpath which led to the building containing Huts 3, 6 and 8.

There were lights in the hut, but the blackout blinds were still drawn, for Bletchley Park stayed dark at night, not wishing to make use of the Dim-Out regulations. He entered the long central corridor of the hut and his ears were instantly assaulted by the noise of the bombes not unlike a battery of one thousand clicking knitting needles. He turned from the corridor and into Hut 6. Hamish McCrae sat at the desk at the end of the hut looking over sheets of paper which Service knew to be decoded and translated German signals. Seeing McCrae engrossed, Service walked softly across the hut and stood by a large, dark-coloured machine of a type known affectionately as a 'bronze goddess'. A bronze goddess could extract data from memory banks with staggering speed, could cross-reference with equal rapidity and solve complex mathematical problems. They had been shipped over from the United States in great secrecy, having been manufactured there by a company called International Business Machines. Benjamin Service was in fact standing next to the world's first computer.

Presently McCrae put the sheets of paper down and looked up at Service, smiled and said, 'Benjy.' He was a young man of odd appearance, a curious mixture of awkward late adolescence and middle age. He had residual traces of acne and was prematurely bald. He was also quite brilliant. It was McCrae who, in 1940, deduced from German cyphers which reported that less than half of their aircraft were serviceable and that spare parts and fuel were not getting through to the airfields in France, that the RAF had won the Battle of Britain. This at a time when to observers and combatants the battle seemed to be at its height. And it was McCrae who, in 1943, organized Hut 6 so that it continually intercepted Afrika Korps signals and ensured that the decoded and translated signals were received by Montgomery before Rommel received the originals.

'Much ado about something?' asked Service.

'Nothing special here.' McCrae tapped the sheets of paper which lay on the desk in front of him. 'Pretty routine. This one here is from army engineers requesting fuel. The same unit sent a similar request eight hours ago, so have a dozen other units.' He leaned back in his chair and stretched his arms above his head. 'A clear pattern is being established: the Germans have a logistics problem. They can't get enough fuel to their forward positions, either a transport difficulty or because they have not got the fuel in the first place. It's been like that for most of the day, the forward units have advanced so far so quickly that the supply lines have been broken. We sent the information off to Downing Street and to SHAEF . . . but what they'll do with it is anybody's guess. Ignore it, most likely. Was it not you,' he asked in his rich Glasgow accent, 'who warned them of the attack in the first place, Benjy?'

'Well, I informed them of a large build-up in the Ardennes with Germans bringing their vehicles up at night and without headlights. I didn't put an interpretation on it. That was up to them.'

'Still, a man with two glass eyes could have seen the preparations for an attack. Such a shame, because the Yanks are getting creamed. The German hasn't pushed forward like this since he went into Russia. Can't last, though, because he's run out of petrol coupons, the Hun has.'

'We'd better not be wise after the event.' Service took out his packet of cigarettes and offered one to McCrae.

'No, you're right.' McCrae accepted a cigarette and Service lit it for him before lighting his own. McCrae coughed. 'Benjy, what are you giving me?'

'It's a new fag, Hamish. Fifth Avenue, American Style.'

'Benjy,' McCrae pleaded, 'did they no' have any Players?'

'No, so I thought I'd try these.'

'Aye, I wish you'd not try them on your friends. They're awful, but I'll not waste it.' McCrae looked at his pad and turned back a few pages. 'We've been getting some curious cyphers at intervals today.'

'Yes?'

'Aye, mostly it's just been the same depressing catalogue of the Hun reporting lightning advances against piecemeal resistance and ending up with a request for fuel, but there has been the odd reference to Operation Grief.'

'Grief?'

'I looked it up. It's German for Gryphon, the mythical winged creature, a winged lion, not usually malevolent according to legend, but if the Hun has unleashed one it's up to no good, I'll be bound. There's also reference to a unit called the 150th Panzer.'

'Doesn't ring a bell.'

'No previous record. It's got to be a new unit. That's not significant, the whole German army is being reconstituted. What is interesting is that many individual units are identifying themselves as belonging to the 150th Panzer, and these units are stretched along the whole front in the vanguard of the attack.'

'Panzer units don't split up.'

'Exactly, Benjy. But the 150th Panzer has been leaping up and down the front as though it could fly.'

'You mean you think the 150th Panzer is undertaking Operation Grief?'

'That's about it, Benjy. But one thing is certain: whatever 150th Panzer is, it's not tanks.'

Petra Oelkers slipped out of the flat on the Potsdamerplatz and walked rapidly towards the U-Bahn station. The subway was crowded. It was impossible for her to tell if she was being followed, though she went past her stop and then caught a train travelling in the opposite direction to try to identify anybody who might be following her. She looked at the people in the subway train. She had great sympathy for the Germans, not just because she was half German herself, but also because she saw how the German people were suffering in the war. She longed for the

Allied victory, was working for it, but that did not prevent her feeling an affinity with the Berliners, with the Germans. The Berliners had not asked for war, it had been forced upon them, just as it had been forced upon the Parisians and the Londoners.

She glanced about her again: these people with worn and haggard faces, who smelled badly because of the shortage of soap, who were thin because of the shortage of food, which of these was her enemy? This woman who seemed lost in her thoughts and who was wearing black, probably for her sons and husband; this old man in a young man's uniform with fear in his eyes; this boy in a man's tunic dreaming of glory? And their city, once a beautiful city, now mostly rubble and hollow buildings, what damage, what destruction. The people in England wouldn't crow so much if they knew what terror bombing was, if they could see what was meant by a fire storm. And this old man and this boy, they were the Volkssturm who were shortly to defend Berlin against the best Allied armies.

She left the subway near the Stettiner Bahnhof and walked down Invalidenstrasse and into the Chausseestrasse. Rubble was piled high along the roadside, the tramlines were twisted and buckled, reaching for the sky where they had been severed. She turned down a side street and entered the maze of streets behind the Chausseestrasse. Here the going was more difficult. The civil defence had not the resources to attend to the destruction in the back streets, and devoted their time to fire-fighting and keeping the main thoroughfares clear. Petra struggled down the roadway, climbing over rubble, avoiding a hissing gas pipe, skirting a car which had been blown on its side and burnt out, sickeningly still with four charred corpses inside. Eventually she turned into the entrance of a tenement stair, the street door of which had long been blown off, climbed two silent flights and tapped on a narrow door. There was at first no answer. Only after her third insistent knock was the door opened a fraction of an inch and the old man with whom she had recently walked by the Kleiner Wannsee recognized her and said, 'You're mad, mad.'

'I was not followed,' she whispered.

'You don't have to have been followed. They watch this house.'

'No, they don't. Let me in. Hurry.'

The door opened wider and Petra slid inside. It was cold and dark, the furniture had been covered in sheets to protect it from the grit which floated in the city's air. Again the man said, 'You're mad.'

She could scarcely see his face. 'War is about taking risks.'

'Not this sort of risk. This is not a risk. It's recklessness. The Gestapo . . .'

'I have information. Vital information.'

'We have done our job, Petra. The Third Reich is crumbling, you have always done as I said, do so now. Go west to the house I showed you and wait until the front passes you. Emerge when you are behind the Allied lines. I shall go north and await the Russians.'

'There is a development,' she said insistently.

'The new front? I read about it in the *Völkischer Beobachter*. They make it read like the war is starting again. Don't worry, it is just the Reich in its death throes. That is no reason to come here. I am surprised at you.'

'There's something else.'

'What else?'

'I don't know. But we must transmit.'

'Impossible, especially if we do not know anything. Petra, this is ludicrous.'

'No, it's not impossible. We can do it tonight at eight o'clock, before the raid, if there is one tonight. They'll still be monitoring the wavelength.'

'What information do you have?'

'Something called Grief.'

'That is all?'

'Except that it's secret. Heinrich told me and then swore me to secrecy.'

'Where is he now?'

'At the Chancellery. On duty.' She stepped a little closer to him, pressing her argument. 'We must send an alert, just twenty

87

seconds, perhaps less. We have not sent a signal for some time, the Nazis can't still be listening.'

'No. It's too near the end to take chances like that.'

'We must. How else can London know if we don't tell them.'

'No.'

'Yes, yes, yes.'

'And I say no.'

But eventually the signal was transmitted.

It was received at SOE, London, and simultaneously in Hut 6, where Service was still chatting to McCrae over Horlicks and a packet of Huntley and Palmer's biscuits. McCrae had had a busy shift, having received, decoded and logged over fifteen hundred cyphers since he came on duty. Just after 7.00 p.m., as he was writing up the log prior to the night watch relieving him, the Wren monitoring the radio receiver raised her hand. 'Sir,' she called.

McCrae looked up. 'That's funny. We haven't had a peep out of agents' waveband for weeks.' Then, addressing the Wren: 'That's incoming, I presume?'

'Yes, sir. SOE have just transmitted the ready to receive.'

McCrae stood, but Service, who was nearer, said, 'It's all right, Hamish, I'll get it.' He left his seat and walked to where the Wren sat taking down the message. When she had written it she tore off the sheet of paper from her pad and smiled at Service. Her blonde good looks reminded him again of the girl he had known, once, a long time ago, before the war, in another world. He was shaken by the emotion the Wren aroused in him, a feeling he had not known he harboured. He thanked her and returned to McCrae's desk and handed the paper across.

'The Gryphon again,' said McCrae, reading the message. Then he read it out in full. 'Alert. Claws of the Gryphon are in Paris. Message ends. Oboe.'

'Who's Oboe?'

'I don't know offhand,' said McCrae, 'but I think it's one of our Berlin agents. Time they wrapped up and got out.'

'Claws of the Gryphon are in Paris,' said Service, slowly. 'What is this Gryphon? It's leaping all over Europe.'

'Your guess is as good as mine,' replied McCrae. 'And that I'm afraid is the level we are operating at. The only thing we can do is send a message to SHAEF. What shall I say? Alert for Subversives in Paris? We also have to keep Downing Street informed.'

'It's as clear as we can make it. Secret classification, I should think,' said Service. 'Hardly seems to merit Ultra.'

Service left Hut 6 and walked back down the drive of Bletchley Park, showed his identity once again to the same sergeant of the Intelligence Corps and walked the few hundred yards to the house where he had been allocated a room. The rain had stopped, the air was cold and crisp. It was not an unpleasant walk to not unpleasant quarters, far preferable to his first accommodation in the hectic early days when he was obliged to share a double bed with an Aberdeen graduate who didn't wash, that on top of a six-mile cycle trip to and from Bletchley Park.

In his room Service washed, changed, climbed into his striped pyjamas and lay in bed with his hands clasped behind his head.

It had been a full day. He only had one day off each week and was pleased to feel that this time he had used it well. But it wasn't the day in Cambridge he thought about, it was the smile he'd received from the Wren, the blonde Wren with striking features. He had not had a serious affair throughout the period of the war, probably a good thing too, going by the sombre Ministry of Health advert in that day's edition of *The Times*, which alerted the public to the danger of venereal disease. 'The only blot on our wartime health record,' it said and advised that, although the disease could be cured if caught early, 'clean living is the only answer.'

There had been a girl before the war, quite briefly, but very richly and sweetly. A half-German girl with blonde hair whom he had met when he attended meetings of the Labour Party in Toynbee Hall in the east end of London and to whom he had been engaged. After her sick father had been arrested and interned on the Isle of Man under Regulation 18B she had left

London abruptly and gone to her mother in Oxford. Then she had written to him, sending back his ring, postponing their wedding 'for the duration', and telling him that she was joining the First Aid Nursing Yeomanry, 'FANY for short,' she had said. After that there had been no contact for a long time. None of his letters was answered, but eventually her mother wrote and told him she had gone to Canada.

An owl hooted from somewhere in the grounds quite close to his billet, and below his window he heard the boots of the Home Guard sentry crunch on the gravel. He'd thought about Petra often in the early days, though less and less as he became pressured in his post. For weeks now he had all but forgotten her until today, first during the train journey and then later when the Wren smiled at him. The owl hooted again. Odd war, his war, he thought. Front line fighting in a manner of speaking, yet fighting where the owl could hunt undisturbed, and the only hard reminders of the war being fought were the tape on the windows and the sound of the sentry walking underneath.

HOFF

Ernst Hoff had never ceased to wonder at the suddenness of dusk and dawn in the tropics. He understood the reason for the phenomena well enough, but having spent all his life in northern latitudes with slow dawns and long dusks, he never failed to be thrilled by the sudden explosion of sunlight in the tropical morning, and by the nightfall which came like the drawing of a blind.

He stood in his shirt and shorts on the verandah of the bungalow and looked out across the ocean, with the moon's reflection running across the surface. He searched the sky for the Southern Cross, and, finding it, looked again at the ocean and listened to the gentle hiss of surf on the beach. They were out there, somewhere, eleven of them, Class IXs, large boats, two hundred and fifty feet long, and at that moment Hoff imagined them to be charging across the surface of the ocean as close to their maximum speed of seventeen knots as their diesels would allow. During the daylight they would submerge and travel at a sedate seven knots on the electric motors. They had come from Hamburg via the Cape of Good Hope to pick up a cargo of latex and he would return on one of them, his job as naval liaison officer completed.

Hoff took his pipe from his pocket and filled it with a British tobacco called Player's Navy Cut, which had been given to him by his Japanese hosts. It was harsh to his taste, but he was nevertheless grateful for the gift. He took a taper from the holder which stood on the verandah table and lit it with the flame in the Tilly lamp. The U-boats had been expected that day. They might arrive tomorrow, or perhaps the day after. Insects danced crazily around the lamp.

He turned and glanced through the window, really just a hole in the side of the bungalow with shutters on either side. The woman they had given him was sitting in the rattan chair filing her nails. She was dark-haired, large-breasted, and had a slim waist. Once she might have been pretty, but the years had taken their toll, the years and the poor diet, for even when allowed full Japanese rations, Europeans become drawn and wasted. Hoff crossed the verandah to the chair, sat and again looked out to sea, pulling on his pipe. Presently the woman joined him on the verandah. She knelt beside the chair, leaning on the arm, and allowed her robe to fall open revealing the fullness of her breasts. He knew she was enticing him, doing her job as she saw it, but he would not go with her again. He had been lucky, very lucky. The Japanese doctor had been able to spare a little of the captured penicillin, but what he had spared seemed to have worked as the awful burning in his groin had slowly faded.

'My favourite part of the day, this,' said the woman. 'Cool after all that heat.'

'Sure is,' said Hoff reluctant to encourage conversation, but he had lived with the woman for six months and knew her well enough to know that she wanted intercourse; social if she couldn't have sexual.

'Tickles me how you talk like a Yank,' she said.

'That's where I learned my English,' he replied. 'At the American University of Cornell. They have very strange universities in America. They take themselves so seriously.'

'Do they?' she said, urging him on. Talk, talk, let's talk.

'If you are a freshman you must wear a badge to show your status.'

'Go on?' faking surprise.

But she has heard this so often before, Hoff thought. 'Yes, and freshmen cannot walk in certain parts of the grounds and they cannot date girls of the university. It is a very strange community, with formal rules for relaxation as well as work and study. There is a university in the Netherlands where students may slap the face of any student who is in the year immediately below them, but even they know how to relax. American students do not seem to me to be able to relax, they are made to feel too self-conscious. Mind you, they are more civilized than the German students who form duelling societies and scar each other with rapiers.'

'Poor things.' Not really understanding.

Hoff thought her pathetic. Once she had told him her lifestory. From the age of fourteen she had survived by letting men treat her like horseflesh, and now there was little future for her because the cruellest of diseases was eating her away from the inside.

'They do not know of any other way,' he said. 'Many are privileged and don't realize how well off they are compared to other Americans. I am still surprised when I think of students owning Cords and Lincolns.'

'I never 'ad a mbtor,' she said. 'Been in them lots of times. Did it – you know, it – the first time in the back of a car. He was a fat salesman from Dartford and 'e give us a threepenny bit. Well, that was me on me way. Did you like America?'

'No. I was not popular in the university. It is very important to be popular in America,' replied Hoff, still trying to grapple with the image of a fat salesman and a fourteen-year-old girl fumbling and groping in the back of a car. 'I was what the other students called "a grind", meaning I worked too hard. I was not a "good sport". A good sport is I think an English expression which was adopted at Cornell. A good sport dresses well, he is popular among his fellows, he is good at sporting events, but especially he is good at track.'

'Track?'

'Athletics.'

'Oh yeah,' she said, 'we done 'fletics at school. Some lines painted on the yard. We called them tramlines, but it was really the 'fletic track.'

'I was not good at track or any sport for that matter.' He patted his stomach. '*Mein Bauch*. It was even larger in those days. Besides, I was too keen on my studies. As well as "a grind" I was called "a grub". Sometimes a "wet smack".'

'Wet smack,' she sniggered. 'I like that.'

93

'Well, I learned the Japanese language. That was the reason I went to the United States, so I am satisfied.' He leaned forward and tapped ash from his pipe into an ashtray which stood on the verandah rail.

'And that's why you come to Malaya,' she said, ''cos you can savvy the lingo?'

'Sorry?'

'I mean because you understand the Jap language.'

'Yes.'

'You know, you're the best thing that's happened to me since the fall of Singapore. After Singapore fell I was tossed from one Nip to the next. First it was just the officers, then it was the rest. Even so, it was better than bein' in the camp wiv' all them la-di-da bitches. Then they sent me here. It's been like livin' proper and you don't seem to want ... I mean, beggin' your pardon, like, you don't work me hard at all, just keeping house really ...'

Which, thought Hoff, is exactly why I kept you. You are preferable to a native woman, your presence, even yours, Paddington Daisy, could soften a house for another European more effectively than that of a Malay *Untermensch*.

'You'll be going soon?'

'Yes, perhaps even tomorrow.'

'To Germany?'

'Eventually. To Hamburg.'

'That's where you came from, is it, 'Amburg?'

'No, I am a Berliner.' There was pride in his voice. 'We are not especially high born, but the Hoffs of Berlin are an established family.'

'Never been abroad, well, not till I came here. I got some stokers to smuggle me on ship, work my passage, you know.'

'Really?' He was genuinely surprised. 'Is that what you did?'

'Yes. I wanted to get to 'Stralia. I talked to a 'Stralian in a pub in King's Cross. Told me you could walk into the outback and just pick up lumps of gold as big as your fist. I nearly made it too, but I was discovered on the ship and they put me ashore at

Singapore. I was savin' for a passage to Darwin when the Nips arrived at the back door.'

'Ah, a stroke of tactical genius,' said Hoff, poking the charred tobacco in his pipe bowl.

'We let the bastards walk in. We outnumbered them three to one and we were defending. They didn't come from the direction they were expected, so what did we do? I'll tell you what we did. As soon as they knocked on the back door instead of coming from the sea, we dropped the bloody flag.'

'It's the new order,' said Hoff. 'The Axis powers will soon meet each other. A bond of military might stretching from Europe to Asia controlled by Japan and Germany.'

'You a Nazi?'

'Yes,' he said, surprised by her familiarity.

'Will a Nazi be taking your place?'

'No. No one will be taking my place. My usefulness here is finished. I shall be returning to Germany with the U-boats.'

'What will happen to me?'

You, thought Hoff, will probably be shot by the next Japanese who sleeps with you when he discovers your illness. Either that or they will return you to the women's camp, where you will eventually go mad as the disease attacks your brain. But he said, 'I don't know. It is not a matter for my voice or authority.'

'No,' she said. 'No, suppose it's not.'

They came three days later, six huge Class IX U-boats, five of the original eleven, Hoff discovered later, having been sunk by enemy action at intervals during the voyage. The submarines turned into the bay in line ahead formation behind a Japanese escort vessel, and tied up in two rafts of three at the small jetty. They were immediately refuelled and the cargo taken aboard. Hoff and the Japanese officers entertained the German officers in the camp commander's bungalow, and half way through the reception Hoff excused himself and walked down to the jetty.

He had never before been so close to large numbers of the Allied prisoners, walking skeletons who laboured two at a time to carry the phials of latex, wolfram, and opium, down the jetty and on to the submarines. Many were unsteady on their feet as they walked back up the jetty having rid themselves of their burden. He smelt for the first time the halitosis, the stench of unwashed bodies, the smell of stale urine and excrement, the smell of the open sores. But beyond that was a smell he had experienced only once before when he visited a relative in hospital for the incurables which lay deep in the country far away from Berlin. He felt embarrassed at his starched white uniform, for these Europeans were skin and bone in loincloths. Hoff noted how distressed the German sailors were to see the condition of the Allied prisoners, and was pleased to see that they stood apart, refusing to fraternize with the Japanese guards. He knew that on the homeward journey he would be asked by the sailors what was meant by Aryan Supremacy, when Germany was allied to a race of *Untermenschen* which treated Aryans in such a manner. He would have no answer for them.

The next day, on the first of the ebb, Hoff stood on the 'conservatory' behind the conning-tower of U-195 and rested his hands on the barrel of the 37mm. As U-195 nudged stern first into the Straits of Malacca, Hoff looked at the wide sweep of the bay which lay just along the coast, north of Penang, and which had been his posting as liaison officer for Operation Monsoon. To Hoff's mind, it had always been indefensibly uneconomic. The purpose of his stay had been concluded rapidly with the arrival of the U-boats and had brought with it an anti-climactic feeling. He looked at the huts, the prisoners' compound, the thin strip of beach with the jungle behind, and at Paddington Daisy standing on the verandah of the bungalow, frantically waving a white handkerchief.

On his return to Germany in September 1943, Hoff was posted to the naval attaché in Berlin. It was an enjoyable posting, hê was able to visit his family and could fish the stream which ran behind his mother's cottage which lay beyond the eastern suburbs of the city. In Berlin, he was also able to correspond speedily with his brother who was serving with the Wehrmacht in Norway.

In mid-1944, he too was posted in the Wehrmacht.

'It's not a bad posting,' said the Hauptsturmführer. 'There are worse. I have known whole ships' companies quickly changed into an infantry unit and marched to the east. You at least stay in German-occupied territory, if not in the Fatherland itself.'

'But this,' Hoff pleaded. 'I am not a fighting man, I will be discovered.'

'We are all going to be fighting men sooner or later,' said the Hauptsturmführer. 'And if they do discover you, then they will cut your throat. It happens from time to time. That's why we give you two weeks in each camp.'

'But I have no experience, no direct contact with the enemy, except once in Malaya, some European prisoners . . .'

'Then you have had a lucky war,' said the officer drily. Hoff had noticed the man seemed pale and emaciated, probably from a stomach wound. He did not pursue his protest.

'So I have two weeks in each camp.'

'Yes. It should be easier for you because you have at least lived in the United States.'

'For three years, yes, but that was before the war.'

'That is more experience than your predecessors had. Some could barely string together a coherent sentence in English.'

'And they were detected?'

'Oh yes, you all are in time. A careless word, a phrase uttered in anger, anything might give you away. Nobody can keep up any deception forever, but you should fare better than others.'

'What is the average life expectancy?' asked Hoff.

'I don't think anybody has bothered to work it out,' replied the officer. 'I should think about six months, or about twelve camps. Those who survive to reach their tenth camp are doing well indeed.'

'Six months,' echoed Hoff.

'We will provide you with the uniform of a Lieutenant in the American Navy. There are not many North American seamen in the camps, so you should enjoy a latitude not possessed by your predecessors, who impersonated Allied soldiers or airmen.

97

Your ship was torpedoed off Iceland two months ago, it was an escort vessel, the USS *Digby*.'

'What if I should meet another man from the ship, I mean, what if there is –'

The Hauptsturmführer held up his hand. 'There were no survivors,' he said with a marked degree of impatience. 'But be assured the vessel did exist, the U-boat captain noted the number painted on her bows. We will furnish you with details of the American naval procedure, principal ports of the east coast, the name of your Naval Academy – we have located an obscure one in Florida – and your service history. Your personal history you make up for yourself, but do draw heavily on your three years in the United States. You have until tomorrow to learn it all. Your transport to the first camp will pick you up at 0600.'

'You have given me little time to prepare,' stammered Hoff. 'I am unused to such haste.'

'Time,' said the Hauptsturmführer, 'is something that Germany does not have a great deal of. Time is something we cannot give you, so please remember the penalties for not being diligent in the assumption of your new identity.'

Hoff stood, preparatory to leaving.

'Please,' said the officer, who remained seated. 'Please do not see your new rôle as unimportant. Prisoners of war have become a great asset to Germany, our possession of them may be vital in peace negotiations. They must be contained. That is all.'

Hoff's first camp was in eastern Germany. He arrived with a group of five other prisoners, all British Army officers, swaying in the rear of an open truck. They had driven through the night with Hoff huddled against the rear of the cab, mulling over the character he had decided to play, quiet, but friendly when spoken with. He feigned sleep for most of the journey and listened to the talk of the British officers. He was gratified to hear that they were preoccupied with escape. It seemed that it was going to be easy to eavesdrop on escape plans and he felt he could survive easily enough by being the fat Yank sailor, friendly in a quiet sort of way. It might even be fun. The conversation had died as the night dragged on, with the British officers ending up sitting as close as they could to each other, their hands plunged into their battledress pockets and their collars turned up, nodding their heads in fitful sleep. The two guards in the rear of the vehicle remained constantly alert.

In a grey, still morning the lorry pulled up outside the prison camp. Two perimeters of wire, machine-gun posts at intervals, guards' quarters outside the wire, long wooden huts inside the wire. Hoff stepped down from the truck and looked about him. The camp seemed to be in a hollow in a valley, pine trees stretched away in every direction. It seemed an unlikely place to escape from, no town, or train, or roads, save for the narrow forest track. And it was hundreds of miles from either front. Hoff and the other five prisoners fell in beside the truck, calling out as the Wehrmacht officer read their names. The double set of gates were opened and the prisoners entered the compound. The other prisoners approached them, with an odd mixture of eagerness and caution which amused Hoff, and began to press for war news. 'Jerry's licked,' Hoff overheard. 'Huns on the run.'

A soldier with a moustache and medal ribbons on his tunic approached Hoff and, after some confusion, shook Hoff's hand with his left hand, his right arm being missing and the sleeve of his jacket folded up and fastened to the shoulder with a safety-pin.

'Ewart-Lowe,' said the soldier stiffly.

'Sorry,' said Hoff.

'The name, Ewart-Lowe. Major. East Yorks Light Infantry.'

'Oh, Hoff,' said Hoff. 'Earl Hoff.'

'Earl?'

'That's it. Lieutenant, US Navy. Pleased to meet you.'

'Oh, of course.' The soldier stiffened. 'Earl, you see, I thought perhaps . . .'

'Sure thing, Ewart,' said Hoff enthusiastically, grinning the 'good sport' grin he'd first noticed among the track types at Cornell.

'No!' snapped the soldier. 'Do try to understand, Hoff. Ewart-Lowe is my surname. Ewart is part of my surname.'

'Oh,' said Hoff. 'Sure do apologize.' He continued to grin. 'You have one of these ...' He drew his finger horizontally through the air.

'Hyphens,' said Ewart-Lowe. 'That's the trouble with you Yanks, you're officers and you're not officers. I think you'd better call me Major.'

'OK, Major. But you can call me Earl.'

'Earl,' echoed the major with distaste. 'Show you round the camp?'

'Sure thing,' smiled Hoff, finding it pleasantly easy to slip into Americanisms. Cornell, the bleachers, weekending, nickel and dime stores, all came flooding back.

'Where were you captured, er, Earl?' The Major broke into a brisk stride and Hoff had to give the occasional skip to keep pace with him.

'Grand Banks,' said Hoff.

'Where?'

'Off the coast of Newfoundland. Torpedoed.'

'Oh, bad luck. Western Desert myself, dammit. How did they get you back here?'

'The U-boat picked me up. Later I was transferred to the depot ship they kept in mid-Atlantic which was dressed up to look like some rust-bucket Spanish freighter, the El something.'

'Scheming bastard, the Hun is, Hoff. Got to watch him. Have to get out and get that intelligence back to our side.'

'Any chance of escape?' asked Hoff, who had given up walking briskly, with the occasional skip, and was now unashamedly running beside the striding major.

'Not much,' replied the Major. 'There's a few old tunnels, but they don't go very far, rock everywhere just a few inches under the surface. No way under the wire, either over it or through it.'

'Sure got it wrapped up tight,' said Hoff.

'If the bastards hadn't, we wouldn't be here,' snarled the Englishman, suddenly stopping and leaving Hoff to run on for a few paces before turning and rejoining his guide. 'Right. Huts one to six down this side. Seven to twelve on the other. You'll be in hut twelve. Latrine over there, cookhouse and mess hall over there. Breakfast in half an hour. This is the parade ground. In hut one you'll find the SBOs.'

'SBOs?'

'Senior British Officers. You report to the SBOs with the other new boys at 1030 hours.'

'Why?'

'Just report, Hoff.' Ewart-Lowe nodded and then walked smartly away.

At 1030 Hoff reported to hut one. He was met by a stern-faced subaltern who saluted and showed him into a room in which three bulky middle-aged officers sat behind a table. There was a chair in front of the table. Hoff sat on it.

'Take a seat,' said the officer who sat in the centre. Hoff smiled awkwardly and then glanced out of the window. He saw a guard walking slowly on the far side of the wire.

'We now have to convince ourselves that you are the genuine article,' said the senior of the Senior British Officers after Hoff had given his name, rank and service number.

'Not a stool pigeon,' said a second officer.

'A what?' asked Hoff.

'A Hun,' explained the third officer.

'Like a plant to see if there's any escape attempts going on.'

'Exactly,' said the first officer.

'Questions and answers, terrific!' said Hoff, leaning forward and grinning a good sport grin.

'Oh my God,' sighed the Senior British Officer, putting his hand to his forehead.

Hoff survived the fortnight in the first camp. He kept himself to himself, but, as he planned, was amicable if approached. He spent much of his time doing freehand drawings of a warship on Red Cross parcel wrapping paper, which he titled 'USS *Digby*. Sunk by enemy action off the Grand Banks, 7.21.44,' and which he insisted on giving to the other prisoners. He thought he was accepted by the others as much as an American sailor could hope to be accepted by British soldiers; he did not feel that he was being excluded from conversations; and, most importantly, he did not feel under suspicion. The trick, he realized, lay in not asking questions, not pressing for details of escape plans. On the morning of the fourteenth day he was separated from the rest of the prisoners at the end of the morning roll-call and was driven back to Berlin, where he was able to report the camp safe from tunnelling activity and the prisoners having no immediate plans to escape by other means. As he went from camp to camp Hoff polished and embellished his act. He continued to do freehand drawings of the USS *Digby* and hand them out as tokens of friendship. It proved an aspect of his personality for other prisoners to talk about, an endearing eccentricity. Some said he was a little shell-shocked.

At the beginning of December 1944 Hoff was sent to a prison camp composed wholly of American servicemen. He was ordered simply to learn, learn American terms of phrase, and note the interests and preoccupations of American troops. Miraculously, he felt, he was able to survive the fourteen days and was able to report that most American terms of phrase were obscene, that the American troops were obsessed by the insurance value of Betty Grable's legs and who might win the next world series, while their preoccupation, he reported, lay in what they were going to do after the war. Half were going to study under the GI Bill and become hot-shot lawyers someplace. The rest intended to make their pile in war surplus.

In Berlin the Hauptsturmführer said, 'You are unhappy in this post?'

'Yes,' Hoff replied, 'if the truth be known. But I wouldn't like that to be interpreted as a complaint. I am a loyal Nazi.'

'That has never been in doubt, Hoff. In fact we have been pleased with your performance. You may have more aptitude for active service than you realized.'

'If that is true I am pleased to be of any use you may think suitable, Herr Hauptsturmführer.'

'Good, Hoff. You may be aware that all American-English-speaking Germans have been invited to volunteer their services to Standartenführer Skorzeny, one of our more dashing soldiers.'

'Certainly, Herr Hauptsturmführer, his capturing of Mussolini was the work of a military genius.'

'As was his rescuing of the Hungarian leader Admiral Horthy. Skorzeny's reputation, together with the fighting conditions of many of our troops, is such that hundreds of men have been offering their services, more than I believe Skorzeny needs.'

'Indeed, Herr Hauptsturmführer,' replied Hoff, fearing what was to come.

'I am surprised that you have not applied.'

'Why, sir, as you said Skorzeny is a soldier of such dash, why' – Hoff patted his girth – 'I am pleased to think I have been useful in this post, I am pleased to think that I may have an aptitude for direct contact with the enemy, but I am hardly the physique of a stormtrooper.'

'You may well be right, Hoff, but I would have thought that the decision was not yours. These are dark times for Germany and a gesture of enthusiasm would not have come amiss.'

'Herr Hauptsturmführer . . .'

'There is, I believe, a solution. Many of the men who have flocked unfalteringly to Skorzeny's side have only a smattering of English, though it is sufficient for the most part. Having said that, the Standartenführer wishes to have a small unit for a purpose that is not disclosed to me, which is comprised of men whose American-English is as faultless as can be managed. Men who have spent their formative years in America and who returned to Germany at the outbreak of war, for example.'

'I was there for just three years, Herr Hauptsturmführer.'

'As a student of linguistics, yes, I know. You are a gifted linguist and your command of American-English is sufficient to enable you to survive in a camp of American prisoners of war. Your information about turns of phrase and preoccupations has been well received by Standartenführer Skorzeny, who used it to good effect in the training of his group, the 150th Panzer. Standartenführer Skorzeny needs a man who can speak faultless American-English and who is well versed in the previously mentioned preoccupations of American troops. I have been asked to locate such a man who I understand is a last-minute replacement. I take it you volunteer readily.'

'Herr Hauptsturmführer . . .'

'Good. You leave this afternoon. Here are your orders and travel warrant. Report to Standartenführer Skorzeny at Friedenthal by 1300 tomorrow.'

It was at Friedenthal that Ernst Hoff met Schweitzer and Genscher.

Chapter Four

Sooner or later, Conner knew, he'd reach the American lines. The road was narrow, snow-covered, the snow indented with ruts left by the half-track. On either side of the road the pine trees grew thickly. Over all a thick fog hung like a shroud, stubbornly refusing to shift. Frequently rockets would fly overhead in low salvoes, each making a distinctive woosh-woosh-woosh sound. They flew from his left to his right so he assumed that he was walking in a southerly direction, maybe south-east, towards the town called Bastogne. And on the road, somewhere ahead, was an outfit in a half-track shooting up their own kind.

The cold gripped him mercilessly. He still clenched the glove between his teeth to prevent the air from frosting his lungs and the ungloved hand was thrust deep into the pocket of his battledress. Conner gripped the strap of his carbine and began to run at a slow but steady pace, forcing the blood to pump around his chilled body. Sooner or later he'd reach the American lines. He had to.

He managed to maintain the run for nearly an hour before faltering and resigning himself to a modest walking pace. Nevertheless, the run had achieved its aim, and Conner could feel his heart pounding harder and stronger and he could again feel his feet, ice cold, in his boots. He started to look for a suitable bivouac, even though he guessed there was another three, maybe three and a half hours to daybreak, because he wanted to avoid sleeping in the snow. He was a city kid and was unsure of himself in the country and he'd heard about guys who had gone to sleep in the snow and had just not woken up. He was searching on his left and right and seeing nothing but pine trees in the fog when he heard the unmistakable click-snap of a rifle bolt. Conner stopped, standing motionless. There was a still, heavy silence, a silence that Conner could almost hear.

'That's good,' rasped a voice which sounded like coal falling on glass. 'Stay still and drop your carbine.' The heavy voice said car*been*. Tennessee, thought Conner. He'd spent a summer in Tennessee. He let his carbine slip to the snow and turned around.

'I didn't tell you to turn around,' said the voice from the fog.

'I'm turning anyway,' replied Conner. 'Show yourself.'

'You an American?' asked the voice, which itself was as American as sweetcorn.

'Well, I'm not Chinese,' said Conner. He stooped to pick up his carbine.

'Don't touch that piece, boy.'

But Conner touched the piece, waited for a moment, and since the treeline remained silent, picked up the carbine and stood, addressing the trees. 'I don't know who you are, friend, but you'd better be at least a captain if you're going to call me "boy", boy.'

There was a second spell of silence. Conner heard somebody whispering, the sound of crunching snow, and then the trees parted at two points, one to his left the other to his right. Two GIs emerged, advancing on Conner, rifles levelled. One was a well-built sergeant who eyed Conner coldly. There was a sudden movement behind him. Conner turned and three more guys stepped from the trees and into the road. They stood in a circle around him, the track stretching away in either direction, the trees on either side and the fog above them.

'Nobody teach you to salute when you approach an officer?' Conner snarled at the men, turning as he did so.

'Just don't seem to be certain who's who any more,' said the big sergeant and then added, 'sir.'

'Who are you?'

'Oh, we know who we are all right,' replied the sergeant. 'We'd just like to know who you are, sir.'

'What the hell, Sergeant,' snapped Conner. 'In case you hadn't noticed, I happen to be the officer around here ...'

'Sure sounds American,' said one of the GIs as the group began to relax their hold on their rifles.

'That's because I am an American,' Conner retorted angrily. 'Who else would I be?'

'Kraut.' The sergeant spat chewing tobacco into the snow.

'Kraut!'

'Kraut,' repeated the big sergeant, shifting his weight from one leg to the other but keeping his rifle pointing unwaveringly at Conner. 'Sir, krauts are operating men in American uniforms.' Conner had the impression that the sergeant was playing it out for as long as he could, he was top snake until Conner proved his I/D. Conner reckoned the sergeant had about five seconds to the big step-down, but he was shaken by what the sergeant had said. 'I think I already met some,' replied Conner.

'How come they let you go?' The big sergeant was aggressive, accusatory.

'I got into the undergrowth. Second time they didn't know I was there.'

'Second time?'

'Second time,' said Conner. 'I saw them shoot up a jeep.'

'You did nothing – sir?' the sergeant growled. 'Too far away, I guess?'

'No.' Conner remained calm. 'I was right on top of them.'

'Listen, sir,' said the sergeant. 'Just who are you? Where do you come from, sir?'

'Conner's the name, David Conner. I come from Brooklyn.'

'Outfit?'

'106th Infantry. The Golden Lions.'

'That's a new one on me.'

'We've just come up the line. We've been here four, maybe five days.'

'Right into a war.'

'That was the idea,' replied Conner. 'But I expected to be chasing krauts, not the other way around.'

'I don't know nothing about Brooklyn,' said the sergeant suddenly. 'That's in Washington DC. Right?'

'It's part of New York City, New York. Stop playing games, Sergeant. You want to know if I'm an American.' Conner bent slightly and put his hand into the pocket of his leggings and pulled out a fistful of dog-tags. The sergeant's jaw dropped a little. 'Every one a dead man, as well you know, Sergeant. Two from the jeep I saw shot up earlier tonight, the rest are from my platoon. That good enough?'

'I guess . . .' The sergeant lowered the muzzle of his rifle.

'So who are you?' Conner pushed the dog-tags back into his pocket.

'Baumgardner, sir. Sergeant. Fourth Infantry Division, sir.'

'So prove to me that you're an American.'

Baumgardner's hand went up to the collar of his battledress. He tugged it open and pulled out his dog-tags. 'Well, I got these.'

'And what else?' Conner knew that if the sergeant and the others were German he'd be a heap of butcher's meat, but he seized the opportunity to enforce his authority.

'A letter from home, sir.'

'Where's home?'

'Tennessee, sir.' Baumgardner replied in his homely, utterly authentic accent.

'Next state to Louisiana, right?' said Conner.

Baumgardner hesitated and looked uncomfortable. Behind him Conner heard one GI snigger and another said, 'Old Baumgardner, he don't even . . .'

'OK,' snapped Conner. 'I guess we're all OK.' He shouldered his carbine. 'I got shot up a couple of days ago, came round to find half my platoon gone and the other half dead. So what's your story?'

Around him Conner could sense the GIs relaxing and he saw safety-catches being eased on. The men began to shoulder their carbines and drew closer into a tighter group. One guy took out a pack of Chesterfields and offered them first to Conner, who accepted a cigarette, then he passed the pack round. Then he

108

went from man to man with a Zippo lighter, cupping the flame with his hand.

'Night patrol,' said the sergeant.

'Sir.'

'Night patrol, sir,' repeated the sergeant. 'Came round a corner, road was full of krauts, opened up with spandaus, they're real pisscutters. Lost our officer and half a dozen guys. Wandered around. Got lost in the fog. Came across two guys from the Engineers who were running around the trees like a couple of silly squirrels. Took our number up to twenty-two. Finally got through to our HQ.'

'That is where?'

'Was St Vith. Christ knows where it is now.'

'OK.'

'HQ couldn't tell us what was happening, but they gave us an alert about krauts in American uniforms infiltrating our lines. Couldn't tell us any more.'

'Do you still have the radio?'

Sergeant Baumgardner shook his head. 'Not since yesterday. Came up against a bunch of krauts, mean, mean krauts, fighting like demons. SS I reckon. Turned 81 millimetre mortars on us; they're big, but big. Radio operator had his legs blown away and the rest of him filled up with shrapnel. Radio wasn't much good after that. Christ, I wasn't but a hop 'n' a skip away from him and I didn't even get scratched. Somebody was smiling on me then.' Baumgardner paused, suddenly deep in thought.

'What then?' Conner brought him back to reality.

'We were pinned down and the krauts poured shit on us from every direction. Took our numbers down some, a few of us slipped away. Just what you see here.'

'All Fourth Infantry?'

'Yes, sir. Those two Engineers were blown away.'

'Where are you making for?'

'Well . . .' Baumgardner faltered. 'I guess we don't know. We don't know what's happening. We don't know exactly where we're at . . . I guess we were hoping to make contact with our kind . . .'

'Well, you've made contact with at least one of your kind, Sergeant. I was heading south to Bastogne.'

'Yeah, there's a garrison there,' said one of the GIs. 'I was talking with this guy . . .'

'It's down the road this way?' said Baumgardner.

'Certainly is,' nodded Conner. 'It's not all that's down there. There's a half-track down there, krauts in American uniforms with American equipment. It was them that I saw shoot up the jeep.'

'No kiddin'?'

'See these tracks? I reckon they were made by the selfsame half-track.'

'I see them.' Baumgardner nodded. 'Would this half-track of yours have come past here maybe three hours ago?'

''Bout that. Maybe less.'

'I reckon we heard it. We were down in the valley. You can't see it through the fog, but these trees are only a hundred yards deep, the ground falls away after that into some kind of gully. We were in there scrambling around in the rocks when we heard a tracked vehicle. That's how we figured there was a road up here.'

'That sounds like my half-track,' said Conner.

'OK, boys.' Baumgardner raised his voice. 'Let's get down there and blow away a half-track.' He turned and began to walk away.

'Sergeant!' Conner stood motionless. 'Aren't you forgetting who's in charge here?'

'Sorry, sir. I guess I was used to . . .'

'Well, get unused to it,' Conner said icily. Then, 'OK, boys, let's get down there and blow away a half-track.'

Baumgardner smiled. Conner thought he was about forty years of age; old for a GI on active service.

You've always got a weapon. A pen, a spoon, a box of matches. There's always something you can use, something on your person, something in the room, always, always, there is something you can use. When you use it, go for his face, particularly his eyes. A blow to the face is more dispiriting than a blow to any other part of the body, and an attack on the eyes is more disabling than an attack on any other organ.

She had picked her way through the rubble in the side street and, as she turned into the Chausseestrasse, she heard a car start behind her. It began to crawl along the kerb and she had to fight to prevent herself breaking into a run. She remembered the things she had been taught in Camp X all those years ago, an age ago, and her fingers coiled around a pen she kept in her coat pocket. The car followed her for a hundred metres and then accelerated past her, turning into Invalidenstrasse with a squeal of tyres. It was a black Mercedes saloon, with two men in the front seats.

She felt more alone, more vulnerable, after seeing the car than she did when the man in the tenement apartment had told her he was leaving if she was insisting on such foolhardiness. She had said she was insisting; he had said, well, there's the transmitter, damn you. Then he had left the house, to travel north and to await the arrival of the Russians, just as he had planned, except that he was leaving earlier and, she felt, probably more thankfully than anticipated. She did not blame him for leaving, but none the less harboured feelings of being deserted and betrayed. She now had no cover, no family friend who was wounded in the last war, no reason to visit this part of the city, just to the north of the centre, and more important, no deft skilled hands to tap out the Morse messages. Instead she had to use her own, clumsy and slow after so many years away from the Morse key.

Her war had been one of constant nagging fear, worry and trepidation. Now, for the first time, and in what was evidently the war's final months, she felt intense and immediate fear for her own life.

The narrow room was silent. It was not an unpleasant silence, but a peaceful quiet as each man immersed himself in his thoughts. It was the only way to cope with the waiting.

Schweitzer, who would not allow himself to sit too close to the stove, nor permit himself to lie on his bunk except during the night, sat stiffly at the table. He smoked a cigarette and dreamed of glory. He dreamed that if he returned to Germany he would continue to serve with deeds of even greater daring. But he had another dream, a dream which inspired him, a dream of dying for Germany. A dream in which the SS Generals and, yes, even the Führer himself, would gather at his graveside and reflect on the great soldier he had been and what glory he might have brought to the Reich had he not made the ultimate sacrifice.

Hoff sat at the other end of the room, a blanket pulled round his shoulders, holding his hands in front of the stove. He too sat and thought and dreamed. He thought of home, the countryside just to the east of Berlin; he thought of his brother in Norway, enduring the harsh winter but relishing the fishing in the summer. He dreamed of the life he would lead after the war; perhaps a teaching post in a university? Hoff felt uneasy with Schweitzer and Genscher, both men of action, men who had killed, often while he had never fired a gun in anger until that day they were stopped by the American Military Police.

He rubbed his hands together. Why had he been selected to volunteer, even as a last-minute substitute, for this lunatic escapade, the details of which he still did not know? The other two, lean and cruel, yes, he could see why they had been selected for reasons other than that they could speak American-English. But he, overweight, a linguist and administrator, what had he to offer? Surely it had been a mistake? He should have told them about his disease, the terrible burning in his groin which having returned, never abated. He considered the possibility of their succeeding in carrying out their orders; slim, he thought. He considered the possibility of their returning to Germany; that seemed infinitely remote. Hoff wondered what he should do, but there seemed to be no solution. He hunched forward a little, rubbed his hands again and tried to forget the furnace blazing in his groin which he knew was to lead to the most terrible of deaths; a rotting mind in a rotting body.

Genscher lay on his bunk. He smiled a gentle, barely perceptible smile which warmed his entire body. For some months Genscher had been convinced that his future and the future of Germany had to follow separate paths. Germany was defeated, that was plain. It was also plain to Genscher that not only would Germany lose the war, but that she would be beaten down and crushed, and that, before the end, many thousands of Germans would die. He knew he had to escape but there seemed to be no opportunity. When he looked forward to plan his future he saw nothing but blackness. But now, lying on his bunk, the blackness suddenly began to disappear, as if a dinner plate that had been held in front of his eyes for so long suddenly broke, and beyond the shards there flooded a vivid stream of light. Genscher smiled smugly, and began to plan.

Chapter Five

Paris, December 18, 1944. The first Christmas after the liberation was approaching and the city enjoyed a euphoria, tinged with sadness at the continuing war.

Floyd turned the jeep down the Rue Merlan and pulled up outside the headquarters of the Military Police. He wasn't feeling particularly well disposed to Christmas or towards the thought of good will to all men and peace on earth or any other idealized crap that gets taken from the shelf and dusted down each year, put in the window and forgotten about come January 6. He burst open the door of the duty room.

'Any blond-haired guys in the cells?' he said.

'Sir?' The sergeant stood and saluted. He was a large man like all MPs and, like all MPs, was turned out to perfection with highly polished buttons, knife-edged creases, brilliantly polished boots. 'Sir, blond, sir?'

'Blond, Sergeant,' said Floyd, walking past the desk and into his office.

'Don't rightly know, sir,' called the sergeant after him. 'The cells were cleared out this morning.'

'What?' Floyd reappeared at the door of his office, and then he relaxed. 'Oh yes, the order came through last night.'

'That's right, sir. All combatants to be liberated and moved up the line. There's some big fight up around the Ardennes. I heard the krauts are breaking out all over the place.'

'Sure looks that way. So who do we have left?'

'In the cells?'

'Where else?' said Floyd in a don't-try-my-patience voice.

'Just the top category prisoners, sir. Murderers and deserters.'

'We haven't arrested anyone for crimes like that in two weeks, have we?'

'Nearer three, sir.'

'You mean you can't make my Christmas by telling me you arrested a blond-haired GI who confessed to murdering a Military Policeman?'

'Afraid not, sir. Is that what happened?'

'Murdered by GIs, yes. We have a witness, not a good witness, but enough to put us on the scent. Some kid was watching from the field while our guys were gunned down and pushed into a ditch. They drove off in a jeep in the direction of Paris. Three men, one of 'em blond.'

'So they're here in the city?'

'We have to assume so, though of course they could be anywhere from here to the Spanish border. We'll have to start checking I/Ds and leave passes for all GIs still in Paris.'

'What are we looking for, sir?'

'Irregularities. Hell, anything.'

'It's a big job, sir. We don't have the resources and, even with the order for all combatants to move up the line, there are still thousands of guys in Paris, guys stationed here, guys in transit, recuperation cases . . .'

'All right, Sergeant.' Floyd held up his hand. He felt weary, but the sergeant was right, of course; it would be like looking for a needle in a haystack. 'I guess maybe we do need more to go on.'

'Blond-haired GI in Paris, sir, be like . . .'

'Looking for a needle in a haystack, don't tell me Sergeant.'

By dawn on the 19th the fog had changed from grey to paper-white. It was virtually a total whiteout, except that the lower trunks of the pine trees, which had escaped being covered with snow, were still visible, like rows of black stumps in a white cloud. Closer to them they could see their boots, they could see the marks in the snow left by the half-track. And they could hear. Conner heard his boots crunching the ice, and he could hear the wheezing of a bronchial chest behind him and guessed it belonged to Baumgardner. He also heard snatches of whispered conversation between two other guys which seemed to consist of one guy mouthing off with vociferous hatred about some 'smart-assed prick', with the other guy occasionally telling him 'not to get sore'. Then Conner heard the sound of a petrol engine. He held up his hand and crouched low. The other GIs did the same. Baumgardner eased up alongside him.

'I hear it,' said the elderly sergeant, taking a scarf from his mouth.

Conner took the glove from his mouth and felt the chill air penetrate his lungs. 'I reckon it's the half-track,' he said.

'Reckon it could be,' said Baumgardner.

Baumgardner's chest sounded OK. Conner turned and saw that the bad chest belonged to a lean-faced youth with bulging eyes and a pointed jaw. He asked, 'Who's the guy with the bad chest?'

'Sweeney.'

'Sweeney ain't fit for combat duty,' said Conner.

'Sure ain't,' said Baumgardner in a manner which stated clearly that if Sweeney's chest condition was anybody's problem, it wasn't one for Sergeant Baumgardner. Then he added, 'Sir.'

'How far ahead?' asked Conner.

Baumgardner made a clicking noise with his tongue and after some deliberation said, 'Hard to say, sir.'

'That's a real useful piece of advice, Sergeant.'

'Yep,' said Baumgardner.

'See, I figure we have a visibility of about twenty-five feet,' whispered Conner.

'Forty-five.' Baumgardner spat chewing-tobacco-stained phlegm into the snow. The brown eased delicately into the white. 'In these conditions you've always got more visibility than you think you have. But you're right, sir. We don't have a whole lot.'

'So when we see the half-track we're only forty-five feet away?'

'Right,' said Baumgardner.

'And committed?'

'Right.'

'So how are we to tell that they haven't met up with more krauts and there's maybe sixty or seventy instead of six or seven?'

'We ain't to tell, sir,' replied Baumgardner in a deadpan voice.

'And how are we to tell they're not our guys?'

'We ain't to tell.'

'Christ!'

'Yep,' said Baumgardner. 'Christ is about it.'

Conner began to edge forward by the side of the road, just on the lip of the treeline. Baumgardner let Conner get about ten feet ahead and then he too began to shuffle forward. Conner moved forward for a full minute, then paused, his eyes searching the mist in the general direction of the sound of the engine. He could make out nothing, nothing but dark tree-trunks at the base of the trees, and the ground near at hand. He glanced behind him and saw the hunched figures of the other guys, obediently following the white stripe on the back of Conner's helmet, trustingly awaiting the decision of the man who was permitted to carry a pistol as well as a carbine. Conner edged further forward. Suddenly it seemed to loom at him out of the mist, a half-track, olive green with a white star on the bonnet. He dropped flat and heard the other guys doing the same. He worked his way backwards until the vehicle had almost disappeared from sight. Conner was puzzled that the half-track was facing towards him, in the opposite direction to which he had anticipated. It seemed to be parked partly off the road, and on a remote stretch of forest track at that, not as before at a junction of tracks. Conner could smell the petrol and hot oil fumes which could not escape the mist and over the smell of the fumes he sensed the rich aroma of coffee being brewed. There were two or three figures moving about the vehicle and one in the cab, sitting under the machine-gun. One of the men by the vehicle was leaning against the front fender and playing 'Dirty Gertie from Bizertie' on a harmonica.

'Convincing bastards,' said Baumgardner who had edged up and sunk down beside Conner.

'Uh-huh,' grunted Conner.

'They've shed a track,' Baumgardner said.

'So they have,' said Conner. 'I thought it was leaning up on one side because it was partly off the road.'

'It is, sir,' said Baumgardner matter-of-factly. 'It's leaning up on the bank and has lost a track. It probably ran up the bank when it lost a track, sir.'

'Why'd they turn around?' Conner desperately tried to move the conversation on.

'Maybe they were returning to their own kind.'

'Gotta be it,' said Conner. 'Getting back to Nazi lines while they're still alive. Murdering bastards.'

'How do you want to handle this, sir?'

Conner thought. Then he said, 'OK. Couple of guys to drop backaways and cross the road to come up on the other side, opposite the half-track. One guy to work forward with a grenade for the driver's cab. One guy to go with him. You and me will work forward from here. Leave the guy with the bad chest, Sweeney, leave him here to cover the back door.'

Baumgardner turned and Conner was aware of the elderly sergeant rapidly but silently moving his arms. When Conner turned, only Baumgardner and Sweeney were still with him. Conner looked at the sergeant with wide-eyed wonderment.

'Been in the field since D-day, sir,' said Baumgardner by way of explanation. 'More or less.'

'Ah,' Conner nodded.

'We need give them five minutes, sir,' continued Baumgardner. 'After that they'll fire when you do.'

Conner belly-crawled nearer the half-track and eased the safety-catch from his carbine. He rested the sights on the side of the head of the man who was playing the harmonica and waited, steadying his breathing until he heard Baumgardner whisper, 'Any time you like, sir.'

The carbine kicked back against Conner's shoulder and he saw the man he had killed lying motionless in the snow a few feet from where he had been standing. There was an instant clatter of small-arms fire as sharp, lurid jets of flame penetrated the fog opposite the half-track. Two more men fell as the bullets kicked up little spouts of snow or ricocheted off the armour plate. The driver reached up for the machine-gun just as Conner saw a small dark object fall in a graceful arc into the cab. There was a dull metallic echo as the grenade exploded, then all was silent.

Conner waited, watching for a full five minutes before edging forward. He stood slowly, and emerged from the canopy of trees and walked towards the dead men. Baumgardner followed him and two guys came out of the fog on the opposite side of the road to the half-track. Conner saw a movement behind the vehicle and raised his gun.

'Easy,' hissed Baumgardner. 'They're our guys.'

They approached the half-track. As far as Conner could make out there were four guys, three on the road and the guy in the cab who looked like he'd been through a meat-grinder. And the smell, the cordite which couldn't escape the fog, the sickly sweet smell of blood, the smell of excrement coming, thought Conner, from any or all of the dead men as they performed their last function in life; known to Baumgardner to be coming from himself, running down both his legs, the way it always did when the shooting started.

'There should be more,' said Conner quietly.

One of the men on the ground moaned. He'd been hit badly in the legs and chest. Blood seeped from both corners of his mouth. The man stared up at Conner with a look which Conner was never to forget.

'You . . . dirty . . .' said the man, then seemed to be racked with pain and breathless.

'Jesus Christ and holy shit,' said a GI behind Conner, who started to speak to the dying man but was stopped by Baumgardner's hand falling on his shoulder. The man, a young GI barely out of his teens, tried to say something, but choked and lay still.

Conner felt weak at the knees. He turned to Baumgardner angrily. 'Why didn't you let me say something, for Christ's sake?'

'Like what – sir? Sorry, buddy, my mistake? Something like that, you mean?'

'We could've taken a request, maybe a last message.'

'Best this way, sir. I reckon he thought we were krauts just like we thought they were krauts. Bad enough looking the reaper in the face, worse if the last thing you're told was that it was a case of mistaken identity.' Baumgardner glanced at the dead men. 'I mean, how'd you like to die knowing you were the victim of a mistake?'

'I guess,' said Conner, feeling frail and faint.

'Tracks!' One of the GIs pointed to the ground. Clearly visible were the marks left by another tracked vehicle which seemed to have skirted around the first.

'They must have passed and left them at it,' said Baumgardner. 'It would have been the normal thing to do if those guys were waiting for a recovery vehicle.'

Conner made twenty feet back down the road before throwing up.

Petra Oelkers sat in the air raid shelter. It was cramped, and, despite the bitter December chill on the streets above, it was hot and airless with too many bodies in too small a space. Most were women; there was the occasional tired old man and hungry child. There were a few whispered conversations; an infant crying. She looked at their faces, the lost, hopeless expressions, the sunken cheeks, the faces of exhausted people with an uncertain fate. A single lightbulb hung from the ceiling, throwing shadows across the Berliners sitting on the benches. Somebody moved, somebody cursed, another tried to sing. This was the worst time, the time between the sirens and the first bombs, the waiting time, and the tension in the shelter could not be overcome.

She turned her thoughts to the mystery of the operation called Grief. It was by now common knowledge that the Reich was advancing its land forces for the first time since 1943 and the *Völkischer Beobachter* was claiming great victories against the Americans and reporting vividly how the enemy front was crumbling before massed Panzer divisions. The news was received with mixed feelings by the cynical and war-hardened Berliners; it was good to take the initiative again, but could it be anything more than a last desperate attempt to stave off the inevitable?

Nowhere, though, had there been mention of the Gryphon, which in some form, for some reason, had somewhere been unleashed against the Allies.

Petra wondered whether the old man had been right, whether she ought to forget about the war, the Gryphon, the battle in the Ardennes, and make her way west, to the safe house. To wait until the Allies arrive and, as the old man said, 'emerge into a free world'. He had left urging her to go westward and reinforcing his warning that he was sure he was being watched.

Petra thought him wrong, but the car following her as she walked along the street that evening had planted a nagging doubt in her mind. She tried to rationalize it. Wasn't that how Heinrich had said the Nazis worked, relying on fear? Sensitive Heinrich, a gentle, cultured man who had been caught up in the false ideology of pre-war Germany and was now trapped in a uniform he hated, with his outpourings directed against Fascism and Nazism – often with the help of a little schnapps. Heinrich had once explained to her how the Nazis kept all Europe under their control just by the use of fear and the unexplained, directed even against the German people. He was right: she had seen how the Nacht and Nebel decree had kept the Germans in a state of fear of the Nazis; she had seen relatives left in a permanent state of anxiety after one of their family had disappeared and had officially been recorded as banished into the night and fog – '*Rückkehr Unerwünscht*. Return not required.' It was how they held down the concentration camps. 'Do you think,' Heinrich had said, after returning to Berlin from a visit to a camp, shaken and utterly revolted, 'do you think we could control 50,000 normal intelligent people with a handful of low-grade SS troops without suggesting to them that there is an informer in every hut?' She remembered him rocking backwards and forwards in the living-room of his flat, bottle in one hand, glass in the other. 'Make them suspicious of each other, divide them against themselves, and they won't unite against the Reich. My God, Germany will one day pay for this.'

She knew now that the technique was very effective; all the car had done was to follow her for a short while, but it had been enough to put her on edge, to frighten her, to sow that awful seed of doubt.

Operation Gryphon: she tried to recall what it was that Heinrich had said that day: 'The claws of the Gryphon are in Paris.' What was a Gryphon? A mythical winged creature. What were its claws? Men, germs, gas? How many claws were there? One, one hundred? Why Paris, why not London, Moscow, Washington? What is at Paris, who is at Paris?

Suddenly the bombs began to fall, very close, the shelter became hushed, the tremors from the explosions caused people's feet to dance on the floor. There was a prolonged rumble which the war-weary and experienced Berliners in the shelter recognized as the sound of yet another fine building folding in on itself, the first of many buildings which would be destroyed that night.

The RAF had gone by 4.00 a.m., but the people remained in the shelter until 8.00 a.m., until it was time to start the daily routine which kept Berlin alive. The Civil Defence needed those four hours to put out fires, stop leaking water mains, to pull down tottering buildings, to clear rubble from the main thoroughfares. Petra emerged from the shelter a little after 8.00 a.m. to a familiar scene: the air thick with grit; a furiously burning building cordoned off to allow itself to burn out; dazed, shocked people picking their way through the streets carrying useless, illogical possessions. One old woman pushed a handcart containing nothing but a mangle. Petra walked through the city towards the Bendlerstrasse. She saw that the bombing had reduced the Goethestrasse to a wilderness, and had exposed the castle-like appearance of the tower of the Malthaekirche, previously hidden by buildings. It occurred to her, as she walked amid the gaunt and the weary people, that the only way she would get information about Operation Gryphon would be to walk up to the Chancellery and ask for it.

She reached Heinrich's flat. It had suffered minor blast damage, the windows along one side had been blown in despite the shutters on the outside being closed. She swept up the dust and glass as best she could and then breakfasted on ersatz coffee and a thin slice of rye bread. She looked out across the city, the rubble, the puffs of smoke, and wondered about the future, not just the near future, whether the Russians would arrive before the Allies, but beyond that to that strange and elusive world called peacetime. She had known peacetime before. For a short period in her adult life, she had lived in a country which was not at war. There had been a young man, a graduate in mathematics. They had met in east London at a meeting of the Labour Party. She remembered with fondness their visits to art galleries, those endless cups of coffee in the milk bars. After they became engaged they had visited his parents and then they had visited hers. He was shy at first, but he had soon relaxed, her mother had liked him. Yet when her father had been interned under 18B and she had felt she had to leave London, there was suddenly nothing to say. When she joined the First Aid Nursing Yeomanry she had sent him back his ring, but she clung to his memory, this lanky, bespectacled son of a country doctor, and was glad that she had shared with him that last peacetime summer, and cherished his memory throughout the war.

By midday Heinrich had not arrived. She lunched on another meal of rye bread and ersatz coffee, though this time she allowed herself the luxury of margarine with the bread. She left the flat and walked the short distance to the slablike Chancellery building, approaching it by the rear gate. She waited while the guards lifted up the pole at the entrance to the rear courtyard to allow a staff car to enter. They then turned to her, two huge men with black uniforms and machine pistols slung on their shoulders. One of the guards said 'Yes?' in an aggressive manner. She thought him curious and a little apprehensive about the young civilian woman who had approached the very nerve-centre of the Reich.

'I have come to enquire about Hauptsturmführer Heinrich Leuger of the Reichsführer SS,' she said. 'He is stationed here at the Chancellery on night duty. He did not return home this morning. I thought, you understand, the raid last night . . .'

'You have papers?'

Petra opened her handbag and showed her identification

papers. She also handed over the letter that Heinrich had given her. This last was completely unofficial, but a letter of introduction by an aide to the Führer carried a certain weight. The guard studied the letter and handed it to the second guard. Petra saw his eyebows raise.

'We will telephone for you.' The guard returned Petra's papers and lifted a telephone which stood inside the sentrybox. He wound the handle, listened, spoke, and listened again. A car approached the Chancellery, the second guard inspected the driver's identification and then lifted the boom. As the car drove into the courtyard, the first guard left the sentry-box and approached Petra. 'Hauptsturmführer Leuger is ill.'

Petra caught her breath.

'I think it is not serious. We can let you enter to escort him home.'

'Thank you.'

'You must not proceed beyond the guard-house. That door over there.' The guard pointed across the yard to a door in the side of the Chancellery itself. 'Enter that door and wait. Someone will meet you. A car will be brought for you.'

'A car?'

'To take you home.'

'That is so kind.'

'I think it is not for kindness that a car has been ordered.'

Petra walked across the courtyard, aware of the curious gaze of people in the rooms of the building which overlooked the rear gate. She reached the guard-house without being challenged a second time and pushed open the door. It was warm inside the Chancellery, and she heard the distant but constant hum of a generator. The guard-room was small and rectangular. A bench ran the length of the room, behind which was a long desk. Beside the desk, hanging on the wall, was a keyboard. Two telephones stood on the desk. There was a second door opposite the door by which Petra had entered. The room was deserted.

Petra waited for a few seconds, hesitating as she felt the insidious worm of doubt grow inside her. So far she had reason to be where she was, but if she was to press home her advantage she had to do so without delay, before Heinrich arrived. Her heartbeat increased, her legs trembled. She began to feel immobilized and forced herself to remember what they had taught her at Camp X; keep cool, keep calm, but act. Never be inactive. She stepped towards the second door which seemed to lead from the guard-room into the very bowels of the Chancellery.

The door opened into a long corridor with whitewashed walls, illuminated by bulbs spaced at intervals on the ceiling. She glanced left and right; the corridor was empty. She turned to her right. The first door she approached was ajar but she heard the clatter of a typewriter. She stepped quickly past the door. The next door in the corridor seemed to be the office of one Karl Blomm, Sturmbannführer of the Geheime Staats Polizei. Petra paused and listened for any sound coming from behind the door. Hearing nothing, she knocked twice. There was no answer so she tried the handle. The door opened with an embarrassingly loud 'crack', as though the panelling had splintered and was catching on the door frame. She caught her breath, but the typist in the next room carried on without interruption. Petra stepped into the office and shut the door behind her.

Karl Blomm of the Gestapo had for an office a cramped boxlike room with a small desk and a small wooden filing cabinet. Behind the desk was a small-scale map of Europe with Germany enclosed by a thick red ribbon held in place by a series of drawing pins. Petra assumed that the red ribbon must indicate the German lines and noted with a pleasure tinged with apprehension that the Russian front was at least one hundred miles closer to Berlin than had been publicly admitted; in fact, according to the map, the Russians were almost on German soil. She also noticed that the pinpricks in the map extended almost as far eastwards as Moscow, as far south as Greece and North Africa, as far west as the English Channel. Karl Blomm had evidently been snipping off excess tape as the front had drawn closer to Berlin, and had not thought it necessary to extend the tape in the Ardennes, despite the boasts in the *Völkischer Beobachter*. There was a telephone on Blomm's desk. She picked it up and wound the handle.

'Switchboard,' said a prompt male voice. Petra knew that the man could well have occasion to speak to the Führer himself during his spell on duty, and his aggressively disciplined manner did not surprise her.

'Personnel,' she said. 'Wehrmacht.'

There was a click on the line. She felt her heart pounding inside her ribcage. Then a second male voice said, 'Personnel'.

'Sturmbannführer Blomm's office,' said Petra. 'Geheime Staats Polizei.'

'Prinz Albrechtstrasse or Chancellery?'

'Prinz Albrechtstrasse,' she said and wondered, oddly, irrelevantly, if Karl Blomm's office at Gestapo headquarters was any larger than his office in the Chancellery. 'Herr Blomm wishes to see the files on every man involved in Operation Grief.'

'But there are two thousand of them.'

'Then the men involved in the Operation Claws of the Gryphon.'

'Claws . . . I have not heard of that . . . Such material must be classified . . . Who is this speaking? Who is this speaking?'

But Petra Oelkers was already replacing the receiver. 'Thank you very much,' she said.

She walked to the door and listened, heard no sound from the corridor and opened the door slowly and as quietly as she could. The corridor was empty. She walked softly past the room with the clattering typewriter and entered the guard-room as a car drew up outside. She stood in the middle of the room and waited for the door to open.

A soldier in the Reichsführer SS entered. He had corporal's chevrons on the shoulders of his tunic. He stared at Petra Oelkers. She held his stare. Then she smiled. 'I have been asked to wait in here,' she said.

'There is no guard?'

'Not since I've been here. Are you our driver, for Hauptsturm-führer Leuger?'

'Ja!' The corporal clicked his heels. Petra nodded in acknowledgement of his salute. For a few moments they stood in silence and then they heard a low groan and a scuffling of feet from further down the corridor.

'I wondered,' Petra said, 'what they meant when they said he was sick.'

'Too much schnapps,' said the driver cheerfully. Petra turned and glared at him. The man drew himself smartly to attention and again clicked his heels.

Heinrich Leuger was carried into the guard-room, supported by two Reichsführer SS Landsers, who were preceded by a strikingly handsome Obersturmführer.

'Fräulein Oelkers?'

'Yes,' said Petra.

'You will please take him home,' said the Obersturmführer. 'You will do what you can to revive him by 1800 hours when he is to report for duty.'

Petra nodded. She found herself genuinely embarrassed.

'You will also inform the Hauptsturmführer that his brother officers are not prepared to cover up his excesses. We have no idea where he kept his schnapps. Alcohol is not permitted in the Chancellery. We will report him on the second occasion.'

'Of course. I had no idea.'

The Obersturmführer snapped his fingers and Heinrich Leuger was dragged into the waiting car. When they arrived at his flat, Petra had Heinrich carried to his bed. When the two Landsers had left, she pushed him on to his side, took his right arm and folded it across his chest with his right hand resting under his head. His left arm she tugged from under his body and stretched out on the bed behind him, as nearly at right-angles to his spine as she could. He was unconscious and reeking of schnapps. Leaving his arms so positioned might, she felt, go some way to stop him rolling on to his stomach or his back, and thus might prevent him suffocating in his own vomit.

She leaned against the wall and looked down at him. The man who loved her, the man whom she had to prevent herself from loving because she lived with him only to betray him.

*

'I gather you started the war in Wormwood Scrubs,' said Service, holding the umbrella so that it covered both himself and his companion.

'Oh yes, yes, right fiasco,' replied the man. He was short and balding. 'We had a basement under the nick and all London knew it, even the clippies on the buses, would you believe? They'd ring the bell and shout, "Next stop for the Secret Service".'

'Yes, I heard that anecdote,' said Service, smiling. 'I have to confess, Charles, I invited you for a drink for a purpose. I'd like to pick your brains, as it were.'

The older man laughed. 'I thought as much. You haven't hardly said a word to me in donkey's years and now you take me for a beer. Mind, I have to confess you've been a deal more civil than some others. What's the picture from Europe? Heavy traffic?'

'Very heavy, nearly two thousand cyphers from eight o'clock this morning until six this evening when Hamish relieved me. The German is still pushing west at a rate of knots, but he's squealing like a stuck pig for more fuel.'

'They'll have difficulty sustaining the advance, then?'

'Certainly, unless they get more fuel. The Americans are beginning to organize themselves, according to a succession of cyphers this afternoon which reported pockets of stiff resistance. The Yanks' main problem and the Germans' main advantage is still the weather.'

'Weather?'

'Fog. Real pea-souper,' said Service. 'Yanks can't put a plane in the air and the Panzers are crashing on while they're still protected from air attack.'

'Grim,' said the older man.

'Certainly is. The Yanks are getting chewed up.'

In December 1944 walls still had ears and the army officer who took out his revolver, pointed it at the head of new arrivals at Bletchley Park, and said, 'If you talk to anyone, anyone at all about the work in this house I shall personally shoot you,' was still at Bletchley Park, still with his gun. However, rules were stretched a little, and 'shop' was occasionally talked when 'ears' and the not-so-dumb blonde were deemed to be absent. The lane from Bletchley Park to the Hare and Hounds at dusk in a December drizzle was just such an occasion.

'Not offended though, Benjamin,' said Charles Pargeter. 'Anything to get out of the lodgings, even on a day like this. Damn place gets so claustrophobic. A stroll and a pint of mild before supper is just what the doctor ordered.'

'Well, I shan't compromise you, Charles.' Service leapt a puddle and then fell back into step. 'I know the score, so if something's not for my ears or eyes just say so and I won't press.'

'Fair enough.' Pargeter strode on like the old soldier he was. His bullish, military manner concealed the existence of a brain which was, as one Bletchley Park member had said, 'as sharp as a tack'.

The muddy grey lane stretched before them; across the square-cut hawthorn hedge the rich brown soils rolled to the skyline. The sky was a heavy blue-grey, except for one section where sunlight had found a gap in the clouds and a beam from the setting sun angled through like a searchlight and played upon the shimmering slate roof of the Hare and Hounds, some three-quarters of a mile ahead of Service and Pargeter.

'Well,' said Service, 'I have personal reasons for asking. There was an incident yesterday night which started me thinking about someone I haven't seen for a long time.'

'I see,' Charles Pargeter nodded approvingly. 'Fire away.'

'Well, I'm leaving for home tomorrow. I have some leave due.'

'You drew Christmas?'

'Hamish McCrae and I worked it between ourselves. Christmas is not so important to him, but he likes to be in Glasgow for Hogmanay. With me New Year is not so important, but I like to have Christmas. It works very well.'

'Indeed.'

'Well, fire away you said, Charles, so the first shot is: what or who is FANY?'

'You are on delicate territory, young Benjamin.'

'I am?'

'FANY stands for First Aid Nursing Yeomanry,' said Pargeter. 'Mind you, if you believe that they'd train linguists and foreign nationals to bandage the warriors you'd believe anything. Is your friend brainy?'

'Linguist,' replied Service. 'German father, English mother. Lived most of her life before the war in Germany. Spoke the language like a native. Looked the part too.'

'Flaxen-haired beauty, eh?'

'Well . . . In a word, yes.'

'I see, and about time too, I might add. How old is she now, do you know? Twenty-six, twenty-seven?'

'Twenty-six,' said Service.

'So she joined FANY?'

'Yes.'

'Do you know where she is now?'

Service shook his head. 'We lost contact at the very outbreak of war. I wrote, of course, but she never answered my letters.'

'Well, I'm afraid it may be a permanent lost contact, Benjamin. Unless you meet up in the Great Hereafter. That's war, son.'

'What would have happened to her?'

'FANY is a front for SOE.'

'SOE? That's Special Operations Executive, isn't it?'

'Yes. She probably went behind the enemy lines. Chances of survival are not high, reducing one in three, so they say. One in three survive training . . .'

'Survive training!'

'It's serious stuff, Benjamin. One in three evade capture, one in three survive interrogation. Actually I'd say the chances are a lot slimmer. The one in three against is just the official line.'

The two men walked on, their shoes scraping on the road surface, their conversation momentarily lapsed. As they approached a mound of concrete blocks stacked at the side of the lane, Pargeter said, 'Always think of that day back in '40, when I pass those blocks. Was that McCrae's deduction?'

'No,' said Service quietly. 'It was one of my few and small successes.'

'What's the story?'

'It was one of Goering's funnies,' replied Service. 'We interrupted a cypher of his which instructed that gliders and troop carriers should practise touching down on narrow concrete strips. I thought it could only mean he was planning to use our road network to provide runways for his airborne troops.'

'Smart thinking, Benjamin.'

'The ministry responded very quickly,' said Service. 'Within a few days there were concrete blocks at quarter-mile intervals at the side of every road and lane in east and central England, ready to be pushed into place if the church bells started to ring. The official line was that they were there to halt tanks because the Ministry of Information felt it would alarm the public and cause panic if the real reason was known.'

'You mean people could cope with the idea of the Hun coming along the road, but the thought of him dropping from the sky was a bit too much.'

'That's it.' Service paused and then said, 'She told her mother that she was going to Canada.'

'As she would. Camp X is where they trained. It's on the northern shore of Lake Ontario, that's where they're put through the mill, Morse, survival techniques, unarmed combat, armed combat, weapons training, parachute descents both into water and on land. It's also at Camp X where they get dished out with authentic clothing.'

'Authentic clothing?'

'Yes. Our agents spent the first few years of the war buying out of the second-hand clothing stores in immigrant quarters in New York and Chicago. Long time before the US was in the war. You see, if you are going to drop an agent into Belgium, for example, it's no use letting her keep her Harrods smalls. She has to be authentic down to the last detail, Belgian linen, Belgian stitching, even the way the thread is used to fasten the buttons to the coat. So the old clothes were bought from the Belgian quarter in New York and put to good use in Camp X. We also bought Belgian suitcases, clocks, manicure sets, jewellery, the lot. For men and women. And we did that for every European country. Very soon, if we wanted to put an agent anywhere in Europe, even the eastern states, he or she would be authentic right down to the newspaper pushed inside the rim of the hat. There's even the story of the rich Dutch woman being relieved of her luggage somewhere between Chicago and Los Angeles so we could send agents to Holland dressed in furs and pearls if we wished. Mostly, though, they went as low-lifers. Well, secretary, tradesmen class. Blended more easily.'

'I see,' said Service.

'I don't have to remind you about the security aspect . . .?'

'Oh, my lips are sealed, Charles. Even more so now that I have a personal stake.'

Pargeter was silent. Then he said, 'Benjamin, if she joined FANY at the outbreak of war, her chances of being alive now are desperately slim. The average life-expectancy of an agent once he or she is behind the enemy lines is anything from six weeks to three months.'

'Oh my God.'

'It depends on so many things. Luck, degree of activity, degree to which you keep your head and remember your training. Most of our agents were in occupied Europe and those that are alive are beginning to come home. We didn't send many to Germany.'

'Is there any way of finding out where she went?'

'Try Hut 3.'

'The Morse receivers. But we also receive Morse in Hut 6.'

'But the Godmother is in Hut 3.'

'The Godmother? You don't mean Miss . . .'

'Dear Miss Stavely? I certainly do. It's no secret that she's been going backwards and forwards to Canada since the war began. What she has been doing is training each new batch of FANY recruits in Morse. Everybody has their own Morse finger, or touch, similar to individual handwriting. Gladys knows them all. She just has to listen for a few moments. In fact, all you have to do is name your girlfriend and Gladys may tell you where she was sent and if she is still operating.'

They were drawing near the pub and had already passed the first outlying farm labourers' cottages. 'Better finish there,' said

Charles Pargeter, quickening his already brisk step. 'Your round, I believe, sir.'

'My pleasure, sir,' said Service. 'I'll talk to Gladys when we get back.'

'Have to be after the festive season.' Pargeter threw Service a sidelong glance. 'You're not the only one to get Christmas leave. She went yesterday.'

'Dare say it can wait.'

'Dare say it will have to,' said Pargeter with finality.

The double meaning wasn't lost on Service, who doffed his cap as they passed the postmistress who was wheeling her cycle towards them.

Chapter Six

Klara Heidler took the train to Lyons. It was a slow, cramped cold, uncomfortable, halting journey. She stood in the corridor between a soldier breathing strong cognac fumes, who managed to sleep standing up, and a young woman who stared dreamily into space. She wiped the condensation from the window and watched the grey-black winter landscape slide slowly by until the glass misted over again. All joviality seemed to be at the other end of the gently rocking corridor, where a group of soldiers sang and passed a bottle about and had encouraged a couple of young women to join them. Klara Heidler seemed to be standing in that part of the train devoted to maudlin or romantic reflection and alcoholic stupor. This suited her perfectly.

The journey to Lyons took six hours. When she emerged from the station, she saw the city of Lyons on a cold, dark evening. A fine drizzle was falling. The lights of the city stretched away in either direction. She stood outside the station and pulled the collar of her coat about her as the cold began to seep through her clothes and wrap about her flesh. Eventually she was approached by a tall man with dark hair. He had, so far as the confusing light would allow her to tell, a sallow complexion. He nodded.

'Mademoiselle Heidler?'

'Yes.' They shook hands.

'Our car is this way.'

It was a black Citroën 15. The man opened the rear door and she slid into the rear seat, old leather, polished with age. He drove the car skilfully with easy fluid movements through the narrow streets of Lyons and out into the country. He said nothing.

They drove south-east towards the Dauphiné. One and a half hours after leaving Lyons, they reached the foothills of the mountains. The driver turned the car off the road and drove along a narrow track which wound steeply up a hillside. Through a break in the clouds Klara Heidler caught a fleeting glimpse of the moon above the trees. The driver turned on to a second track, narrower than the first, and as they drove along it branches from the trees and roadside shrubs scraped the side of the car. The road emerged into the courtyard of an old house from which no light shone. The car halted by the front door of the house and Klara Heidler followed the man into the building. Inside it was chilly with a strong smell of damp.

She was led through the house and shown into a large room. The room was illuminated by two hurricane lamps which stood on an oak table. A log fire burned fiercely. Shutters covered the windows, presumably to prevent light escaping. By the fireside stood a man, short, middle-aged, dressed in a green smoking jacket. She heard the door shut behind her. She and the man had not met before; they looked keenly at each other. Klara Heidler saw him silhouetted against the raging fire which cast dancing shadows on the ceiling and walls. Suddenly, simultaneously, they extended their right arms.

'Heil Hitler!'

'Heil Hitler!'

They smiled, approached each other and shook hands, the man clicking his heels.

'Konrad Morke,' he said. 'It is an honour to meet you, Fräulein Heidler, an honour to serve with you.'

'I'm sure we will work well together Herr Morke. We have an important, no, a vital task.'

'You have news of the offensive?'

'It goes well. Our leading Panzers are now deep into Belgium. The Americans are falling back like frightened children.'

'Excellent.'

'There is panic in Paris, every soldier is being moved up to the front. Some of them have only just arrived from the United States.'

'Again, excellent.'

'But the offensive will only work if we play our part. So we must succeed, we will succeed. We are part of the offensive just as much as the leading Panzers.'

'The Claws of the Gryphon?' the man queried.

Klara Heidler looked into his steel-grey eyes. He was a man of purpose, of resolution. He was a Nazi. She said, 'They are in Paris.'

'Good men?'

'Yes. One especially.'

'When do we strike?'

'Soon. A few days. He will be brought by an American jeep. We have it all ready. Is the house ready?'

'Yes.'

'Secure? I saw no guards.'

'Yes. Wine before we eat?'

'Thank you.'

'The house has been thought of as empty for some time,' said Morke, pouring wine into an ornate crystal glass. 'It once belonged to a so-called Frenchman, one of the richest in Lyons. He left France early in the war, we were informed, to join De Gaulle in London. When we occupied Vichy France we used the house as a rest billet for SS and Gestapo officers.' He handed her a glass of wine. 'Many of the bourgeoisie who made our stay in Lyons so agreeable know of our existence here and have a vested interest in keeping our secret. Since the invasion and the withdrawal of German forces, all France seems to have been involved in the Resistance and keen to denounce collaborationists. The collabos have to protect each other with a conspiracy of silence.'

Klara Heidler nodded her agreement. 'I myself was recruited partly on the basis of my collaborationist activities.'

'The only true resistance, the maquis, were the Communists and it is they who are pursuing every collabo with vengeance. It is the Communists we must fear.'

'But as yet there is no suspicion about the house?'

'No.'

136

'How many men do you have here?'

'Twenty, but most are out of sight at any one time.'

'All German?'

'Yes. The withdrawal from France was not orderly. It was disgraceful, Fräulein Heidler. German troops, even SS, running across fields in a blind panic, throwing themselves into rivers and canals, flinging away their weapons. They split into smaller and smaller groups. Those in central France being cut off by the Allied armies went south-west into Spain, or east towards Switzerland. Many did not make it, many were lynched or pitchforked, some reached this house where I ordered them to stay. In this way we formed our own resistance cell and placed ourselves at the disposal of the Reich.'

'It is a resistance cell which will alter the war for Germany,' said Klara Heidler. 'Germany is defeated, but we can alter her end.'

Konrad Morke glared at her.

'Germany is defeated,' she said again. 'Any talk of victory is futile. If our army can smash its way to the coast and seize Antwerp, we shall seize the only intact port on the coast and split the Allied line. This should cause the Allied politicians to fly at each other's throats in mutual recrimination. If also we can snatch our own prize, then Germany will be in a good bargaining position to negotiate a separate peace with the Allies. When that has been done, Germany can throw all her weight to the east against the Soviets. The alternative is for Germany to be crushed into unconditional surrender, to be squeezed to death from east and west.'

'Germany is defeated,' Konrad Morke said softly. 'You are right, Fräulein Heidler. It is I who lack the courage to face the facts.'

'But the fight must continue. Von Rundstedt in the north and we few in the south can together deliver a devastating blow to the Allies. Both must succeed, both will succeed. What preparations have you made?'

'He will be kept in the basement. He will be given blankets for warmth. I have a camera with a flash, and a developing and printing room. We shall be able to show the Allies photographs within an hour of his being brought here.'

'Good. You have enough food?'

'Enough for four weeks.'

Klara Heidler raised her glass. 'To our success.'

In the dead of night, rain splattered on the window of the small, dimly lit room. Schweitzer lay snoring in his bunk, covered in a layer of blankets. Genscher and Hoff sat in the centre of the room huddled over the stove, blankets draped round their shoulders. They sipped coffee and smoked cigarettes. Genscher looked intently at Hoff and said, 'So how about it?'

Hoff shook his head. 'I don't know. Gee, I don't know.'

'See, you're talking like a dough-boy now, Chrissake. Hoff, you'd pass for an American any time, so become an American same as me. Germany's dead and it'll be a lot deader when the world finds out about the camps and what we did to the Jews and resistance workers. I hated Jews once, but now it's my own survival that matters. I seen a camp one time, I couldn't believe it, and the size, as big as a town. Anybody that had anything to do with the camps is in trouble. I'm in the SS. That'll be near enough. I gotta neck to save.'

'Yeah.' Hoff nodded. 'I saw a train once. Women and kids crammed into cattle trucks.'

'Right. We got into this army. For me it was a big mistake, I should've stayed home, it wasn't so bad, looking back – just a couple of lean years. But there's also Poles, Hungarians, Spanish, Dutch, Frenchies and even a bunch of Britishers fighting with the SS. A lot joined up when Hitler invaded Russia, some big anti-Communist crusade. The Britishers were in prisoner of war camps and were offered freedom in return for joining. They formed their own division, Saint something . . .'

'St George Division,' said Hoff. 'They have a little Union Jack on their landschilds. I met a member of the St George Division once. He was drunk in a bar and was sick as a dog. He just wanted to go home.'

'Up until now there's only been one way out. But now what do they do? They give us American uniforms and a jeep, and they don't just send us across the line like the other mugs, they send us to Paris, safety. And they expect us to continue to fight. They're crazy.'

'It's different for me,' said Hoff. 'I'm not an American. I just spent time there.'

'So spend some more time there.'

'Maybe I could,' said Hoff. 'There's good medical treatment there?'

'The best in the world. You got a medical condition?'

'Nothing that can't be treated,' Hoff replied. 'Had it once before, thought I'd got rid of it.'

'You need American medicine,' said Genscher.

'Guess I do.'

'So you're with me?'

'I didn't say that.'

Genscher jerked a thumb contemptuously at Schweitzer. 'You can't be with him. The guy's mad.'

'I'm not saying I'm with him either. I'm my own man.'

'You can't be your own man for too long, Hoff. They expect us to pull this crazy stunt in a couple of days. Sometime around Christmas. I'll be booked out by then, you'd better come with me.'

'Where are you going?'

'Chrissake, Hoff. I'm going to a place where the air's good, where there's mountains and trout in the streams and there's a little town called Sugar Creek. I'm going home, Hoff. Coming?'

'My home's in Germany. Berlin.'

'Hell, there ain't nothin' in Berlin, Hoff. It's just a few square miles of rubble. I mean, they don't even allow soldiers home leave to Berlin and Hamburg and places like that in case they get too dispirited. Not a lot to fight for if you see what sort of mess your home town is in.' Then Genscher paused. 'You got family?'

'Yes. Mother and a brother. Brother's in Norway.'

'Hell, he's safe enough there. Come back to the States with me and contact him after the war.'

'How do you plan it?'

'I don't know yet,' said Genscher. 'I haven't finalized the details. I'll figure something out, but I have to know whether to plan for one or two.'

'What happens if we stay?'

'We won't be needing any clean shirts in a couple of weeks' time.'

'You reckon?'

'Sure do. Listen, Hoff, this is a strictly one-way ticket. You can't tell me you think they've got any plans for us after the beginning of January. We're expendable. If this boy scout trick comes off, we take the cargo south some place and sit on it; then we're redundant. If it doesn't come off, we're all past caring.'

'So what shall we do?'

'You're in?'

'Yes,' said Hoff. 'I guess I am. Guess you'd better plan for two.'

'Sure thing.' Genscher lit two cigarettes and pushed one across to Hoff. 'Just you and me.'

They were following the road. They seemed to mount the summit of a hill and, as they descended the other side, they walked into thicker and thicker fog. There were occasional 'holes' when they would emerge into a dull overcast day and walk on for a few hundred feet before plunging again into the grey, freezing fog. Conner knew that Baumgardner was keeping pace with him and he could hear Sweeney wheezing with his bad chest, despite the fact that he had copied Conner's example of breathing through a glove clenched between his teeth. He didn't know the whereabouts of the others. He stopped and Baumgardner, numb with cold and weary with lack of sleep, stumbled into him.

'Calling a halt,' said Conner, taking the glove from his mouth. The cold was sapping energy from his body to such a degree that even speaking just become an effort.

'Jesus,' growled Baumgardner. 'It's colder than Christ on the Cross.' Sweeney joined them, ambling out of the mist sounding like bellows that had been shot full of holes. Then one by one the others appeared, walking zombie-like, getting to the dangerous stage where they didn't care if they lived or died.

'Gotta keep together,' said Conner. 'Don't lose sight of the man in front of you. These are survival conditions. You get lost in this fog and wander into the forest, you're a dead man.'

'When do we stop, sir?'

Conner didn't know who asked the question, the words just came out of the fog. 'We don't,' he said back at the fog. 'There's no shelter. We lie down in this, we won't wake up. Got to watch each other, don't let the guy in front of you sleep. Next last guy in line keep watching the last guy in line. Don't let him fall behind.' Conner held his watch close to his eyes. 'It's coming on 1500 hours, be dark soon.'

'Won't make no difference no how,' growled a voice.

'The hell it won't.' Conner addressed the small group of men. 'It'll get colder, a lot colder, or maybe you don't remember last night. We got to chow up and keep moving. Keep alert, remember that half-track full of krauts up ahead.'

'Chow up on what?'

'K-rations. Eat them cold. Start eating now and keep eating on the move.' One of the GIs started to mouth off, but Conner was already walking on down the hill, chewing on a D-bar.

It was the longest night Conner had experienced. Darkness came early and stayed late. The temperature dropped to twenty degrees below freezing, or so he was later informed. The small party dragged on through the night, putting one numbed foot in front of the other. Throughout the night they heard the irregular beat of the engines of the doodle-bugs flying westwards. Nobody spoke, they just kept their eyes on the guy in front. Occasionally Conner lifted his watch and flicked his Zippo lighter just to find that the minute hand had crawled on another twenty minutes. Baumgardner followed Conner, setting an example by following the guy in front. Behind Baumgardner, Sweeney was considering going to sleep and letting his legs carry on without him.

0300 hours seemed to Conner to be the nadir of the night. From then on it was an easy cruise towards the dawn. He began to walk with a little more grit since the worst of the night seemed to be over, he began to look forward to the dawn, never giving up his faith that the dawn would bring warmth and perhaps their arrival at their own lines. In the event the only thing to change was the temperature, which rose a little as darkness left. It had been just eighteen hours since they had shot up the American half-track, yet it seemed like an event from another lifetime. He walked on, denying himself and the others any rest. To rest, even for ten minutes, would freeze up the joints and allow them to fall asleep. None of the men complained. He thought that maybe they were just too tired to care.

At about 1000 hours, Conner became aware that he was walking towards an object. He was very close, just a few yards away. He stopped, aware of his senses sharpening. The dark shape became a man who looked towards Conner. There was a moment's silence. Conner heard the man yell 'Krauts!' He pulled the glove from his mouth and shouted 'Cover!' Conner and the GIs dived into the snow and heard the heavy coughing of Thompson machine-guns ahead, heard the bullets ricochet off the frozen trees around them. They held their fire and eventually the Thompsons died, their echoes bouncing away into an unseen ravine.

Baumgardner was the first to speak. 'Bunch of trigger-happy jerks,' he snarled loudly for all the men to hear, since it was after all Sergeant Baumgardner giving his opinion. Conner lay on his stomach and raised his upper body on his elbows, cupped his hands to his mouth and yelled, 'We're Americans.' '. . . cans . . . cans . . . cans' went echoing away.

'What unit . . . it . . . it . . . it?'

'One-o-six . . . ix . . . ix . . . ix. Some guys from the fourth infantry . . . ry . . . ry . . . ry.'

'So where you from?'

The owner of the voice eventually proved to be a short, stockily built lieutenant. He wore the rounded helmet and olive green battledress of the Airborne forces. He nodded at Conner.

'Guess you've run into krauts dressed as our guys too?' said Conner.

'Sure have,' replied the lieutenant. 'Regular shooting-gallery once we wised up.'

'Come across one of our half-tracks full of krauts?'

'Nope.' The lieutenant shook his head. 'Can't say we have.'

'We were following it,' said Conner. 'Must have turned off someplace.'

'There's more tracks in this bunch of woodlands than there are streets in downtown Detroit. Could've turned off anywhere.'

Conner saw men begin to gather behind their officer. 'What's the situation here?' he asked.

'Little short of desperate,' grinned the lieutenant. 'We have krauts in the north, we have krauts in the south, and about any minute now we expect krauts to come right on down this road. Which is why you guys nearly got chopped up. You got close because we were listening out for Panzers.'

'Where is this?'

'About ten miles north-east of Bastogne. Couple of miles behind us is Task Force Rose. I guess you'll be welcome.'

'Task Force Rose?'

'First obstacle between the krauts and Bastogne. Guess you won't know, but we're making a stand at Bastogne.'

'That's all we need,' said Baumgardner.

'You'd better report to Captain Miller.'

'We haven't slept for two nights,' Conner complained impulsively and instantly regretted doing so.

'So join the club, Lieutenant,' replied the officer of Airborne forces. 'You could stay here if you want. We're actually first in line, but nobody counts us on account of the fact that we don't have a lot of life-expectancy when the King Tigers come rolling on down the road. We're just here to give some warning.'

'I guess I was edgy,' said Conner. 'Sorry. I guess nobody's getting any sleep.'

'Forget it.'

'I guess we'll go and report. What size is Task Force Rose?'

'Seven Shermans who don't have a cat in hell's chance against the new kraut tanks, one company of green infantry, one company of tired infantry, and one scratch company made up of stragglers.'

'Captain Miller is commander of the scratch company?'

'That's it. We hold this bridge . . .'

'There's a bridge here?' Conner stared into the fog.

'Well, there sure as hell was when we arrived yesterday. If it wasn't for the fog you'd get vertigo. One hundred and fifty feet straight down. We hold it as long as we can, then blow it and fall back and join you. So don't get trigger-happy when you see guys in olive green running at you. We ain't Wehrmacht, we're Airborne.'

'You got it,' said Conner. 'Say, remember, should this half-track approach . . .'

'Thanks for the warning, and say you go easy, friend. We had a couple of motorized stragglers through yesterday, spoke of a massacre of our guys up near some place called Malmédy, came across it while dodging German columns.'

'That right?'

'Hundreds of our guys stacked up like cordwood.'

'Christ,' said Conner. 'These guys are playing to win all right.'

'We'll radio through and tell Rose to expect you. I guess they're getting edgy, they'll have heard our guns a while back.'

'Thanks,' said Conner. 'Say, what date is it?'

'Wednesday, December 18th. Mind how you go.'

It was 6.00 p.m. before she could get away, having first coaxed a sick and frail-looking Heinrich Leuger out of the flat. She took the subway to the Stettiner Bahnhof and walked to the Chausseestrasse, then turned down the side street to the old house, picking her way across the rubble. She saw a light flashing from a basement on the other side of the road and thought it must be someone who was still trapped, desperately trying to attract attention. She investigated and found the light was in fact a flickering flame, part of an inferno raging in the basement which had probably been a coal cellar.

Petra went on her way, slowly, carefully, not wishing to risk a broken ankle. She reached the house, glanced round and, seeing no one looking at her, slipped inside. She climbed the stair to the second floor and let herself into the flat. Stealthily she crept to the room where the transmitter was kept, disguised as a suitcase. She picked it up, rested it on the table and switched it on. The soft red glow began to shine from the bulb as the valves warmed up. She slipped on the headphones, sent the short pre-transmission signal and a moment later heard the distinct dash-dot 'ready to receive' signal. Then she sent the message: 'Operation Gryphon is two thousand strong. Operation Claws of the Gryphon is highly classified.' She repeated the message twice.

No black Mercedes saloon kerb-crawled behind her this time, but, as she walked from the house back towards the subway, she could not shake the unnerving conviction that she was indeed being watched. She even felt that the old man who handed her the ticket at the subway station was looking at her knowingly. As she stood on the platform she tried to calm herself. She'd been in the field for four years, far exceeding her own optimistic expectations. Now, after years of transmitting material often of the highest grade, she could not lose her grip. Not now. She glanced along the platform, lit with a row of bulbs set high in the wall just before the roof curved. A few people stood there, either old or very young, everybody else being in the army. The Reich had even cleared hospitals by raising battalions of infirm soldiers. There were deaf battalions for men who were hard of hearing; 'mogan' battalions for men with special dietary needs, and the prisons had been emptied and penal battalions formed. Those who were not in the army, like the old men and women who stood on the platform with her, worked a gruelling seventy-hour week. The end was near, the quiet on the eastern front could mean only that the Red Army was massing for its final drive on Berlin. She could soon be back in England, to pick up the threads of her life again. She felt she would like to live the post-war years in England, the country in which she had been born, her mother's country. That clever sensitive boy with the gentle manners would have forgotten her by now, but there would be others. It was so near, she couldn't lose her nerve now. She'd come this far, she had to see it through.

Her reason for not being fully employed in Germany's war effort was that she was a mistress, the possession of an SS officer who worked in the Chancellery. There was one other person on the platform who seemed to be young and in good health. He wore a dark coat with a homburg pulled low over his eyes and whenever she turned and looked at him, it was to see him staring at her.

Not now, not after all these years.

Chapter Seven

'We have to think this out clearly. We have to know what we are doing.'

'I am thinking,' muttered Genscher. 'Keep your voice down, the guy's probably awake.'

Hoff glanced across the room at the bunk beds. Schweitzer lay on his side covered with a crumpled blanket. He seemed to be breathing softly. Hoff nodded to Genscher.

'So the first problem, as I see it, is to get out of these uniforms. If we don't, we get stopped as deserters.'

'If that happens,' said Hoff, 'and they find German underclothing . . .' He drew a finger across his throat.

'I know, Hoff, I know. So we need clothing. Civilian clothing.'

'Not so easy to come by.'

'We'll get it. If we don't buy it, we'll steal it; but we'll get it.'

Hoff sighed, 'We'll buy it with what? Steal it from where? Get your feet on the ground, Genscher, will you?'

'They're on the ground and firmly planted. How much money have we got?'

'Two, three hundred American dollars. Counterfeit, of course.'

'Of course, but they'll pass.'

'So we buy some clothes. How do we do that without raisin' suspicion? I mean, we're serving soldiers, we don't walk into clothes shops and walk out as civilians.'

'We'll get clothing, believe me.'

'All right, what then? Where do we go?'

'We're DPs, displaced persons, there's thousands of them all over Europe. We speak German so we say we're Belgian. The

Belgians speak French and German, because for the last two hundred years Belgium's been tossed between France and Germany and after the last war a bit of Germany was given to Belgium. So we can say we're German-speaking Belgians.'

'So what then?'

'Simple. We just go.'

'When?'

'Now, Hoff. This instant. We walk down the stair, into the garage, into the street and away.'

'Just like that?'

'You know a better way?'

'I guess I don't.'

The two men rose from their seats by the stove, Hoff moving his bulk quietly, and Genscher, wiry, weasel-like, leading the way. They had reached the bottom of the stair and were about to open the door and step into the street when Schweitzer said, 'I wouldn't if I were you.' Hoff and Genscher turned. Schweitzer was standing at the top of the stairway and pointing a Colt automatic at Genscher's head. He said, 'One more step and I fire.'

So Genscher said, 'Go screw yourself, Schweitzer.' He opened the door and stepped into the street. Hoff followed without looking back at Schweitzer. It was only the second time that Genscher had seen the street in which stood the lock-up. It was a tree-lined avenue in a residential quarter. He took in his surroundings as quickly as he could, looking for some landmark, maybe even a guy giving out bundles of civilian clothing.

Schweitzer came tumbling out into the street, ran past Hoff and grabbed Genscher by the arm. He threw a right which caught Genscher squarely on the jaw. Genscher staggered backwards, but recovered quickly and sufficiently enough to kick Schweitzer in the groin. Schweitzer bent double and Hoff clasped both his hands together and brought them down on the back of Schweitzer's neck. Schweitzer, much to Hoff's surprise and delight at his own prowess, collapsed heavily.

Genscher picked up Schweitzer's Colt and slipped it into his tunic pocket. Could have been nasty, he thought, if the street had been full, could have been an obstacle. But it wasn't full, it

148

was deserted, except for him and Hoff. As they reached the end of the street and were about to turn the corner, Genscher glanced back and saw Schweitzer staggering back into the lock-up.

Genscher and Hoff turned into a wider, busier thoroughfare. It was a cold, dull, afternoon. Most people walked with their shoulders hunched against the chill, and few bothered to give the two GIs a second glance. Those who did smiled at them, the liberators.

'You know,' said Genscher, 'for the first time in five years I feel like a free man.'

'For the first time in my life I feel like a criminal,' replied Hoff, who walked half a step behind the small, eager Genscher. 'I have deserted. I cannot go back. I can only go forward. I hope you know what you're doing, Genscher.'

'Trust me, trust me.'

'Where are we going, Genscher, where now?'

'I don't know Hoff, and I don't care.'

In the event they went to a café and bought coffee and rolls with the counterfeit dollar bills, which were snatched greedily by the proprietor.

The telephone rang, the sergeant reached forward and picked it up. He listened for a few moments and then said, 'OK' and replaced the receiver. He left his desk, knocked on Floyd's office door and entered. Floyd stood by the filing cabinet, on the top of which stood a small Stars and Stripes on a miniature flagpole. He looked at the sergeant and raised his eyebrows.

'Got a report of a brawl, Captain Floyd,' said the sergeant, reading from the note he scribbled. 'Three of our guys.'

'Three guys?'

'Yes, sir. I wouldn't normally bother you with this incident, but the three deserters who murdered our guys . . .'

'Yes, Sergeant, that's good thinking.' He turned from the filing cabinet. 'Where is this incident?'

'Er . . .' The sergeant glanced at his notepad. 'Some place, the Rue St Josèphe, which is in some district called Drancy.'

'Drancy, that's a new one on me.' Floyd crossed to the map of Paris which hung behind his desk. He consulted the directory of streets in the bottom left-hand corner. 'Plenty of Rue St Josèphes,' he said, 'but none in Drancy. Where is Drancy?'

'Way up north of the city,' said the sergeant. 'What the hell are our guys doing up there?'

'That, Sergeant, is something we are going to find out. Get a detailed map of the city and pin down Rue St Josèphe, Drancy. I'll come on this one myself.'

Klara Heidler returned from Lyons, took a taxi from the Gare de Lyon to her apartment, washed, changed and left immediately in her Citroën for the Rue St Josèphe. The first thing she saw upon turning into the avenue was Captain Floyd of the United States Military Police and three of his men. They were talking with an elderly woman whom Klara Heidler recognized as living on the opposite side of the road to the lock-up. She slowed involuntarily as her stomach suddenly felt hollow. Collecting herself, she drove on and calmly pulled up outside the lock-up. As she got out of her car she could feel the MPs looking at her. She shut the lock-up door firmly behind her. In the upstairs room she found Schweitzer sitting on the edge of a bunk, nursing his head in his hands.

'What the hell's happening?'

Schweitzer looked at her. 'Genscher and Hoff deserted.'

'They did what?'

But Schweitzer just groaned.

'You didn't go after them?'

'I did. I couldn't stop them.'

'Somebody must have seen you. There are Military Policemen in the street.'

'They must not find me!'

'Neither must they find the jeep. You are not the only one who could lose out of this, Schweitzer. On your feet, quick, we have about thirty seconds.'

They had about ten, but Klara Heidler didn't open the door

to the insistent knocking until she was satisfied that everything that could be done was done.

'I'm sorry,' she said, 'I was upstairs.'

'Ma'am.' Floyd raised his hand to his brow in the form of a half-salute. 'I'm sorry to disturb you, but we have had a report of American soldiers on these premises. We'd just like to check it out, ma'am.'

'That's absurd,' said Klara Heidler. 'I am quite alone.'

'Ma'am, American soldiers were seen to enter this door. Just a few minutes ago there was a brawl outside this door and one American soldier was seen to return inside. We'd just like to check it out, ma'am.'

'But I assure you . . .'

'We'd like to check it out, ma'am, if only for your own safety, ma'am.'

Klara Heidler stepped aside, as if wearied by Floyd's deadpan insistence.

'You live here, ma'am?' Floyd stepped through the door and into the garage.

'No, I'm renting it. I will be turning it into a studio. I am an artist.'

'An artist, ma'am. Yes, ma'am.' Floyd glanced round the garage. He noticed that it was large enough for two cars, with one vehicle parked at the further end completely covered with tarpaulin. He went up the stairs. Klara Heidler followed. The room at the top of the stairs had a table, chairs, a stove, bunk beds, a lavatory off to the left. The room was empty. 'Guess there's been a mistake,' he said, knowing he hadn't the authority to search the building without the presence of a civilian policeman, or firm evidence of the presence of American troops.

'The old woman I saw you talking to,' said Klara Heidler. 'She has a little problem.' She lifted her elbow. 'Sometimes she sees little men running in the road, sometimes for her there are giant – how you say? – beetles walking on the wall, and –' she shrugged her shoulders in the classic French manner – 'for her sometimes there are American soldiers fighting with each other.'

'OK, ma'am,' said Floyd. 'We just have to check these things out.'

Klara Heidler threw the bolt of the door behind him and sank against it. Slowly Schweitzer emerged from under the tarpaulin which covered the jeep.

'Fools,' hissed Klara Heidler. 'Utter fools. Is this the quality of German soldiers?'

'I think one at least did not think he was German. The other I think has no stomach for a fight,' Schweitzer said stiffening to attention.

'And you, Schweitzer, are you a good German? Or do you too change your allegiance as the future of your country changes?'

'I do not!'

'Those swine will pay for this. I shall make them pay.'

'This mission, will it proceed?'

'Of course, Schweitzer. Except that now we are two, instead of four. So each will have to work twice as hard. Soon we will strike, just as the offensive in the Ardennes is poised on the brink of success. Then we shall unleash the claws of the Gryphon. It will be a great day for us, a great day for Germany.'

In the jeep Floyd was puzzled. Sure as hell there was no GI in that building, but there was something odd about it all the same, something he wouldn't forget about, just something to slip on the back burner for a while.

'So what did you see, and don't say your hand in front of your face. You said that last time.'

'Sir, there's fog, and there's mist, and there's trees, and snow and ravines and a lot of dead GIs and a bunch of krauts runnin' around in our uniforms, sir. At one time or another I saw most of that, sir.'

'That doesn't help a whole lot, Conners.'

'Conner, sir. Just Conner.'

'Well, that still doesn't help a whole lot.' Captain Miller pressed his fingers to his eyes together at the bridge of his nose and then shook his head vigorously. 'Jesus, they say the trick is not to think about sleep then you don't need it so much. It ain't easy.'

'Sure isn't,' said Conner.

'You lose any men, Conner?'

'Some. All of my platoon one way or the other but I think some escaped.'

'Hope so, Conner, but I wouldn't put more'n a dime on it. The 106th took a real maulin'. We were monitoring the transmission a couple of days ago. None of the brass in 106th seemed to know what was happening. A whole bunch surrendered, that's for sure.'

'Hey, what chance had we?' Conner appealed to Miller, feeling the need to defend his division. Then he realized he had little to defend. The 106th existed as a division only on paper; it was less than six months old, it had an invented yellow and blue badge and a name some clerk made up, the Golden Lions, like it was a name which had been earned way back, as though it had fought in the Indian wars or in Mexico. The 106th had no corporate identity and its men were drawn from all over the USA, so when the pressure was on, it could not even identify with one particular state or region. 'We just weren't ready,' said Conner. 'A few months more and maybe we could have put up some defence.'

'It was just bad luck, Conner. We weren't expecting anything like this.' Miller leaned back against the tree-trunk around which he had piled sandbags, the sum of which and their location constituted his command post. 'The 106th didn't do any worse than some battle-smart divisions that have been in the line since D-Day. Thing is, though, that now we're getting organized it's the battle-smart ones that have survived. I don't recall seeing any other guys with those lapel badges and wearing neckties. Tell you one thing, though; yesterday we captured a couple of German drivers who told how their convoy was shot up by a group of GIs wearing neckties and led by a big officer. It's not the first time we've heard of this group. So there's some of you still out there fighting. Did you guys really go into line with those neckties?'

'General's order, sir,' said Conner.

'It applies to us as well, but, Christ you wear neckties to smart parties, not to do battle. Guess that was just the 106th being green. Guess you'd better think of it as a total wipe-out, Conner. You close to anybody in the 106th?'

'No, I don't reckon I was, sir.'

'Good. That's a good way for a fighting man to behave. Be a good buddy, be a good leader. But don't make too many friends.'

'Yes, sir.'

'So you brought in some men?'

'Yes, sir. Sergeant and four men of the Fourth Infantry Division.'

'Fourth?'

'Yes, sir.'

'Good, that gives our little private army a bit of backbone and a touch of class.'

'It does?'

'Conner, you would not believe the clerks, cooks, stenographers, walking wounded that comprise a good percentage of Task Force Rose, many of whom are today going to fire a rifle or machine-gun, maybe even use a bayonet, for the first time in anger. Mostly we are small arms, we have a few mortars, and we have seven, I say seven, Sherman tanks presently lined up like ducks in a shooting gallery. Most of the men are survivors, stragglers, a few shell-shocked; we have not worked together as a unit before, the men hardly know the NCOs, the NCOs hardly know the officers, the officers, like you and me, Conner, hardly know each other. Such is Task Force Rose. Task Force Rose is today supposed to stop, all by itself, a German attack comprising King Tiger tanks, Panzer grenadiers and Waffen SS storm-troopers. In addition we have the added complication of krauts in American uniforms. If nothing else, it's going to make us suspicious of each other, just when we have to rely on each other. You want promotion, Conner?'

'Sir?'

'Nothing. I thought maybe you might want my job.'

*

The attack came at 1000 hours on Wednesday, December 18. The first Conner or any of the others on the southern flank of Task Force Rose knew of the attack was when the Shermans fired explosive shells which eventually set something in the mist brilliantly ablaze. The Shermans were supported by small-arms fire and a battery of three howitzers situated behind the tanks seemed to fire blindly into the fog. All around him Conner could hear safety-catches being eased off, accompanied by a rustling, scratching sound as men tried to squirm closer to the ground. Conner knew each man was anxiously, nervously peering into the fog, all too aware of the skirmish going on behind him. 'Hold your fire,' Conner whispered. 'Don't get edgy, wait until you see something.'

The American fire lasted for about five minutes and then ceased abruptly. An eerie silence descended on the area, a silence which threatened to break at any moment. Conner and the men around him began to cough as the cordite fumes, unable to escape because of the fog, seeped across the ground from the centre of Task Force Rose's position and reached the outlying positions.

'We beat 'em off.' The voice belonged to a man who was lying near Conner.

'Don't you believe it, sonny. That was just a recce. They were just probing our positions, testing our strength. When they attack you'll know all about it.' The second voice came from further away, close enough to hear clearly, but when Conner tried to make out the speaker his eyes couldn't penetrate the murk.

'Cheerful son of a bitch, ain't you,' said the first man. 'So what happened to the guys guarding the bridge?'

'Quiet up!' snapped Conner. But he thought the man had a point. Conner never did find out what happened to the Airborne troops who were supposed to blow the bridge when the enemy appeared. Perhaps a half-track had come slowly out of the mist . . .

An hour after the first attack, the Americans heard a rattling, clacking sound, above which was the sound of hard-working petrol engines.

'Light tanks,' said a voice from behind Conner. 'They're not King Tigers. I heard King Tigers, sounds a bit like a freight train in a tunnel. They're not King Tigers.'

The tanks approached the American positions on the road, then halted, and began to fire smoke shells into the American lines. The shells exploded with a dull thud throughout the width of the American positions and sent out thick orange smoke which, like the cordite fumes, was prevented by the fog from rising. Men started to cough and wheeze violently. Conner snatched his glove from his hand and held it between clenched teeth, not this time to prevent his lungs being frosted but to form a primitive gas mask. He pressed his face to the ground and scratched at the frozen leaves in a desperate attempt to release more oxygen. Somehow he clung to the ground and resisted the temptation to run in a blind panic searching, gasping for breathable air. Somehow he managed to breathe, just enough to prevent himself from suffocating.

Inexplicably the German tanks did not press home their attack, probably, Conner later reflected, because they could not see the effect they were having. Slowly the smoke dispersed and the men began to take deeper and deeper breaths. The tanks were heard moving again, this time not rattling on a metalled surface, but crashing through vegetation. Conner listened keenly, trying to make allowances for the fog distorting the sound, and also for his own anxiety, which had always allowed him to imagine the worst. The tanks, Conner guessed there were about six in all, seemed to be driving a course southwards through the woods parallel to the American line. They continued southwards well past Conner's position and then turned west, coming to a halt due south of Task Force Rose.

'Runner!' Conner shouted over his shoulder.

A GI crawled up alongside him, his eyes, Conner noted, still streaming from the smoke bombs.

'Inform the Commander that German tanks are stationary to the south of our position. I'd estimate about half a mile away.'

'Sure thing, sir,' replied the GI in a manner which dispelled completely any fear Conner had about the water in the man's eyes indicating fear. Conner heard the man making his way towards the command post with a steady, stooping half-run, half-walk.

The battle entered on a second lull. This time the silence lasted for nearly two hours. All the men could do was listen and wait and smoke cigarettes, ensuring that the flame of their lighters and the glow from their cigarettes were concealed behind cupped hands. The nervous chatter which had followed the first probing reconnaissance of the Germans did not occur again. The Americans remained still and silent. Nobody needed to be told that the Germans were moving into position, ready for the onslaught. A few minutes after 1300 hours a second group of tanks was heard approaching the American lines. To Conner these tanks did indeed sound like a slow freight train in a long tunnel but, to his everlasting relief, they swung to the opposite end of Task Force Rose's position, some half-mile from where Conner lay.

Almost immediately the second group of tanks was in position the Germans opened fire, and Task Force Rose seemed to Conner to be taking fire from three different directions. He pressed himself to the ground as the tank shells wooshed overhead, barely, it seemed, inches above him. Occasionally a shell would explode against the frozen rock-hard trees and send shrapnel thudding to the ground. Most shells landed near to the centre of Task Force Rose. Men shouted; those who had been hit screamed in agony. One Sherman took a direct hit and exploded with a hollow metallic ring.

'Enemy to the front!' yelled a soldier who lay behind Conner and who began firing his Thompson. Conner looked up and saw men running towards his position, less than a hundred feet away, emerging out of the fog in white winter battledress with helmets which curved down over the wearers' ears and neck. Conner swore; that was some GI doing his job for him. He ought to have seen them, he'd damn near lost the battle all by himself. 'Let 'em have it!' he yelled in his fury, though he knew it was an unnecessary order, the Thompsons were already coughing regularly, reassuringly, the carbines cracking rapidly, and the tall powerful men in white were falling in their dozens. One GI frantically threw a grenade which landed closer to the Americans than to the oncoming Germans and gave a momentary advantage to the latter. The Germans pressed hard, running suicidally into the fire thrown up by the American small arms. Many fell, catapulted backwards as the bullets tore life from their bodies. Conner himself accounted for three. But still they came, like a white-crested wave flooding out of the mist, stumbling through the trees, tripping over the bodies of their fallen comrades, closing on the Americans all the time, the dead falling nearer and nearer to the muzzles of the M1s and Thompsons. Conner clipped a fresh magazine into his carbine and, without aiming, fired in an arc across the front of the advancing SS stormtroopers. Someone dropped to the ground behind him and yelled, 'We have orders to withdraw.'

'Thank Christ,' said Conner. Then he shouted, 'OK, fall back, fall back, fall back.'

The withdrawal was a scene of confusion bordering on panic. The GIs threw grenades into the advancing stormtroopers and began to inch back over the stony wooded ground, firing from the hip. Conner's group retreated to a position previously held by the armoured infantry and came across the American dead, shellholes and corpses strewn everywhere. They pushed on west, located a road and met up with stragglers from the armoured infantry. Many were dazed, shocked, one man kept chanting, 'They chewed us up, they chewed us up. Christ, they chewed us up.'

Conner looked behind him. He saw the fire from two burning Shermans dissipated in the mist. The remaining tanks were holding their ground, making no move to retreat, firing rapidly. 'What about the tanks?' yelled Conner, addressing no one in particular. 'Why ain't they falling back?'

'They got orders to hold,' a sergeant of armoured infantry replied.

'That's crazy.' Conner watched almost in tears. 'They're taking fire from all sides, they have no infantry support. It's suicidal.'

'Go tell that to the General, sir.' Then the sergeant turned and spat on the ground.

The group moved eastwards. Behind them a Sherman exploded, bellowing bright orange flame. Then a fourth tank was hit and Conner watched as the driver struggled out, his clothes and hair on fire. He staggered into the mist, a blazing animated automaton, before mercifully being cut down by small-arms fire. Then the tank from which he had escaped exploded with such force that the turret blew off and fell to the ground some seconds later with a resonance which rang through the forest. The remaining Shermans began to move backwards away from the high ground. The northernmost tank took a direct hit in the side and a vicious horizontal jet of flame shot out of its hull. The surviving Shermans turned around and lumbered towards the road, lobbing high explosive shells behind them into the German positions as they went.

The column of retreating GIs, with the wounded riding on the Shermans, reached Bastogne an hour and a half later. They passed the hastily thrown up fortifications and hull-down Shermans about a mile outside the town and walked into the square at the centre of Bastogne. It was already a town under siege. Conner joined a shuffling line which was passing a field kitchen and was given his first hot meal for three days. He went to a washing facility and soaped himself from the waist up, suddenly impervious to the cold. Then he shaved, savouring each refreshing stroke of the razor. In the Divisional HQ he found space at a table in a bustling room and wrote up his report.

'Not been inactive, have you?' said a clean-looking major reading over Conner's submission. The major smiled. He had an arm in a sling. 'Bit different from what they taught you to expect?'

'Some,' conceded Conner.

'Well, I've been in North Africa and I came ashore on D plus one and I haven't seen anything like it. I guess we're both learning, but you seem to have done well.'

'I don't know how you can say that, sir.' Conner nodded at the pile of dog-tags he had placed on the major's desk. 'Ten of those guys were part of my first command, I don't know what happened to the rest; two were murdered by Germans dressed as GIs, the remaining four guys we shot up thinking they were krauts.'

'That's just the German tactic working.' The major winced slightly and put his right hand up to his left, bandaged, shoulder. 'There've been instances of our guys shooting each other up all over the place. Just yesterday there was an incident. Two men dressed as infantry officers made their way across our lines, got through two sentry-posts, but the third sentry got suspicious and shot them. Turned out the lead guy was one of ours all right, but the guy behind was a kraut holding a gun on him.'

'Jesus.'

'We're wising up rapidly. Looking like an American isn't enough now we know what the krauts are up to; we're getting to tell the real thing from the cheap imitation. You think these guys in the jeep that came past your position before the main attack were German?'

'I reckon,' said Conner. 'They were miles from their unit and looked pretty fresh, at least the one I spoke to looked fresh. These things only become significant later. Then, we didn't know about this tactic. This guy even looked like a German, blond, blue eyes, driving straight out of the German lines. Christ, I should have seen it, a blind man could have seen it.'

'Well, like I said, Conner, don't worry about it. These guys have done all the damage they're going to do, they're probably cold by now anyway. Once we discover them, krauts in our uniforms aren't a good life insurance risk.'

'I guess not.'

'But again, like I said, Conner, you did well. You avoided capture, you made your way back and you rounded up stragglers.'

'They made their presence known to me, sir. Sergeant Baumgardner held them together.'

'So you say in your report, but you brought them home. They were lost; you knew where you were going. And you took part in the action of Task Force Rose. That gave us a valuable five hours.'

'What's the situation now, sir?'

'We're surrounded. Bastogne has Germans on all points of the compass. They have us bottled up while their main thrusts push west, one to the north and the other to the south of us. We can't tell yet whether they're going to try to take us out or whether they're happy to keep us contained. But whatever it is, we're strictly defensive, and with no chance of a drop until the weather lifts.'

'I understand.'

'Guess you could use some sleep.'

'Too right.' Conner grinned.

'Try the hotel across the square. It's been requisitioned as an officers' billet. You'll have to share your bed, and I don't just mean with other human beings, but what the hell.'

Yeah, what the hell, thought Conner as he slumped on the edge of a double bed in which already lay two other men. He was asleep before his head touched the pillow.

'You say,' said Schmitt when the Untersturmführer had finished speaking, 'that someone telephoned and asked for the file on the Operation Grief personnel.'

'Yes, sir!' The Untersturmführer stood rigidly to attention.

'And that this person was a woman?'

'Yes, sir!'

'Quite high born, you say?'

'I think so, Herr Schmitt. She did not sound like a woman who hangs around the beer halls.'

'I see. She asked for the file on Operation Gryphon?'

'Details of the personnel to be exact, Herr Schmitt. She asked for them to be sent to the office of Sturmbannführer Karl Blomm in the Prinz Albrechtstrasse. It was not an unusual request, often we send personnel files to the Gestapo, though I did think it strange that the caller should refer to Sturmbannführer Blomm as Herr Blomm, and I am afraid I may have been a little indiscreet.'

Hans Schmitt's eyes narrowed. 'Go on.'

'Well, sir, my reaction, as I recall, was, "What, all two thousand of them?" or "There are two thousand of them," or something similar.'

'I see what you mean,' said Schmitt. 'Still, as I understand it, that particular operation is over, it was effective only immediately prior to our main advance.'

'I am much relieved, Herr Schmitt.'

'But it was an indiscretion.'

'Yes sir. Then . . .'

'There's more?'

'Yes, sir.' The Untersturmführer stammered nervously. 'The caller said that she would just like the files on the personnel involved in the Operation Claws of the Gryphon.'

Hans Schmitt suddenly gripped the edge of his desk. 'What did you say?'

'Sir, that the caller . . .'

'I heard you the first time. What did you say then?'

'I asked her to identify herself, I asked her security rating.'

'You know of the Operation Claws of the Gryphon?'

'I do not, sir. That is to say, I know no details. But it is one of a number of operations in respect of which I am obliged to ascertain the identity and security clearance of anybody making enquiries about that operation.'

'I see. So in the space of less than one minute this female caller found out that Operation Gryphon involved two thousand men, and that there indeed is a highly secret operation known as the Claws of the Gryphon.'

'I'm afraid so, sir. I took the liberty of telephoning Sturm-bannführer Blomm and asking if he authorized such a request . . .'

'And?'

'He knew nothing of it.'

'So there's a spy in Berlin.'

The Untersturmführer remained silent.

'You did well to report it to me, Grass.'

'Thank you, sir.'

'But had you not informed me I would have found out anyway and I would have personally arranged your transfer to the Russian front.'

'Yes, sir.'

'Dismiss.'

As the man left his office, Schmitt reached for the phone which stood on his desk. He dialled an internal number and, when his call was answered, said, 'Rademacher, is that you? Good. Will you come to my office, please? Yes, now.' Schmitt replaced the receiver and began to drum his fingers on his desktop, but stopped when he heard Rademacher's footstep in the corridor. 'Come in,' he called, before Rademacher tapped on his door.

Rademacher entered the room. He was dressed in a grey suit, was plump with full cheeks. He was tall and well set and always seemed to wear wartime austerity well, so well in fact that Schmitt had long suspected him of black market connections. Rademacher was twenty-seven years old and had proved himself to be quite ruthless.

Schmitt said, 'Rademacher, there is a spy in Berlin.'

Rademacher looked at him enquiringly, took out a packet of Red Cross Virginia cigarettes and offered one to Schmitt. Now where, thought Schmitt, did he get hold of those? But he took one just the same. 'Someone has been asking Personnel about Operation Claws of the Gryphon.'

'Whatever's that?' Rademacher proffered his cigarette lighter.

'All you need to know is that it is highly classified.' Schmitt lit his cigarette.

'Thank you,' said Rademacher, extravagantly and pointedly allowing the flame of the lighter to burn before making use of it to light his own cigarette.

Schmitt let the remark ride. 'The informant reports that the enquiry was made by a woman.'

'It's been known before. Frankly, many of their best agents were women, especially the Soviet women. Hardest to crack, higher pain threshold.' Rademacher glanced disapprovingly around his superior's office and sniffed at the bareness.

'Our informant further reports that this particular lady seems to be German and quite high born.'

Rademacher raised his eyebrows. 'A German female?'

'Apparently.'

'So she is a traitor as well as a spy.'

'That is for you to determine, Rademacher.'

'Why? Because I too enjoy a lineage of certain distinction?'

'Merely, Rademacher, because I am allocating this task to you; because, although I do not personally like you, I think you are good at your job.'

'Thank you.'

'And also because of a chance remark you made yesterday about observing a woman walking along Invalidenstrasse shortly after a radio transmission ceased.'

'Oh, that woman. One of our listening-posts picked up a Morse transmission, but we only got one direction on it, we had no time to get a cross-bearing. It could have come from anywhere within a certain area, and there are Wehrmacht installations within that area, so the transmission could have been legitimate. Morse is often preferred by the army these days, telephone lines are invariably severed by the bombing.'

'I know, I have tried . . . but never mind.'

'Following the transmission I drove around the area, but because of the rubble in the side streets I could only drive on the main thoroughfare. I saw one or two people, mostly making for the shelters, one was a striking figure of a woman, very Aryan, heading towards the subway. She must live in the area because I saw her again, this time on the subway platform.'

'Which area is this?'

'By the Stettiner Bahnhof.'

'Then you will follow up these observations,' said Schmitt.

Chapter Eight

'It's mad,' said Schweitzer. 'Utter madness.' He sat in the front passenger seat of Klara Heidler's Citroën, slowly pulling on a Gauloise and looking at the imposing rear side of the Palace of Versailles. Military Police stood at the gate and also at the entrance to the palace, which still managed to glow in the dull December sunlight. A squad of Marines was drilling at the extreme right of the palace's courtyard. Schweitzer watched as a black staff car approached the palace from the Avenue de St Cloud. It halted at the gates and the MPs inspected the credentials of the driver before waving it on into the courtyard.

'Beside the palace are caravans, tents and vehicles which comprise Supreme Headquarters Allied Expeditionary Forces,' said Klara Heidler, 'about fifteen hundred men. In the palace itself the Supreme Commander has an apartment. No, it is not madness, Schweitzer, it has been fully thought out.'

'It is still mad,' said Schweitzer with a gleam in his eye. 'So mad that it might work.'

'It will work, Schweitzer. I must not fail.'

'Except that now I go alone, without the assistance of Genscher and Hoff.'

'You will be better off without them,' Klara Heidler said coldly. 'If they had not been loyal Nazis they would have been no use. I think it is as well that their treachery was revealed sooner rather than later.'

'So I go one night near Christmas?' Schweitzer turned to her. He looked at her face, a hard face, a purposeful face, but with furrows on her brow and bags under her eyes.

'Yes,' she said. 'Perhaps the twenty-sixth or the twenty-seventh. Between one and two a.m. It is a bad winter so you should enjoy a certain assistance in that respect. Then we go to Lyons in the jeep where we shall keep him in custody.'

'Who will decide on which date I shall go?'

'I will. I will watch his movements. I have watched him driving with his English mistress whom he calls his personal assistant. We need to be certain that he is in the palace. But like I said, it will be soon after Christmas, and on a night of bad weather.'

'I do not go in these?' Schweitzer lifted the lapel of his grey civilian jacket.

'No. You wear your American uniform.'

'I go right up to the front door and ask him if he wants to come drink a beer or two with me?'

'Don't be flippant.' She fixed him with a glare. 'I told you that this has been carefully planned. There is an entrance in the wall which runs by the gardens at the front of the palace . . .'

'Then this is the rear?' Schweitzer nodded towards the building.

'Yes. This small entrance is used by gardeners and other workmen.'

'And you have a key, of course.'

'It is never locked.'

'All right, but once inside I'm still a million miles from the target.'

'One of your generals, General Patton . . .'

'One of my generals?'

'You are in the American army aren't you?'

Schweitzer smiled.

'He said, never tell a man how to do something, tell him what to do and he will surprise you with his ingenuity. So you, Schweitzer, will surprise me with your ingenuity.'

After a pause, Schweitzer said, 'It's good to feel that someone has faith in me.'

'You were chosen for this. You have proved yourself on the Russian front.'

'As did Genscher. He is now proving himself in Paris. Hoff too.'

'We needed men of fighting quality, good speakers of American-English and good Nazis. Sadly, Genscher and Hoff did not fulfil the last requirement. But to the matter in hand: I can tell you that the gate is about half a mile from the palace itself. I can also tell you that the grounds are patrolled by armed guards with dogs. Nearer the time I will tell you exactly which apartment to make for once you have reached the palace.'

'Weapons?'

'A Colt revolver with a silencer. A knife, aniseed and ground pepper for the dogs. Aniseed to hide your scent, the pepper for the dogs' eyes if they should still find you.'

'Thank you,' said Schweitzer with an air of forced patience.

'You will also have bad weather, the dead of night, and surprise on your side.'

She started the car and drove east along the Avenue de Paris, before turning north towards Paris. The traffic consisted mainly of military staff cars and light army vehicles. Rain began to fall and Klara Heidler worked the windscreen-wiper lever backwards and forwards. She said: 'You must do all you can to capture him, you must assure him of his continuing welfare. You must tell him that if he doesn't come with you, you must shoot him dead, and indeed if he refuses to accompany you, then you must assassinate him. But remember, to assassinate him is poor compensation. You must do everything you can to kidnap him. Germany's bargaining power depends on it.'

Genscher and Hoff waited in the café until nightfall, spending useless money freely. They ate a simple though wholesome meal which seemed to have been prepared with care by the proprietor's wife, and the proprietor pressed a complimentary bottle of wine on to the two big-spending Yanks.

'We need civilian clothing.' Genscher swilled the wine round in his glass. 'That's the next step, Hoff, clothing.'

'If you say so, Genscher.' Hoff prodded his food. 'You know, the French don't eat as good as they used to eat.'

'No? They still eat better than we did in the SS.' Genscher

leant back in his chair. 'Do the Frogs always serve up each course on the same plate? We had the soup and cleared that and then along came the stew ladled into the soup bowl.'

Hoff smiled and shook his head. 'No, I think there's a bad shortage of crockery in Paris at the moment.'

'I see. Anyway Hoff, tonight we get civilian clothing.'

'How? I mean what happens if we screw it up?'

'You they shoot. Me –' Genscher shrugged '– I was coerced into it, I took the first opportunity to escape, I'm trying to make my way home to my kin in Wisconsin . . .'

Hoff's jaw sagged. 'Me they shoot, you they don't. How do you work that out, Genscher?'

'You shot one of those MPs, remember, out on that lonely road, the ones we pushed into the ditch. You let him have it in the guts, Hoff, remember? I was in the back of the jeep. I didn't do nothing.'

'What am I going to do?' Hoff appealed to Genscher. 'I just saw him as an enemy. It was only after you'd got me to thinking, but I'd forgotten that . . .'

'You never forget shooting a guy close up,' said Genscher. 'No, you're in a mess, Hoff, you need to stick by me. You do what I tell you and it'll work out.'

'Yes,' said the big man, looking trustingly into Genscher's steely eyes. 'I'll trust you, I'll go along with whatever you say.'

Outside an army six-wheeler rumbled northwards. The windows of the café rattled.

'So tonight we've got to get ourselves some clothing. Then we go west.'

'How do we get the clothing? We have to think of that now.'

'We have to find somebody who's about our size and borrow their clothes; is all.'

'That won't be easy, Genscher.'

'So we persuade them.'

'OK, OK.' Hoff was weary. 'So we start looking.'

'That's right, Hoff. We start looking.'

'Reckon we could start looking right here.'

'Huh?'

'The proprietor, he's a little guy like you. I reckon you're about the same size.'

Genscher glanced across the floor of the café and looked at the proprietor, who smiled at him. Genscher smiled back and then turned to Hoff. 'You know,' he said, 'you could be right.'

'Maybe we could get a little of our money back at the same time?'

'Taking to this style of living like a duck to water, ain't you, Hoff. But sure, sure, and anything else they've got that we could use.'

'When do we do it, then? Now while there's nobody else here, or later tonight when they shut?'

Genscher glanced around him, the wooden chairs and round tables, the brass gas lamps on the wall. 'Now, I reckon, these places never shut. Only not right now, we'd only be seen through the window. We go round the back, there's got to be a back entrance.'

Hoff and Genscher stood and walked towards the door, the café proprietor crossed the floor and opened the door for them, thanking them for their custom. The sudden coldness of the night gripped them and their breath hung in the air. They walked to the end of the block, turned down a side street and found the back alley. It was a narrow passage between two brick walls, thickly overgrown. Genscher began to force his way through the garbage and the shrubs, picking his way, inch by inch, along the passage. Hoff followed, often stumbling. It took them fifteen minutes to reach the rear of the café. Genscher tried the gate. It creaked open. In the gloom he saw piles of kitchen refuse and a fat cat scuttling away into the dark. The smell of cooking wafted across the yard. Genscher walked up to the rear door. He looked up. The building rose for four storeys above the café, most rooms seemed to be in darkness, save for one lighted room on the third floor. 'I'm not too happy about that light,' he said when Hoff joined him. 'Could be tricky, especially if the dame shrieks.'

'Let's just get on with it,' muttered Hoff. 'I'm beginning to get edgy.'

Genscher pushed the back door. It opened easily, but rang a bell which was attached to the door frame. He stepped back into the gloom, and whispered, 'I'll grab him, you get in and grab the woman.' Before Hoff could protest the proprietor opened the door fully and peered into the gloom, holding a towel across his arm. He stepped into the yard and Genscher grappled him to the ground. Hoff ran into the house. The proprietor's wife stood in the passageway. He saw the look in her eyes flash from surprise to recognition to betrayal to terror. Then he hit her. Hard.

Genscher came into the building and saw the huge frame of Hoff standing over the woman's crumpled body. He knelt and felt for her pulse. 'Jesus, Hoff,' he breathed.

'I only hit her once, Genscher,' Hoff protested, standing awkwardly as if not knowing what to do with his huge hands.

'Holy Mother of Christ, man, what did you use, a baseball bat?'

'I didn't mean to . . .'

Genscher stood and peered through the gap between the two curtains which separated the kitchen from the dining area. The café was still empty. 'We're in luck,' he said, turning. 'Thank Christ they're not busy. But we have to hurry.'

'What do I do, what do I do?' Hoff was agitated. He kept looking at the woman.

'OK, you turn down the gas in the dining area. There's three lamps, turn them down and blow them out. Lock the door and switch the sign round to say the place is closed. That might give us a few hours to get clear of the city. Then empty the till, and don't forget to lift the till drawer to get the big bills. We need francs as well as dollars.'

Without waiting to see Hoff move, Genscher went up the narrow flight of stairs which led from the kitchen. There was just one bedroom upstairs, just that one room. That's all, sleep upstairs and work downstairs, and not taking in much by the look of the threadbare carpets and cheap fittings as shown by the flame of Genscher's lighter. If he was a little more sentimental, he thought, maybe he could feel sorry for the old couple. But then maybe not. This was better than working in a coal mine and if this is how they had spent the last five years, getting by with no great comfort but no great hardship, then they had had a lucky war. There were two wardrobes, the first contained dresses and skirts, the second belonged to the man. Genscher took a suit, a couple of shirts, socks, underclothing, a pair of shoes and a raincoat. Ten minutes later he went downstairs and saw Hoff looking down at the woman with horrified fascination. He started as Genscher appeared.

'Relax,' said Genscher. 'It's me.'

'Where's your uniform?'

'I left it upstairs, what the hell. I don't want to be no French civilian carrying round US army battledress. We have to blend, Hoff.'

'I've got to carry around a battledress.'

'We'll fix that, only next time don't hit them so hard. Did you get the money?'

'Sure.'

'OK, give it, I'll carry it.'

Hoff hesitated.

'If we have to dump your uniform we have to dump it quick. We don't want to hang around emptying the pockets.'

Hoff handed over the money. There was not a great deal, mostly it was the counterfeit bills they had used to purchase their meal.

'Did you close up the café?'

'Yes,' said Hoff.

'So let's go.'

They took the métro to the south side of the city.

'Suburbs are safer,' said Genscher. 'The city centre's full of MPs.' The train rattled slowly southwards. Hoff, sitting next to Genscher, towering above him, feeling too large and conspicuous in battledress, could only grunt in agreement. They left the train when Genscher felt that they had gone far enough beyond Concorde, which he deemed to be the centre of the city, alighting at Pasteur, having already changed at Opéra and Madeleine. They emerged into a built-up area of high tenements and small *tabacs*. The first thing they saw was two MPs sitting in a highly polished jeep. They faced away from the train exit.

'Got any more bright ideas?' hissed Hoff.

'Jesus, what is this place?' said Genscher.

'We were safer in the old neighbourhood.'

'No, we weren't. When the café proprietor comes round and finds he's a sudden widower, the streets back there are going to be crawling with lawmen. When they find my uniform the place is going to be crawling with MPs as well. We're safer here.' Genscher was jostled by a man who lumbered past him smelling heavily of wine. 'We just keep on walking, find a quiet street and wait until some big guy comes along.'

'But look at them, Genscher. They're all small, we'll never find a big guy. What am I going to do, what if those MPs turn around? Can't we hurry on, maybe run for a bit?'

They didn't find a big man until close on midnight. He was a lumbering overweight man with a beret, a cape, and a cheap cigarette which was drooping from his lip and burning only on the underside. Hoff and Genscher looked at each other and nodded. The man walked towards them, but did not seem to notice them. They let him pass and then followed him, just a few paces behind. The man walked along the main thoroughfare for about half a mile before turning into a dimly lit lane. Genscher glanced around him. There were vehicles on the main street, but no pedestrians close by. 'Now,' he whispered. 'Hoff, go, Hoff. But not so hard this time.'

'You're not going to help me?'

'No, you great lummox, I'm keeping lookout, he's carrying a weight of booze anyway. Go on, quick!'

Hoff walked after the big Parisian and disappeared into the gloom. Genscher lit a cigarette and stood on the street corner. He took the lighter away from the tip of the cigarette just in time to see a jeep full of MPs cruising down the main road. He turned and saw Hoff and the big Parisian struggling in the centre of the side street, clearly visible from the main road. The jeep drew level with the entrance to the side street, Genscher heard one of the MPs yell, the jeep braked, reversed, and drove towards the fight. Genscher began to walk away. As he did so he heard the dull thud of what could only be some MP's night stick coming down on what could only be Hoff's lumbar region.

Genscher took the métro back to the centre of Paris and found a bar full of servicemen. He bought a beer with a counterfeit ten-dollar bill and sat next to a group of fresh-faced GIs.

'Hi,' he said.

'Hi,' replied the nearest soldier with a genuine smile. A child, thought Genscher, a mere child.

'You boys just out from the States?'

'Yes, sir. You American?'

'Sure am, from Wisconsin.' Genscher sipped his beer.

'No kiddin'?' The group turned, interested.

'Yep. I'm from Silver Creek, Wisconsin. Heard of it?'

'Can't say we have, sir,' said a dark-haired boy. 'We're mainly out of Texas.'

'Fine place,' said Genscher. 'I was down in Fort Worth one time.'

'Yeah? Hey, terrific.' A fair-haired boy grinned. 'What are you doing in Paris, sir? If you don't mind me asking.'

'Sure don't, son,' said Genscher, thinking quickly. 'I'm a correspondent, yeah, that's what I am, a correspondent.'

'No kiddin'? A newspaperman?'

'It's the real thing, son.' Genscher felt himself growing into the role. 'I'm a war correspondent. I write the stuff that the folks at home read in the newspapers. After it's been censored some, of course.'

'Censors, yeah,' said the dark boy. 'My mom wrote that my last letter home was half cut away by the censor.'

'Gotta be careful what you say, son,' said Genscher. 'Don't want to give away any military secrets.'

'You been up the line, sir?'

'Sure.'

'Is it as bad as they say right now? They say it's a real bitch and we're going up any day now.'

'That's a military secret you just let out, son. You gotta be thankful I ain't no German.'

The GIs laughed except the speaker, who looked embarrassed.

'But it's just like they say,' said Genscher. 'It's everything you heard and worse. When I was up there the krauts were tearing lumps out of us. Unit I was with got overrun. I lost everything, combat gear burnt, I/D gone . . .'

'You lost your I/D?'

'Wouldn't credit it, would you?' said Genscher.

Outside the remote villa in the foothills of the Dauphiné the man paced up and down. He was nervous. He clutched a Walther in a clammy palm. It was a cold night and he shivered, despite his leather greatcoat. He scanned the area in front of the house, infuriated by the swaying trees which threw dancing shadows everywhere. A figure approached from his right. He spun and aimed the pistol.

'It's I, Klaus,' said the man who approached. 'There was somebody out there.'

'I think it was nothing,' said Konrad Morke.

'The dogs do not bark at nothing, Herr Morke.'

'This time they are mistaken.'

But again the dogs began to bark.

'They bark at shadows,' said Morke.

'I do not like it, Herr Morke. I think the villa is not safe.'

'You are an old woman, Klaus.'

'I am certain they are barking at someone.'

'They are excited.'

'Again, I insist. The villa has become unsafe. This is the second time this month. I think, the others too, we think it is time we fled into Switzerland.'

'No!' Morke turned angrily to him. 'That would be desertion. While Germany is still fighting and while something is asked of us, we stay. I am returning inside. I have had sufficient of this nonsense.'

Klaus Fiesler followed him, insisting, 'I am right. You remember in the old days I could smell Communists. I could smell the Lyons maquis. I tell you I can still do so. We are not safe here.'

'It is safe. That is all. *Sieg Heil!*'

Morke entered the villa and went to the rear of the house. He descended a flight of stairs into the cellars and opened the door of a small room. He checked that the iron-framed bed had been made up as he had instructed, and saw that the small stove had been fired. It gave out little heat and indeed served only to take the edge off the chill in the room. There was a small amount of coal by the stove, sufficient to keep it burning for a few hours, but insufficient for the occupant of the room to start an inferno. Manacles were folded neatly at the foot of the bed, where there was also a chamber-pot. He left the room, throwing the two heavy bolts across to lock the door behind him.

He then went to a small room further along the cellar corridor and, taking a key from his pocket, unlocked the door and let himself in. He looked around him and in the dim light from the gas lamp in the corridor began to make out certain objects. One million Swiss francs, ten million, one hundred million? It was impossible to put a value on the articles in the room: oil paintings, jewellery, ornaments in silver and gold. All looted from Lyons and the surrounding area by Morke and others, who, risking their own execution, decided to keep it for themselves. Even so, the contents of the small room were less than a hundredth of the treasure shipped from Lyons to Germany during the Occupation.

Morke looked at the valuables and thought about what Klaus Fiesler had said. What if the Communists were getting curious about the villa? He would need something for himself, something easily carried, easily changed into hard cash. The jewellery, for example. Morke selected what he felt to be his fair share, given his senior rank and the years he had been of service to the Reich, and shovelled the stones and rings, bracelets and necklaces into a canvas sack which he wrapped in a waterproof SS poncho. He left the room and later that night carried the package out into the wilderness at the side of the house and buried it shallowly near the roots of an upturned tree. Perhaps over the next few days he would take a few more items, he wouldn't be greedy, he'd leave some for the others, he would leave the oil paintings, for example, but he'd take sufficient for himself.

Chapter Nine

There was a mist, a light white mist, which was thickest in the meadows, especially near the stream. Closer at hand the mist condensed on walls and clothing. Underfoot there lay a thin film of ice which cracked easily when walked on. Two men stood in the driveway of a modest detached house at the edge of their village: they were both well wrapped up against the cold; one was youthful, the second middle-aged. They stood admiring a gleaming black sports saloon which stood on the gravel drive, just below the front door of the house.

'It's really generous of you,' said Benjamin Service. 'You ought not to have done so. An MG, no less.'

'Nonsense,' replied the older man. 'I'm pursuing a policy of getting rid of my money while I'm alive. It's no damn good to me when I'm dead and I want some say in how it's spent.'

'But this is really too much.'

'Well, if the truth be known, it's partly your mother's idea,' said Robert Service. 'She thinks it'll help you bring the young ladies home. It's a 1940 model, been on blocks since '41.'

Benjamin Service nodded. 'Yes, I dare say I'll have to think about a future pretty soon.'

'The war is nearly over. Can't last much longer.'

The two men turned from the house and walked down the driveway towards the road.

'Could be another year,' said Benjamin Service.

'As long as that?'

They turned right, towards the village.

'Well, yes,' Benjamin replied. 'Germany is not defeated yet, not by a long chalk. She's still fighting hard.'

'But the newspapers give the impression that it's nearly over. For heaven's sake, the government allows lights in houses now. Since November we've had a light in our house, so long as the curtains remain closed, and even the street lights are on for a few hours after dusk. Anyway, how was London?'

'Foggy, a real pea-souper, wet and icy. People in their offices were sitting in coats and scarves. Streets full of servicemen.'

'What's playing where?'

'Didn't stop to look. Got off the train at Paddington, took the tube to Waterloo, got the train to Bournemouth. Had to wait for an hour so I walked around a bit. That's when I saw the typists and clerks working in outdoor clothing and the servicemen all milling around.'

The two men halted to allow an American jeep to turn from a side road into the main road. There were two men in the jeep and as it swept around the corner the driver yelled, 'Merry Christmas!' Robert Service raised his hat and Benjamin Service waved.

'We'd better press on and have a couple of pints before the Yanks come in from the base. Otherwise we'll get squeezed out,' Benjamin suggested.

'No, we won't.' His father refused to quicken his pace. 'They've all gone.'

'All?'

'Practically all. The only ones left now are the chaps like those. I gather they're supposed to look after the camp, but, as far as I can see, they have a whale of a time driving jeeps about, usually at breakneck speed. The rest went to Europe on D-day, or so we heard. They took heavy casualties, I believe. It's an unnerving feeling to think that so many of those boys we got used to seeing around the village may now be dead or badly wounded.'

In the lounge of the Green Man, Benjamin Service shook hands with one or two villagers who recognized him, bought drinks at the bar and carried them over to where Robert Service had occupied a table near the open fire.

'Merry Christmas,' said Benjamin, raising his glass.

'Your good health,' Robert Service replied.

'So how are things?'

'With us or with the village?'

'Both.'

'With us they are well, thank you. The practice has been quiet, mostly because the war is keeping people healthy. Rationing is a good thing and should be kept on. One or two babies delivered over the last few months, some of them quite an odd colour.'

'Still soldiering on, then?'

'Oh yes. I'll have to keep the practice going until the end of the war, delay my retirement. There's a shortage of GPs at the moment, all the medical people are in the services. When the war finishes there'll be a flood of people wanting a country practice, so I'll be able to leave with a clear conscience. Buy a cottage and a bit of land, south Devon, I think.'

'Lovely. And the village?'

'Well, like I said, it's been quiet since the Yanks went, but not like it used to be. We can't go back, we're well in the twentieth century now.'

'Merry Christmas, Doctor.' An elderly man ambled past their table.

'Merry Christmas,' Robert Service acknowledged. 'So, what's the news? Henry Debbage, the harvester, was killed in France.'

'That's bad.'

'Yes, I don't think Sam will last much longer. He's pining away. Somebody else had to come and take in the harvest in these parts this year.'

'I didn't know Henry was fighting. Agricultural workers are in a reserved occupation.'

'He volunteered. Wanted a bit of the glory, wanted something to tell his grandchildren, I dare say. And poor Mrs Johns . . .'

'Not another son?'

'I'm afraid so. John, also in France. She's had a hard war, poor woman. First she lost her eldest son in North Africa, then her husband was recalled to sea, you remember. Now John's gone. There's just young Freddie left. Mrs Johns is just a shadow of her former self, no spark at all now.'

'Did they volunteer like Henry Debbage?'

'Yes. That's what makes it difficult for her. All her sons could have had a safe war by farming. Instead, they volunteered. Oh, and Ted Chambers came back from the Navy, invalided out. Lost a leg when his ship hit a mine. I don't think that there's any other news.' Robert Service sipped his beer. 'So tell me, when are you going to get married?'

'I don't know. Some time, I suppose.'

'What happened to that German girl you brought home before the war?'

'Half German. English on her mother's side, and on her birth certificate, as I recall.'

'Lovely girl. They still talk about her in the village. What became of her?'

'She joined a medical unit of some description. They shipped her out to Canada and, well, we just lost contact.'

'I see. Well, your mother and I both hope you'll find another girl and settle down. It's going to be a brave new world after the war, you and the new Europe can start out together.' He drained his glass. 'One more, I think, and then we'll walk back. Village GP can't be seen to be overdoing it. Anyway, I'm hungry and we have a goose for lunch.'

'A goose!'

'Ssshh! Keep your voice down, some people are having two rashers of bacon and boiled potatoes for their Christmas meal.'

After the meal, the Services listened to the BBC Home Service special broadcast of *The Journey Home*, and then the news which, as most often, was read by Alvar Liddell. Later Mrs Service hid behind a two-day-old copy of the *Daily Telegraph* and, with the help of probably one too many sherries, kept muttering, 'That's true,' 'That's correct.' Benjamin Service turned to his father and said, 'I think I'll go and pay a call on Mrs Johns.'

'Now? It's cold out.'

'I'll take my car.'

'I think she'll appreciate a visit on Christmas night. You might care to take her some goose?'

Benjamin drove slowly through the village getting used to the feel of the MG, savouring the rich smell of leather from the seats, and the smell of polished wood from the coachwork, both scents penetrating the mustiness of a car which had been laid up for three years. In the village square, the church choir had gathered to sing carols and for the first time in years were allowed the luxury of a lantern. Service slowed and wound the window down. The chill air nipped his face, but he enjoyed hearing the choir as they sang, 'Hark, the Herald Angels Sing'.

Mrs Johns welcomed him into her cottage and pressed a glass of port into his hand as he gave her the slices of meat from their goose. In her parlour she had photographs of her husband and sons, cheery, bronzed men, Englishmen, proud in their uniforms. Mrs Johns's speech was slightly slurred and Benjamin Service guessed that she had probably drunk much during the day, and eaten little. She was also, as Robert Service described, thin and wasted.

'Thank you, Master Benjamin,' she said as he expressed his sympathy in her loss. 'First it was Paul, then Jack went, now it's John. There's just young Freddie left.'

Service reached forward and patted her hand. He noticed that Freddie's photograph was kept separate from the photographs of Mrs Johns's husband and other two sons.

It had got so cold in the night that Conner's entire body had grown numb. He sat huddled in a foxhole with a scarf wrapped round his neck and over his mouth, with his hands in gloves pushed deep into his tunic pocket and his carbine resting in front of him, muzzle pointing to the sky.

He had spent the last seven days attached to the so-called 'Snafu' Company, which was based in the centre of Bastogne, in the square which was bordered by tall thin houses with sharply angled roofs. 'Snafu' Company picked up any job that didn't fall within the responsibilities of other companies. So Conner spent December 19 siphoning fuel from vehicles, leaving no more than two gallons in each vehicle so that if the vehicle took a direct hit the fuel wasn't lost as well. The excess fuel was stored around Bastogne in dumps not exceeding fifty gallons. On the 20th

'Snafu' Company drove extra ammunition out to 567 Field Artillery Unit, an all-black unit who had exhausted their ammunition, sometimes firing at the German tanks at point-blank range, often sighting down open barrels at the oncoming Tigers. The area in front of 567's position was just a graveyard of Nazi armour, with German dead littering the concrete hard ground. The next day the Germans laid down a three-hour barrage on the foxholes in front of 567's position, then the stormtroopers broke through and machine-gunned and bayoneted the unarmed artillery men until they were driven off by the 101st Airborne. 'Snafu' Company went up the line and plugged the gap and Conner saw that, despite the barrage, there were still about three hundred German dead around 567's position.

That night he and a few others drank a potion known as Malmédy Skull Pop; it comprised snow, vanilla essence and industrial alcohol. He remembered little of the incident.

On the night of December 22 the Germans had launched a strong attack on Team Browne's position at Senochamps. Team Browne managed to repel four separate German attacks, but at the cost of heavy casualties. That night the order came down from Battalion HQ that no howitzer or tank was to fire more than five shells per day. The next day, Saturday, December 23, just before dawn, the Luftwaffe bombed the American troops who huddled together in the freezing conditions. Shortly after that the men with whom Conner found himself, believing that the dawn would bring a large-scale German attack, began to shake hands with each other.

The dawn of December 23 did bring something and if Conner ever wanted to believe in God or miracles he would remember that day, because it dawned bright and clear with unlimited visibility. The freezing fog which had been of such assistance to the German advance had suddenly cleared. It was to be a temporary break in the weather, lasting only until the afternoon of Christmas Eve, but for the first time in the Ardennes Offensive the Allies were able to get planes into the air, German positions around Bastogne were bombed and strafed, and supplies were dropped from transports which flew straight and steady through the German flak. Gliders dropped inside the perimeter bringing with them medical supplies and four invaluable surgeons. Years later when Conner, by then an Assistant District Attorney in the city of New York, was researching the siege of Bastogne, he was to discover that during the brief period of good visibility the RAF and the USAAF between them put more than 4000 planes in the air.

The fog returned just before dusk, welling up like smoke from the ravines, and the GIs once again settled down in freezing near-zero visibility and waited. Just after midnight some GI shouted, 'Hey, it's Christmas. Merry Christmas everybody.' Somebody else replied, 'What's merry about it?' Then there was silence until 6.45, when one of the heaviest German barrages of the siege fell, this time aimed at the south-western defences. Conner heard the woosh of incoming shells just in time to roll himself into a ball at the bottom of his foxhole. The shock from the exploding shells travelled through the soil and had the effect of 'punching' him at whichever part of his body happened to be in contact with the ground. The noise was deafening and the frozen soil thrown up by the shells rained down like shrapnel. The barrage lasted for one and a half hours and then lifted, suddenly. There was a silence of about thirty seconds and then Connor began to hear men shouting to each other. He stood in his foxhole, head and shoulders above the ground and made out the heads of other GIs, all staring out towards the woods from which they knew the German troops must soon be coming. He also saw the mess left by the bombardment; craters where there had once been foxholes, corpses where there had once been life. Behind him in the command post, the company commander yelled, 'Prepare to receive infantry.'

'And armour,' said Conner to himself, freeing the muzzle of his carbine from soil. He felt his heart pounding in his ribcage and he felt a hollowness and a coldness caused by something other than the temperature. 'Christ, I'm scared,' he said. 'I'm scared, I'm scared, I'm scared.' He was evidently not the only one, for he heard the guy in the next foxhole saying his rosary.

The Germans didn't attack until thirty minutes after the barrage had lifted. They came out of the fog, running hard, first one stormtrooper in a snowsuit, then two, then ten, then a hundred, all big men, firing from the hip as they came on, just as their comrades had done when attacking Task Force Rose. Conner didn't wait for the order to fire, he levelled his carbine at the approaching Germans and squeezed the trigger rhythmically while moving the gun from left to right. Many other GIs were doing the same and the SS stormtroopers, running into a withering small-arms fire, began to fall, almost as if given the order to lie down. But still they came on, running out of the fog. Then the Panzers appeared, King Tigers and Panthers growling out of the fog, coming on over the open ground at thirty miles an hour. Behind him Conner heard the sharp 'crack' as the tank-busters fired on the approaching tanks. The first tank to be hit, a Panther, threw a track and slewed round, remaining in the battle as a stationary gun platform, raking the American lines with machine-gun and shellfire until two infantry men with a bazooka knocked it out. A Tiger took a direct hit while only fifty yards from the American lines. It burnt fiercely, forcing the German troops who had been following it to give it a wide berth, thus exposing themselves to the American machine-guns. A third tank fired on a tank-buster and probably hit the ammunition; Conner clearly recalled it exploding with such force that the explosion had the effect of momentarily halting the fire on both sides.

Still the stormtroopers came on, overrunning the outlying American position, machine-gunning the men in the fox-holes. The second and remaining tank-buster took two shells in quick succession and ceased firing, leaving the Americans only bazookas to deal with the Nazi armour. Conner fired indiscriminately and heard the bullets sucking the air about him and, not for the first time in his war, felt the near-psychic sensation of bullets missing him by a fraction of an inch.

A Panther lurched out of the mist and drove a course which Conner realized would take it right over his position. He kept firing until the last moment and then shrank as the tank came

184

tearing through the ice-hard snow, closing on his foxhole. He heard an explosion and then heard one of the tank's tracks rattle against the underbody of the monster. The Panther slewed round and the good track came to rest half covering Conner's foxhole. He realized at the time that it had probably saved his life. He heard the tank continue to fire both shells and its machine-gun, until it was jolted by a second explosion and became quiet. Through the gap between the tank track and the lip of his foxhole, Conner watched the SS stormtroopers overrun the second line of the American defences, taking and inflicting horrific casualties, and pit themselves against the final American line on a ridge overlooking the German advance. The Germans pushed forward determinedly, but Conner thought he detected a faltering in their advance. Then he saw clearly that the Germans were indeed falling back, still firing as they backed down the slope, still falling in large numbers under the grim American fire. Conner waited until the firing ceased and then, using his bayonet, began to chip away the snow and soil at the edge of his foxhole, digging a gap big enough for him to squeeze through. He dug frantically, knowing that the German troops would be regrouping prior to a second attack. Eventually he had cleared a gap of sufficient width and he tossed his helmet out before him to alert the shaken and nervous defence to his existence and nationality.

Then he called, 'American. I'm coming in.'

Someone answered, 'I see you, buddy. Come on home.'

Conner pushed himself out of his foxhole and, picking up his helmet, ran in a stooping manner to the American line, jumping over both American and German dead. He leaped into a slit trench.

'Mr Conner!'

Conner turned and looked into the big, beaming face of Sergeant Baumgardner. They shook hands warmly and vigorously.

'Always knew you'd survive, Mr Conner,' said Baumgardner. 'You have a lucky streak in you.'

'You reckon?'

'Sure do. I can recognize one of life's survivors.'

'I draw great comfort from that observation.' Conner reached for his cigarettes and handed one to Baumgardner.

'I sure need this.' Baumgardner drew deeply as Conner held the flame of his lighter to the sergeant's cigarette.

'Think they'll be back?'

'Sure to be.'

'What have we got?'

'Just what you see.'

Conner saw a small group of men, less than two hundred, stretched out along a ridge which was perhaps a quarter of a mile wide. Just behind the ridge a field kitchen was being set up and the smell of coffee was already drifting incongruously across the battlefield.

'This is all?' he said.

'We sent for reinforcements, but we had to use a runner, that means a guy in a jeep, because the bombardment took out our communications. We lost our tank-busters and we're down to three bazookas. We lost two-thirds of the company in the attack, but, apart from that, we're in good shape.'

'I reckon the krauts could have broken through them?'

'Sure, sure they could. We couldn't have lasted another couple of minutes. If they'd've continued their attack they'd have been half way to Bastogne by now. But that's war, I guess, never knowing what the other guy's reserves are.'

'I guess,' said Conner.

A man's scream pierced the thin air. Conner looked up.

'That's Mr Boyle, the company commander. He took one in the guts. They wrapped him in a mile of bandage and it just kept turning red. Soon as they wound a new bit round it just changed colour. The medic reckons he can do something for him if he can get him to the field hospital in Bastogne. The scream's healthy enough.'

'Healthy?'

'Sure. If a guy's strong enough to scream like that he'll pull

186

through. It's the guys that don't feel anything after they've stopped a bullet that don't make it.'

'I guess,' said Conner again. But it didn't make the man's screams easier to listen to.

'Better chow up, sir,' said Baumgardner. 'We don't know when the next opportunity will be.'

The Americans consolidated their position on the ridge and a detachment of glider infantry were brought in as reinforcements. Conner took charge of a detachment which combed the first and second American lines, bringing in the wounded of both sides and taking the dog-tags from the dead GIs. He and his unit spent the remainder of the day on the ridge waiting for the SS stormtroopers to come running out of the mist. But they never came. In the distance, behind them, the Americans heard the rattle of small arms and the dull thud of exploding shells and were later to find out that the Germans succeeded in penetrating the perimeter at three points during that day, though they were never able to exploit their success and drive to Bastogne. The south-western perimeter, where Conner was, remained quiet after that single bloody engagement at dawn which left hundreds of dead, Americans and Germans alike.

The men on the south-western perimeter saw action only once again that day, an odd incident at about 1600 hours, just as darkness was falling. The sound of German armour was heard, the Americans nestled behind their guns and bazookas. The German armour revealed itself to be a column of six Panthers carrying stormtroopers in white battle tunics, but far from driving towards the Americans, the German tanks wandered into the clearing, driving in front of and parallel to the American lines. The Americans opened up with their small arms, the storm-troopers fell from the tanks like confetti, and the armour turned and accelerated away, disappearing into the night and the fog.

The night was filled with the sounds of engagements to the north of Bastogne, but the south-west remained silent. Occasionally a doodle-bug was heard flying overhead, but directly in front of Conner's position all was still and quiet. Eventually he shrank back from the ridge and, using the flame from his cigarette lighter, read his watch face. It was ten minutes after midnight.

He had survived Christmas Day, 1944.

Chapter Ten

The story travelled around Bastogne, told by one GI to the next, of the way those six Shermans came on, lunch-time Boxing Day, barrelling down the road just like those kraut positions didn't exist, rattling, swaying, chewing up the road, straight into the perimeter. Conner never tired of hearing the story of the relief column's breakthrough from the south. The Germans were not able to close the gap in the Bastogne perimeter and over the next forty-eight hours reinforcements of men, equipment and supplies were brought in and the wounded evacuated. On December 28, Lieutenant David Conner was arrested.

Conner was still with Snafu company, by then plugging a hole in the northern perimeter. He nestled in the foxhole, watching the dusk fall. He listened to the rattle of small arms over to the east which he knew by now most likely meant a GI had probably seen something move in the forest. He also listened to the welcoming rumble of the American artillery which had once again taken the offensive. It was about 1600 hours when he heard a scuffling sound above and behind him. He twisted and looked up. A large coloured sergeant crouched casually on the edge of Conner's foxhole. A few days ago, a few hours ago, the man would have lasted a little under thirty seconds. But now he crouched as calmly as if he were on the back stoop at home. He was even smoking a cigarette with the tip pointing towards the last known German positions.

'You want to get yourself blown away?' Conner squirmed deeper into the foxhole.

'Nope,' said the soldier, drawing deeply on the cigarette.

'Why don't you just shoot yourself?' gasped Conner. 'Christ sake, you're doin' everything else for the enemy.'

The soldier pulled on the cigarette again. Then he flung it away. 'It was all finished anyways,' he said.

'You want something?' said Conner when the soldier seemed content to hover on the edge of his foxhole all night.

'Yep,' said the soldier. 'You, sir.'

'Me, sir?'

'You Mr Conner, sir, Lieutenant David, of the 106th?'

'Yes.'

'I have to take you in, sir.'

'In where?'

'HQ, sir. I've told your sergeant already.'

'You make it sound like I'm being arrested.'

'Could be about it, sir.' The coloured GI spat on the ground. A star shell exploded, illuminating the area as clearly as the recent daylight. The soldier sat conspicuously in the glow. 'Any time you're ready, Mr Conner.'

Conner waited until the star shell had died before scrambling out of the foxhole and walking crouched behind the coloured soldier who strolled towards his jeep.

In Bastogne the Divisional Commander said, 'Don't ask me, Conners.'

'Conner,' said Conner.

'OK, Conner, but still don't ask me. Here, you don't believe me, read it yourself.'

Conner grasped the sheet of paper. It was a clear enough request: 'Compliments of the Officer commanding US Military Police, European Forces, to the Officer commanding Bastogne garrison. Ref. Conners D, Lt, 106th. Please release above officer into the custody of US Military Police for immediate escort to Paris.'

'They got your name wrong,' said the Divisional Commander, 'but it's you all right, there isn't another Conner or Conners or O'Conner or O'Conners, Lieutenant D. in the 106th.'

'I don't understand.' Conner appealed to the senior officer behind whom stood the Military Police.

The officer shrugged. 'Don't ask me why, but it's obvious they want you. Maybe it's your dark past catching up with you.'

'I don't have a dark past, sir.'

'Whatever it is, the order's clear. Incidentally it's triplicated in case you're considering doing something stupid with it like ripping it up and eating it. Once saw a guy do that. They let him finish and then showed him the two other copies. He had a bad case of indigestion after that, Conner.'

'We'd like to press on, sir,' said the Senior MP. 'The request is for the immediate release of Mr Conner and we'd like to make the drive during the dark, sir. The road is safer then, sir. Lots of German stragglers, sir. Tanks and infantry.'

'OK.' The Divisional Commander took the copy of the order from Conner. 'Better get movin', Conner. Best of luck, son.'

The Senior MP addressed Conner. 'Will you leave your carbine here, sir? I'll also have to relieve you of your automatic, sir. The latter may be returned to you, sir, if we have to defend ourselves between here and Paris, sir.'

Benjamin Service returned to Bletchley on Boxing Day evening. He had driven back via Oxford, nursing the MG along, gradually reintroducing life into the long dormant machine. The journey from Dorset to Bedfordshire took six hours and used up an entire month's supply of petrol coupons. He turned into the narrow gravel drive which led to the house in which he had been billeted. After a wash and change and an evening meal he took his cycle from the shed and cycled to Bletchley Park.

The common room was decorated with holly and ivy and mistletoe, and somebody had been able to dig up some pre-war decoration which had been strung over the fireplace. Service greeted the others in the room and poured himself a glass of claret. He had timed his arrival well; ten minutes to go before dinner. One of the first people he saw when he entered the room was Gladys Stavely. She too, he realized, must have returned that day from Christmas leave. She was sitting on the long settee which stood in the centre of the room facing the open fire. She was sipping wine and leafing through a copy of *Blighty*, 'the magazine which laughs its way to victory'. He sat next to her.

'Hello, Benjamin,' she said stiffly.

'Miss Stavely.'

'You know, Benjamin,' she said, putting the magazine aside. 'Throughout the war we, shall I say, the elders of Bletchley Park have grown accustomed to being a little out of touch with the goings-on among the majority of our staff, the majority being those aged between eighteen and thirty-five years.'

'Oh really, I didn't . . .' stammered Service.

'We have got used to not being party to the gossip,' continued Gladys Stavely. 'We have got used to being expected to put in a token appearance and nothing more at the functions organized by the dance committee, and then to retire with dignity, only to be kept awake half the night listening to you – I believe the expression is "Whooping it up". We have become accustomed to the sound of Wrens tiptoeing along the corridor to the rooms belonging to those men friends billeted here in the house, and we have grown used to the sound of bedsprings and other noises which seem to follow shortly after the nightly migration of those same Wrens.' She sipped her claret. 'To these things, Benjamin, we have grown accustomed, and I might also add that the deference shown to the aged has also not gone unnoticed, nor unappreciated.'

'Miss Stavely . . .'

'Now it is Boxing Day night, young man, and it is indeed the season of goodwill, but I cannot help but notice that in the corner by the bookcase is a pretty young second officer Wren who has recently joined us and is longing for someone to go and talk to her, and behind me I detect young men engaged in frivolous, but I dare say entertaining, conversation. So I do wonder why young Benjamin Service, who has not spoken a word to me all these years, except in passing or in the course of his duty, should come and sit beside me?'

'Well, Miss Stavely,' Service began, 'I confess I have a request to make of you.'

'Of me?' She seemed genuinely surprised.

'Well, yes. I'd like you to tell me the name of one of our agents in Europe.'

'Mr Service!' said so loud that the general hubbub of conversation halted for a second or two, and heads turned towards the aghast 'godmother' of Hut 3.

'I'm sorry if I've shaken you, but I did want to grasp your attention,' Service continued when the conversation in the room had resumed.

'You have done that all right!' Miss Stavely, with her silver hair done up in a bun, was not amused.

'An agent has been transmitting from Berlin.'

'So I understand.'

'You haven't heard the transmissions yourself?'

'I have not.'

'So you could not yet identify the sender?'

'Not without hearing the transmission. Even if I did hear the transmission, I doubt whether it would be in order for me to name her to you, Mr Service. What is your reason for wishing this information?'

'I have a personal reason.'

'I see. Well, sympathetic as I am, Mr Service, I think that's a poor and a somewhat selfish reason for asking me to compromise myself.'

'Yes. I appreciate I'm putting upon you, but if you listened to the next transmission and I gave you a name, would you be prepared to say whether that was the name of the operator?'

'This information will not go beyond you?'

'Most certainly not if the answer is "yes", because I have a personal interest in her safety.'

'Her safety. I see.'

'Yes, it's a girl I knew before the war. It's more than a million to one chance that it's her. We lost contact at the outbreak of war when she joined the FANY. It was only recently that I discovered that FANY wasn't a medical unit, and she spent her childhood in Berlin, so it would be logical to send her there.'

'There are only three female agents in Berlin.'

'Would one be called Petra Oelkers, code name Oboe?'

'Yes,' said Gladys Stavely stiffly. 'One would.'

Benjamin Service gripped his wine glass, 'My God, she's alive still, after all this time.'

'She may not be, Mr Service. Don't allow your hopes to be raised.' Gladys Stavely would not allow her face to show any emotion. Inwardly she was delighted for Benjamin Service, but feared the next few months. 'She may have been caught months, years ago and forced to reveal her code name. That has happened. She may also have been "turned", that has also happened, especially with agents of mixed parentage like Oboe. I can only tell if it's her when I listen, she had an endearingly clumsy Morse finger, as I remember.'

'But there is still the possibility that she is alive?'

'Yes. But if she is in Berlin she is in grave danger. She should come out and make her way west. She'd be home by now if she hadn't moved to Berlin.'

'She wasn't posted to Berlin?'

'No. She was dropped in Holland in a field near Eindhoven. She worked in Holland and, in the course of events, had the opportunity to go to Berlin.'

'In what circumstances?'

'I only know what she told us. Are you sure you want to know? You may be hurt if she means a lot to you.'

'Yes.' Service nodded. 'I want to know.'

'We gather she took up with a German officer, in the SS actually. He was posted to Germany to a position in the Chancellery. We didn't order her to go, she volunteered. So we had an agent as close as we could possibly get to the Chancellery. She made contact from Berlin, sent some good material. Then her transmissions ceased earlier this year and we thought she had been eliminated.'

'Now you say the call sign Oboe is being used again?'

'Yes.'

'She's done amazingly well to survive. The life-expectancy of agents even in quiet areas is only a matter of months.'

Later they walked to Hut 6. In the hut the bombes were working feverishly, clicking loudly. Hamish McCrae raised a hand in greeting as Service and Gladys Stavely entered the hut. 'Hello, Gladys,' he said when they came within easy hearing distance. 'To what do we owe the honour?'

'A kind invitation from your colleague, here.' Gladys Stavely nodded towards Service.

'From Benjy? He must want something, Gladys. Be careful.'

'He's come clean.'

'Really.' McCrae grinned at Service. 'Honesty does become you, Benjy.'

'So what's happening on warring planet, Scotsman?'

'Been some Christmas in Belgium. The Yanks and Jerries have been clawing each other apart. Real hard fighting – some of the hardest, sticking the heed on each other for days on end. There's a town I've never heard of before, Bastogne. Just here.' He tapped the map on the wall behind him. 'It's been under siege for about a week. Yesterday the Jerries attacked in force, no Christmas truce for these guys. They penetrated a few places as well, according to their situational reports. All the Jerry reports spoke of heavy resistance and heavy casualties.'

'Some scrap, then?'

'Not half, Benjy. The overall picture is that the German advance is slowing up and they're in a state of confusion. No field commander wants to continue advancing, but the top level order from Adolf, who seems to have taken charge of the campaign, is that the advance is to continue. As far as we can tell they're bickering like children.'

'What slowed the advance?'

'A combination of factors. Terrain didn't help them. Deep gorges running across the direction of advance meant that their army has to funnel through half a dozen bridging points, and there's such congestion it sounds like Bank Holiday Monday in the park. It's bitterly cold and the snow is slowing them up, but they've used the fog well; it's still thick, but it cleared briefly yesterday and our aircraft gave them a pasting. They don't have enough petrol, that was clear early on from their cyphers. We got that information off, you'll remember, and it has obviously been transmitted to the Yanks who started to burn their fuel dumps as they retreated. That caused the Hun a bit of a headache, because the cyphers indicate that they had intended to use captured fuel to continue the advance.'

'Nice stroke.'

'Yes, and once the Yanks recovered from their surprise, they organized themselves and the Jerries have had to fight for every inch of ground. I believe the decoded cyphers we sent off yesterday made good reading in London and Paris.'

'Bastogne still under siege?'

'No, according to a cypher we intercepted this afternoon, an American column broke through from the south splitting the German forces and forcing a supply corridor. Bastogne's become a salient.'

'So it's the beginning of the end, if I can paraphrase Winston.'

'I doubt if he'll mind.'

'You haven't heard any more from Oboe, which is what Miss Stavely and I really came to enquire about?'

'No, we haven't, Benjy,' replied McCrae, noting a look of concern in Service's eyes. 'Nothing has come through since you've been away. Nothing more about the Gryphon either. That seems to have died a death.'

'Just thought I'd ask. Well, we'll leave you at it, Hamish.'

Service turned to Gladys Stavely. 'Would you care to join me for a drink in the common room, Miss Stavely?'

Petra Oelkers walked slowly down the Potsdamerplatz towards the apartment she shared with Heinrich. She looked about her in dismay. The city she had once loved and had come to love again was badly ruined. It had been a city of fine buildings; now it was just rubble, and dust forever hung in the air, getting in the eyes, teeth, hair and clothing. It was a city of constant klaxons, of discarded hoses which lay like tentacles. The radio played light dance music in an attempt to bolster the spirits of Berliners, but there was no escaping the fact that this was the end for their city. Perhaps, she thought, perhaps a new city might rise from these ashes, but the Berlin of her youth was dead, already decaying.

Heinrich was in the apartment when she arrived. She found him struggling into his uniform, having managed to wash and shave but unable to get rid of the bloodshot eyes and, she guessed, the heavier than usual hangover. On the floor of the apartment were his beloved records smashed in pieces and the gramophone lying on its side.

'A bomb?' she said, then realized they had not been like that when she had left the flat that morning, and that there had been no raid during the day.

'I smashed them,' he said, swaying as he pulled on his black tunic.

'But, Heinrich, your music.'

'What music was there?' He had to force his eyes to focus. 'Grit, grit, grit everywhere, on the surface of the records, inside the gramophone There is no music any more.'

'Oh Heinrich,' she stooped and began to pick up the pieces. It was a futile gesture since the damage was irreparable, but she felt she had to do something. She collected a handful of slivers and put them on the oak chest which stood at the side of the room. 'I'll make you some coffee,' she told him. 'You look like you could do with some.'

He nodded and allowed himself to fall back on to the couch.

'Could you eat?' she called from the kitchen.

He shook his head and managed to shout 'No', though the effort brought him close to retching. 'What day is it?' he asked when she returned with a steaming cup of ersatz.

'St Stephen's Day.' She sat next to him.

'Are you not having anything to eat or drink?'

'There is little left,' she replied. 'I am not yet hungry or thirsty.'

He grunted.

'Do you know that they brought you home again yesterday? They were not well pleased with you.'

'Really?' As if he did not care. 'Perhaps I was having a small celebration.'

'The advance is going well?'

'We are pushing forward, we are driving a wedge between the British and Americans, but . . .'

'But?'

'But we cannot tell him the advance is faltering because we cannot supply our tanks with petrol, and we cannot use captured petrol because the Americans are destroying theirs.' He shook his head. 'You see the difference in our war effort. The Americans can afford to destroy millions of gallons of fuel; we have to make ours from coal, because we now have no oil supply. We cannot tell Hitler that the attempt to overrun Bastogne has failed. We have not told him that the American opposition is stronger than we anticipated. Guderian advanced through the Ardennes in the summer of 1940 and separated the small British army from the French army – that was brilliant. Hitler advances through the Ardennes in the winter of 1944 into a huge Allied army with unlimited reserves – that's madness.'

'He will not listen?'

'He is mad.'

'What is there to be done?'

'Nothing. The fate of Germany rests with a man who directs his army without listening to his military advisers, and who is a gibbering, rambling, imbecile. Germany is being driven down. I can see the end, Petra, I can see Hitler demanding advances on all fronts while our children fight Allied tanks in our streets. We have to withdraw, to pull back from the west, even Skorzeny's men in Paris may have lost their opportunity to strike. But enough. I must go to the Chancellery, I am on duty soon.'

She fetched his coat, a heavy full-length black leather coat, dusty and scratched from the rubble, and helped him into it. She put his peaked cap on his head and screwed it straight. 'When will you return?' she asked as she guided him to the door. 'In the morning?' He nodded and left the flat without a word or a backward glance.

She closed the door behind him and leaned against it. Heinrich, poor Heinrich, a human being in the company of animals. But she had other loyalties and Heinrich had given her valuable information. Skorzeny, a name she had heard before, though she could not recall how or when; and probably most valuable of all, the news that the German army was under the command of an imbecile. Hitler had always been mad, but now he was deranged and completely out of touch. This was high grade material. Of all the information she had ever transmitted, this, she felt, was clearly the most important. If the Allies could be informed of this fracture at the very core of German High Command, then they could press the advance into Germany with greater confidence.

She ate an evening meal of rye bread and eggs which she had bought in the black market. At 7.00 p.m. she walked down the Potsdamerplatz towards the subway station. The subway ran throughout the Christmas period, carrying the factory workers for whom Christmas Day and St Stephen's Day were just a normal part of their gruelling week. The national cause was no longer victory but survival. She knew that many Germans who might have been allowed a half day to celebrate St Stephen's Day would report for work anyway, not asking or expecting to be paid for their overtime. She also knew that the slave workers in the camps were being worked to death. For them Christmas or Hanukah had ceased to exist; when your life-expectancy is down to six weeks for a strong man, then annual celebrations count for little. Outside the Chancellery a group of pale waif-like children with gaunt, drawn faces were singing *Stille Nacht*. She stopped to listen; their singing was carried on the thin air, a pure sound, drifting across the ruins.

She was pleased that she had stopped. As she stood there listening to the carollers, she realized that she was breaking one of the cardinal rules which had been laid down at Camp X: she was being hasty. Few people would be making a journey across the city on this bitter St Stephen's Day night, and for her to journey, unless she was obviously a factory or office worker, would have the effect of drawing attention to herself. She waited until the carollers had finished, handed the choirmaster a few coins and then returned to the apartment. It was not until the next evening, December 27, that she journeyed to the north of the city, climbed the silent stair, and let herself into the silent flat, the furniture of which was draped with sheets. She began her transmission at 2015 hours, in keeping with the pattern she had established.

When she had finished the transmission and received the acknowledgement, she hurriedly concealed the transmitter and was about to flee the apartment when she was chcked by a sense of impending danger. She sat in a chair, not bothering to remove the sheet, and let the air which blew in through the bomb-blasted window play icily about her face. Recently, she told herself, recently she had become panicky, become slipshod. Yesterday she would have been detained and questioned if she had continued her journey; instead she had delayed, and now the Allies had a name in connection with the top secret German operation in Paris, and had information about Hitler's mental state. A few days previously she had felt like running because she thought a man on a subway platform was staring at her. She was frightened that she was losing her grip, losing her calm, and she sensed that she was becoming a danger to herself. She was anxious to leave the flat, anxious to dash down the street to the subway station near the Stettiner Bahnhof. Instead she remained sitting in the flat for an hour, just listening. In that hour she heard somebody, a man she thought, walking in the street below the window, moving as stealthily as the rubble would allow. There was half an hour's silence, then she was sure the same man passed again. Later she heard a car stop at the corner of the street, a door open and close, and then she heard the car drive away. She remained in the flat until the air raid warning sounded, whereupon she indulged herself in a legitimate run to the nearest shelter.

In the cellars of the Gestapo Headquarters in Prinz Albrecht-strasse, Rademacher sat beside Schmitt. Both smoked Turkish cigarettes, distributed freely by Rademacher. There was a dull thud as a bomb fell near by, the lights dimmed and then shone brightly again.

'Close,' said Rademacher.

'Just a rogue,' replied Schmitt, drawing enjoyably on his cigarette. 'They're after the factories again. Odd effect it's having.'

'How so?'

'Well, we've always had difficulty getting labour out to the munitions and aeroplane factories, but now that the terror bombers have demolished the old factories, our skilled workers are forced to take work in the direct war material production factories. It means we can use skilled Germans instead of Poles and Frenchmen, who sabotage whatever they can.'

'That would explain why our production has stepped up. We produced more guns last month than we did during the first half of 1942.'

'It's one of the reasons, but we've still got seven million slave labourers in the Reich. We have to keep our eyes on them, they'll turn against us given half the chance.' Schmitt smoked his cigarette to the butt and dropped it on the floor, grinding it under his boot-heel. He glanced around him; there were perhaps a hundred and fifty people in the cellar, mostly men. There were a few hushed conversations taking place, a luxury which was indulged in on those nights when the bombs were falling some miles away. 'Speaking of subversives, have you made any progress on the female who made enquiries about Operation Grief?'

'A little, Herr Schmitt,' replied Rademacher. 'There was another transmission tonight. We were able to take a bearing on it from the mobile listening post, we plotted it and intersected with the first bearing in the north of the city just behind Invalidenstrasse. I walked around the area this evening, but saw nothing suspicious.'

'I don't know that area well.'

'It's an old residential quarter, tall thin tenements, mostly uninhabited now because of bomb damage.'

'And with two bearings you cannot locate the transmitter?'

Rademacher shook his head, 'We need three. We plot the bearings on a map which gives us a triangle, or a "cocked hat" as we say; the transmitter should be within the boundaries of the cocked hat. We could then narrow it down to one of perhaps four buildings, but not the floor of the building, which in that area could mean we'd have to search anything up to forty flats.'

'So it could take some time?'

'Well, if she transmits tomorrow we could take the third bearing and start doing a house to house immediately afterwards. There is, however, another way.'

'There is?'

'Another course of enquiry to pursue, just so that we will not be idle until she transmits for the third time, may be indicated by the content of her transmission.'

'Oh?'

'Yes. We listened to her transmission. It didn't seem very damaging, gave the name of the officer in charge of Operation Grief and said some very uncomplimentary things about the Führer. She said that he is deranged, that his generals no longer trust him, he is beyond reason, but retains total control of the armed forces. I took the trouble to enquire about the man in charge of Operation Grief and it is indeed who she says it is, Otto Skorzeny. We might, therefore, assume that her information about the Führer is also accurate.'

'I hope not, Rademacher.'

'You have just proved my point.'

'I have?'

'Yes. How long is it since you have seen the Führer?'

'Perhaps one year ago, no, more than that, the autumn of 1943.'

'Exactly. He has shrunk from the public eye; he's withdrawn, moving from command post to command post. Presently he is somewhere in Berlin, probably the Chancellery, and seen only by his aides.'

Schmitt raised his eyebrows. 'I see, I see. So this woman, this highborn German, is an aide to the Führer? My God.'

'Or else she is the wife or mistress of an aide who might be given to indiscretion. That is more likely to be the case, because if she was on the Führer's staff she would not have to resort to the subterfuge of pretending to be an assistant to Sturmbannführer Blomm and telephoning for the information.'

'So we need to seek an aide to the Führer who may, shall we say, present a security risk.'

'I think it might prove a profitable line of enquiry, Herr Schmitt. Would you care for another cigarette?'

Schmitt drew a cigarette from the proffered packet. 'But if she's right, Rademacher, about the Führer, I mean, then what hope is there for us?'

'None,' said Rademacher. 'No hope at all.'

Gladys Stavely unhooked the spare set of headphones and slipped them from her head. She ran down the corridor to Hut 6. Benjamin Service looked up anxiously as she entered.

'Benjamin,' she panted as she reached his desk. 'She has transmitted again. We picked it up on our monitor. It's her all right, Benjamin, same sloppy style.'

For a moment Service said nothing. Then he said, 'Half of me hoped it wasn't going to be her.'

'I think I know what you mean,' said Gladys Stavely. 'You're glad she's alive, but heavens, alive in Berlin, now of all times. Were you close, Benjamin?'

'Yes,' he said. 'I loved her. I still do, even after all this time. We were going to be married.'

'I remember her clearly. She was one of our good ones. I can't imagine how she has managed to survive for so long. She's in danger now, though, she's sending two- or three-minute transmissions, she obviously thinks it's high grade.' Gladys Stavely shook her head. 'She reports that Hitler's off his rocker.'

'We knew that in '39.'

'More so now, she says he's totally deranged but has full control of the army and airforce. It's good material, but like all the other agents, she doesn't know about Ultra – these things.' Gladys Stavely swept her arm and indicated the bombes and the 'bronze goddesses'. 'We knew this already, we've been picking up Hitler's long rambling cyphers for months. The tragedy is she's risking her life by making three-minute transmissions to give us information we already possess.'

'Oh my God,' Service buried his face in his hands. 'The waste, the waste.'

'I'll instruct SOE in London to wait for the next transmission and send her the "don't send" signal. It means "stop transmission, you are in danger, get out quickly", but we transmit a pre-arranged signal. All operatives know what it means.'

'Can I wait with you? I can get someone to cover for me here for an hour or two.'

'Of course you can. Come to Hut 3 at about 8.00 p.m. tomorrow, we can monitor the exchange.'

'Thanks, Gladys.'

'There was another piece of information, you'll get it anyway, but I may as well tell you while I'm here. She also said that a Nazi named Skorzeny is leading the Gryphon Operation. Mean anything to you?'

'Not a thing. But we'll cross-check it anyway.'

Chapter Eleven

Colonel Helmut Kiessling of the Reichsführer SS sat uneasily behind his desk looking up at his visitors, two men dressed in plain clothes, but both wearing similar black leather coats. The taller and younger of the two smirked at him, the older one was more serious.

'Gestapo,' said Rademacher.

'You don't surprise me,' said Kiessling, though he was certainly surprised that the younger of the men should be taking the initiative.

'I am Rademacher. This is Herr Schmitt.'

Schmitt nodded.

'Please, gentlemen,' said Kiessling, indicating vacant chairs standing against the wall of his office. 'Please be seated.' He spoke as calmly as he could, but could not prevent his voice from quavering.

'Thank you,' said Schmitt. Rademacher just said, 'No.'

'As you wish, but you don't mind if I remain . . .'

'Not at all,' said Rademacher quickly.

'How can I help you, gentlemen?'

'You are Colonel Kiessling?' Again it was Rademacher.

'I am.'

'In charge of security here at the Chancellery?'

'That is correct.'

'Ah.' Rademacher began to nod his head slowly.

'There is something amiss?' Kiessling felt himself becoming agitated, he felt a bead of sweat run down his brow.

'Yes,' said Rademacher.

'Well, what?'

'Are you married, Kiessling?'

Kiessling glared at the younger man, stung by his imperti-
nence. Eventually he said, 'I am.'

'Where is your wife?' This time it was Schmitt who spoke.

'In Frankfurt. Our home is in Frankfurt.'

'Do you have a mistress?' Rademacher again, but this time he
failed to surprise Kiessling.

'That question I find offensive.' Kiessling allowed his anger
to show. 'Do you think that in my position . . .'

'Just answer the question,' Schmitt said coldly. 'We don't have
all day.'

'Very well. No, I do not have a mistress. I wish only to return
to Frankfurt and be with my wife. Can you tell me what this is
about?'

'There is on your staff,' said Schmitt, 'a spy.'

'Impossible,' Kiessling shot to his feet. His face initially red-
dened, but rapidly paled.

'It is not impossible,' replied Rademacher. 'It is possible,
probable and, we believe, factual.'

Kiessling sank into his chair. 'I can't . . . No, it's not possible.
They are hand picked, every one . . . to belong to the Reichsführer SS you . . . No, I can't believe it.'

'How many staff have you?'

'The Reichsführer Division itself numbers –'

'Just here, in the Chancellery.'

'Two hundred and fifty.'

'Men and women?'

'Mostly men. There are about seventy-five women.'

'It is the women we are interested in,' said Schmitt. 'Is there
any woman with an accent which, for want of a better expression,
might be described as "high born"?'

'One or two,' replied Kiessling, 'but mostly we are drawn from
the labouring and artisan class, like all SS Divisions.'

'Of these one or two high-born women, who evidently forsook
their birthright to join the new order –'

'Do they have direct access to the Führer?' Rademacher cut
Schmitt off in mid-sentence. He took his cigarette case from his

coat pocket, selected a cigarette, offered one to Schmitt and then tapped his cigarette on the case. 'Do they see him in the course of duty, does he have occasion to talk to them?'

'No,' Kiessling said, staring hungrily at the Turkish cigarettes. 'There are no women in Section One, the section which is responsible for the protection of the Führer, they are all male officers who also function as aides-de-camp, though their primary function is security.'

'Now we progress,' said Rademacher. 'Who is in charge of this Section One?' He struck a match and lit his cigarette.

'Hauptsturmführer Scheill.'

'He is loyal?'

'The most loyal. All my . . .' Kiessling faltered before completing the sentence.

'Exactly, Kiessling,' said Rademacher. 'Tell us about Scheill. Is he married?'

'No.'

'A mistress, perhaps?'

'I think not.'

'I see.' A faint sneer lifted Rademacher's lip. 'We would like to meet Hauptsturmführer Scheill.'

'Now?'

'Now.'

Kiessling lifted the phone on his desk and waited for a few seconds. Then he said, 'Tell Hauptsturmführer Scheill to come to my office immediately,' and put the phone down without waiting for the reply. Both Rademacher and Schmitt noticed how fleshy were Kiessling's hands. Moments later an urgent and brisk footfall was heard in the corridor, there followed a sharp tap on Kiessling's door and Scheill entered. He was a tall blond man, his black uniform was neat, his boots highly polished. Rademacher thought he was about the same age as Scheill, putting Scheill too at twenty-seven years. Scheill stood rigidly to attention.

'These gentlemen,' said Kiessling, 'are from the Gestapo. You will kindly answer their questions.'

Schmitt asked, 'Are all your staff loyal?'

'Of course!' snapped Scheill.

'Unfortunately it is not an "of course" matter,' said Rademacher. 'I wish you to think of all the staff under your command in Section One and then reconsider your answer.'

'There is a spy in Section One,' added Schmitt, anticipating Scheill's protest.

Scheill buckled slightly at the knees.

'Exactly,' said Rademacher. 'The stakes are high, and if necessary you and I will continue this discussion at No. 89 Prinz Albrechtstrasse. To aid your thinking, we can provide you with a little information – clues, if you like.'

'First,' said Schmitt, 'the spy, or perhaps traitor would be a more appropriate word, has access to the Führer's company. In the course of his duty he has occasion to see and probably be spoken to by the Führer.'

Scheill shook his head. 'We all do.'

'Secondly, the spy or traitor is married to or has some other relationship with a woman whose accent indicates that she is of high social standing.'

Scheill's head sank.

'We have succeeded in jogging your memory, I think, Hauptsturmführer.' Rademacher smiled.

Scheill nodded.

'The name!'

'Leuger. Heinrich Leuger.'

'Rank?'

'Obersturmführer.'

'Not Leuger,' Kiessling sighed. 'Of all my staff . . .'

'We in the Gestapo,' said Schmitt, 'have learned never to be surprised.'

'But I would agree with Colonel Kiessling,' Scheill protested. 'Leuger has one of the lowest Party numbers I know.'

'All in the Reichsführer SS have low Party numbers,' explained Kiessling, 'but as Scheill says, Leuger must have the lowest, a three-figure number in fact. He joined the Party in 1933, when he was still at school.'

'One of the first,' remarked Rademacher.

'Indeed,' Kiessling agreed. 'Mine is considered low, being 2583, but Leuger –'

'Is only three figures,' said Schmitt. 'You told us.'

'He, Leuger, is a loyal and a committed National Socialist,' Scheill said unexpectedly. 'He is a good German and can trace his lineage back to Gneisenau. When others of his class joined the Wehrmacht, Leuger joined the SS. I think he was once a favoured aide of the Führer.'

'Once?'

'With respect, sir. The Führer does not now seem to differentiate between aides, once he . . .'

'I see, but still he has a high recommendation?'

'Yes,' said Scheill, 'but Heinrich, I mean Leuger, has a problem. A drink problem.'

There was a heavy silence in the small room broken when Kiessling said, 'This ought to have been reported.'

'I felt I had a loyalty to my comrade,' stammered Scheill. 'Besides, he was able to perform his duties. He has been incapable only on one occasion.'

'You also had a loyalty to the Reich.' Kiessling gripped the arms of his chair. 'Good God, man, do you realize what you have done? You have allowed a spy into the very nerve-centre of the Reich.'

'Leuger has put the entire Reich in jeopardy,' said Rademacher with a noticeable gleam in his eye. 'You, and also you, Colonel Kiessling, may well be deemed guilty by association.'

Scheill paled visibly. 'We warned him . . .'

'You sheltered him!' snarled Rademacher. 'But to continue. Where does Leuger live?'

'He has a room in the officers' quarters, of course, but in practice he lives in his private flat, with his mistress.'

'Ah,' said Rademacher. 'Where?'

'The Potsdamerplatz. No. 27. He was able to get special permission to live out. He has connections and can trace his lineage –'

'All the way back to Gneisenau,' said Schmitt. 'Must you repeat yourself?'

Rademacher smiled with evident relish. 'And his woman, is she equally high born?'

'So I believe,' said Scheill. 'She is a Berliner, though they met when he was serving in Holland. He brought her back with . . .' He faltered.

Kiessling put his head in his hands and groaned.

'Do you see what he has done?' Schmitt said calmly. 'Do you see what you have helped him to do?'

Scheill's jaw began to sag and he rocked unsteadily from side to side.

'Rescue what you can from this, Scheill,' said Rademacher, 'by not breathing a word of this to anyone. No one. Especially not to Leuger. In fact, forget we called. For the time being.'

When the two Gestapo officers had left his office, Kiessling looked at the still swaying Scheill and said, 'You have just sent yourself to the Eastern Front. You have probably sent me, and possibly all of Section One to the same destination. But only if we are lucky.'

Later, years later, the recollection of the incident would still cause Benjamin Service to wake in the middle of the night. On such occasions he would lie still and listen to his pulse until the familiar sounds of his old house reassured him that he was alive. At the time all he heard was the rifle shot; he saw the explosion as the bullet ricocheted off the cottage wall and he heard it singing as it bounced off the wall of the adjacent cottage. As he turned the corner he glanced in the rear view mirror and saw the policeman wrestling with the GI for control of the rifle, he saw the phone kiosk, he saw the station-master standing at the entrance to the booking office, and he saw the train standing on the track just beyond the station.

He had been in a third-class smoker, enjoying as he always did the motion of the train, this time rocking steadily towards Peterborough. It was the morning of December 28, his second day back at work after the Christmas break and he'd drawn lucky by being asked to escort a visitor. An 'escort' was seen as a perk of the job which often got one away from the Park for a day. On this occasion a mathematician from Newcastle University was visiting Bletchley Park, and it was arranged that he should be met at Peterborough. Service left earlier than necessary, hoping to take the opportunity of visiting the Cathedral before meeting the visitor at the station and returning with him to Bletchley. He sat facing forward, and when the train rounded a left-hand bend, enjoyed watching the black engine pour smoke over the landscape.

He had sat in a smoker intending to smoke on the journey, having returned to his favoured brand of Craven A, but he was too worried to enjoy a cigarette; something nagged, something vital yet unidentifiable was staring him in the face, and it was not just that Petra was alive. The train rocked steadily. Service knew that he had all the pieces of the jigsaw, but they would not come together to form a whole. Skorzeny was the key to the whole mystery. Yesterday night he and Hamish McCrae had sent a request for information on Skorzeny, but the reply had not come back by the time Service called at Bletchley Park before catching the 9.15 slow to Bedford for the Peterborough connection. He caught the Peterborough train, found an empty third-class smoker and pondered on the name Skorzeny. It was a name he had heard before and when its significance did dawn on him it did so with a scalp-crawling chill. His sense of slowness and stupidity at not seeing the obvious was outweighed only by the awfulness of the implication. Skorzeny, the brilliant Lieutenant-Colonel Otto Skorzeny, who had snatched Mussolini from the Allies and had also snatched Admiral Horthy when he was about to surrender Hungary to the advancing Soviets, it was he who was in charge of Operation Gryphon. And Gryphon, *Grief* in German, was so close to the German word *greifen*, 'to snatch, to grab'. As for the claws, what did claws do but reach out and grab and tear? And the Claws of the Gryphon were in Paris. Skorzeny's claws were in Paris. The train lumbered through a village station. Before he knew what he was doing, Service had pulled the communication cord.

The train stopped, shuddering and squealing just beyond the

edge of the platform. Service unhooked the leather strap, lowered the window, opened the door from the outside and jumped down on to the track. He ran back to the station buildings, heedless of the heads and shoulders of passengers leaning questioningly from the windows of other compartments, regardless of the guard in the brake van yelling, ''Ere you, we don't stop 'ere,' as he ran past below him towards the sloping end of the platform.

On the platform itself a porter wheeling a barrow halted and looked blankly at Service as he ran by, coat open, scarf flying. The station-master stepped from his office and said, 'Where's the fire, Guv?'

'I need a phone, your phone,' Service panted, and then saw the guard from the train running towards him.

'That train doesn't stop here.' The station-master glanced at his pocket-watch in an authoritative manner. 'I hope you haven't stopped the train to make a phone-call, young man?'

'That's exactly what I have done.' Service heard his own voice rising. 'It's of the utmost importance.'

'Well, I dare say it would be to you, sir . . .'

But Service had turned and fled. At the bottom of the station approach, close to where two American jeeps were parked side by side with the drivers sitting chatting in one of them, stood a phone kiosk. Service wrenched open the door, dialled O for operator and asked for a long-distance call.

'Bletchley what, dear?' said the operator.

Service repeated the number as he watched the station-master wave and then point to him. Turning the other way, he saw a police constable in a cape cycling towards him.

The operator came back on the line. 'They won't accept the call, dear. They said it was classified or something.'

'Just say it's Benjamin Service phoning in, will you,' he said insistently and then spelled his surname.

'Oh, I can't do that, dearie. We've had instructions on account of them fifth whatsits and spies. I mean, you could be one of them for all I know, couldn't you?'

Service left the phone hanging from the hook just as the constable swung his leg over the saddle and rested his cycle against the fence next to the kiosk. He said, 'Just a moment, please, sir,' but Service ignored him and raced to the vacant jeep, slid behind the wheel and pressed the starter button. One of the GIs leapt into the passenger seat. He was a fresh-faced boy who had time enough only to say, 'Hey, buddy, whaddya . . .' before Service punched him. Hard. The GI fell backwards out of the jeep and Service let in the clutch. He drove away from the station just as the rifle cracked behind him. In the rearview mirror he saw the bobby grab the rifle with a where-do-you-think-you-are-Dodge-City expression, and then he was round the corner out of sight.

On the first long stretch of road he saw the second jeep following him, being driven hard. He also saw that the GI in the passenger seat held one hand up to a bloody nose, the other hand held a microphone to his mouth.

Service rapidly grew used to the jeep. The three forward gears were simple enough, but the steering was a different matter, with the vehicle badly understeering. He went wide on the first series of corners but soon learned to 'wind' the jeep in and out of bends. The wind blew icily through his hair, his scarf flew out behind him, the second jeep pursued him grimly. He came to a crossroads and turned left towards Bedford.

It was going through Eaton Socon that he picked up a second pursuer: a black Austin Twelve of the Bedfordshire constabulary. Service almost collided with the car as he tore through the town. Behind him he saw the GIs in the following jeep wave desperately at the police car which turned and joined the pursuit. Then, between Eaton Socon and Bedford, his road was blocked by a US army half-track, two jeeps and two more police cars. He halted. Behind him the second jeep had slowed to a halt, as had the police car. He kept the jeep stationary with the motor turning over, two hundred yards from the road-block, a hundred yards from the following jeep and police car. It was as if a sudden lull had come to a battle and he was aware of things he had hitherto missed: a skein of geese in the sky flying southwards, the build-up of storm clouds to his right. Service gripped the steering-wheel. He could give himself up, but that would involve a long and tedious delay in getting the information to Bletchley, because he would be caught in red tape as the US Army and the Bedfordshire constabulary sorted out the incident. So he engaged first gear and let in the clutch.

As he expected, only the jeep and the half-track were able to pursue him across the open country; two police cars collided at the entrance of the field and the third became bogged down shortly after driving through the gateway.

Service found the jeep handled better on the rough ground than it did on the road. The suspension seemed less spongy, the steering more precise. He drove across the field making straight for the open gate into the next field, ploughed like the first, ready to receive the winter wheat. The heavy clay slowed up the jeeps and gave a strong advantage to the half-track which closed steadily. By the time he reached the entrance to the second field the half-track was only the matter of a few yards behind, pressing determinedly down on the stolen jeep driven by this oddball limey with a long scarf round his neck. Service drove through the gate and into the second field. The gateway was too narrow for the half-track, which demolished one of the posts and flattened a section of hawthorn hedge, but disappointed Service by not seeming to lose any speed following the impact.

Service managed to lose the half-track at the exit of the field. The gateway, mercifully open, led to a narrow minor road, beyond which in a depression was a copse. Service drove to the left of the gateway and then approached it at an angle, the half-track was by now a murderous ten or fifteen feet behind him, lumbering, bouncing, barely in control. Service, braking hard at the last moment, made it through the gateway and on to the road; the half-track didn't. He heard and felt, rather than saw, the monster crash through the gateway, virtually bounce on the narrow lane, and then drive completely out of control into the copse. By the time he glanced in the rearview mirror the pursuing jeeps were stopping near the exit of the field and two GIs were leaping from the vehicles and running down into the copse. He drove on for two miles, just putting distance between himself and his pursuers, and then stopped.

He had vital information and he was lost in the myriad lanes which crisscross Bedfordshire. To get to Bletchley Park, he had only his sense of direction to guide him, all signposts having been removed from crossroads at the outbreak of war. He reckoned himself to be some twenty-five miles north-east of Bletchley, with Bedford about five miles distant, directly between him and Bletchley. He drove back on to the lane and turned left at the first crossroads in what he guessed was the direction of Bedford.

In the event he came upon the town more suddenly than he expected. Driving slowly to attract as little attention as possible, he was beginning almost to enjoy the drive along the lanes when the cottages increased in frequency, then gave way to houses, by which time he was in the suburbs of Bedford. He nosed the jeep forward. Midweek, midday, the streets were quiet. He looked for somewhere he could leave the vehicle, nudging nearer to the centre all the time. The pedestrians increased, the number of vehicles increased, and suddenly he was in the centre of town. Equally suddenly, in front of him was his passport, a slow-moving convoy of US army trucks. Service pressed on the accelerator and tucked in behind the tail truck. As near as he could tell, he was following a convoy of six vehicles which attracted no attention. The trucks turned north. Service, recognizing the main road to Bletchley, pressed the accelerator and swung left, separating himself from the convoy. He'd got through Bedford, he still had transport. It was twenty miles to Bletchley.

He made fifteen miles before the engine coughed, then ran, then coughed again and died. He coasted to the side of the road, thumping the fuel gauge almost hysterically as if he could by magic conjure just one more gallon of fuel.

Service used the last ounce of momentum to carry the jeep off the road and on to the grass verge before starting to run. At first he panted and tripped over his feet. Then he got a stitch in his right side, but ran through it until it disappeared. After the first mile his breathing regularized and seemed to fall into harmony with his legs until his body moved in a steady rhythm. Even so, it took him an hour to jog the five miles to Bletchley

Park. He didn't stop at the gatehouse, but held his pass up to the incredulous sergeant of the Intelligence Corps who just managed to say, 'Very good, Mr Service, sir,' as he ran past. He jogged up the smooth concrete drive which wound round the lake, and ran into the house. With legs like jelly he ran up the stairs to the first floor. He went to an office with 'Director' on the door; it was empty. He ran down the corridor to a second door on which was a notice which read 'In conference, Strictly No Admission'. He pushed the door open and stood panting on the threshold. Twenty faces turned and stared at him. Many of those in the room were in uniform, all were senior officers. The man whose room he had first gone to stood and said, 'Service! Can't you read? What in God's name do you think you're doing?'

Service caught his breath and said, 'Eisenhower. They're going to kidnap Ike. Or shoot him. Kidnap would be my guess.'

RADEMACHER: There is a conveniently empty building just across Potsdamerplatz from No. 27. I'll watch from there and follow her when she leaves.

SCHMITT: You will need the mobile listening-post to take a third fix should you lose her in the dark.

RADEMACHER: It's already in position.

SCHMITT: I should have known you would not be guilty of such an oversight. For myself, I am a little worried about Leuger, he could be embarrassing to take into custody if he has the sort of connections Scheill says he has.

RADEMACHER: He is of the officer class. He will take the honourable way out.

SCHMITT: I confess I was thinking along the same lines. I will wait with you and when you leave to follow the woman, I shall pay a call on Obersturmführer Leuger. He would be no use to us anyway. He's just a drunkard with a loose tongue.

*

'So that's about it,' Genscher said, shouting over the din of the Mack diesel.

'Hey, that's something else, buddy,' replied the driver, a large coloured soldier who had evidently developed the technique of making his voice carry over the roar of the engine without straining his vocal cords. 'That's some story.' He wrestled with the near-vertical steering-wheel as the empty truck bounced over the rough, cratered road. 'Something to tell the folks at home.'

Genscher leaned back in the seat and rested one foot on the dashboard. 'Sure is. I tell you, the worst time was when those krauts broke through our last line of defence, I mean, I wasn't a correspondent by then, I was a regular GI, I'd chucked away my notepad and I'd picked up a Thompson. Felled a couple of krauts, like I said. Maybe more, I don't know, but I saw two go down from my bullets.'

'Regular hero, you are. You thinking of enlisting?'

'Hell, no. I want to get back to the US. I've got a story to write up and file.'

'You sure have,' said the driver.

The road, a grey thin ribbon awash with mud, drove a near-straight line between low Flemish fields towards a dull blue-grey sky. Most of the traffic was flowing in the opposite direction, heavily laden trucks, pushing inland from the coast, travelling in convoy.

'They have to travel in convoy,' said the driver. 'They also have to have guys ridin' shotgun. Too many lorries been ambushed by bands of deserters after food and blankets.'

'No kidding?'

'It's the real thing. They take what they need and sell the rest. Sometimes whole trucks, including the driver, disappear.'

'Hey.'

'But we're OK, north bound, we're empty, ain't nobody interested in us, empty.'

'Reassuring,' said Genscher.

'Did you get scared when your uniform burnt? I mean, one time I saw some guy run into a field kitchen back in Fort Bragg. Hey, man, was he a mess, I mean a mess.'

'Yeah, sure I got marked some, but not bad. The battledress was finished, but a couple of guys got me down in the snow before the flames did any real damage. I came to Paris wrapped in blankets and bought some new clothes.'

'They don't look so new to me, I mean begging your pardon, sir.'

'They're new to me, friend, and they feel pretty good after battledress.'

'Yup, I guess they would,' nodded the driver. 'I can't wait to get into a zoot suit. Mind, I got an easy war, backwards and forwards everyday. I came over on D-day plus two and I ain't yet seen a kraut. I heard them shooting and a couple of days ago I saw a flying bomb come down near Antwerp, but I ain't never seen one. What do they look like?'

'Just like regular guys, only they have different uniforms.'

'These SS guys, they come as tough as they say?'

'Tougher,' said Genscher. 'They're the worst.'

The driver swung the wheel and turned into another road.

'I guess this is you and me home,' he said.

'Guess it is,' said Genscher as the truck swept by a road sign which read: Antwerpen 4 km.

December 29.

Floyd shook his head vigorously. Briefly, all too briefly, the feeling of tiredness, the out-and-out fatigue left him, but flooded back with devastating suddenness. He glanced behind him, the dull grey sky hung heavily over Paris and the drizzle fell steadily. In front of Floyd, on his desk, were documents which were divided roughly into three piles. There was a pot of coffee and stubs of cigarettes in the ashtray. Stale smoke hung in the air.

There was a knock at his door, the sergeant opened and said, 'Lieutenant Conner, sir.'

'Good.' Floyd stood. 'Show him in.'

Conner walked into the room. He was dressed in a mud-and-blood-stained battledress which hung baggily around him, his chin was all stubble, his hair was matted. And he stank, by God he stank. Floyd's nose twitched and he said, 'You smell like you haven't washed for a week.'

So Conner said, 'Funny you should say that.'

Floyd smiled and extended his hand. As they shook hands he noticed a look of relief in Conner's eyes. 'You look worried,' he said. 'Take a seat.'

Conner sat in the chair which stood in front of Floyd's desk. 'I guess I am. You get pulled out of your first quiet period in forty-eight hours and bundled into a jeep with "the MPs want you in Paris" as your explanation, then I reckon you'd be worried as well.'

'Reckon I would. Coffee?'

'I sure could use some.'

Floyd poured the coffee, handed a mug to Conner, and then poured some for himself. 'This has been keeping me going for the past twenty-four hours,' he said, sitting again in his chair. 'Sorry about the way you were brought here, but the MPs are used to handling people like bits of meat, even officers, junior officers anyway. That's how they are trained and in fairness they didn't know why we wanted to see you.'

'You going to let me in on the secret?'

'Sure am, I think you can be of assistance to us.'

'Oh really?' said Conner. 'It's so good to be a nice guy. You don't think maybe you could have told me that in the first place, you know, helped relieve my anxiety a little?'

'So don't get sore about the way you were brought here, Conner. I can't use it.'

'Who's sore?'

'Knock it off. You going to help us or are you going to help us?'

Conner sipped his coffee, 'Guess I owe you for taking me out of the line.'

Floyd leaned forward. 'Just so we understand each other, Conner: you are going to help us. I am not asking you to repay any favour and as soon as we are through with you, you're going right back in the line, so don't play the battle-smart veteran with me. How old are you?'

'Me,' said Conner. 'I'm nineteen. Coming up twenty.'

'Well, nineteen coming up twenty Conner, you have a lot to learn about life and the first thing you have to learn is that you're not important, and seeing a bit of action doesn't give you any special privileges. Before I was an MP I was in the Marines, took a piece of shrapnel from a Jap grenade at a place called Guadalcanal. You may have heard of it.'

'I've heard of it,' said Conner, a note of respect creeping into his voice. Now he'd seen combat he could more easily imagine the experiences of the men who fought in the Pacific theatre. 'The Japs didn't move off the beach, right?'

'Right. The Japs don't know the meaning of the word retreat. It's not in their language. They stuck to their positions in the dunes until we killed them with grenades or bayonets and all the while they just kept their fingers on the triggers, moving the machine-guns from side to side, throwing grenades ...'

'Makes Hell sound like a Sunday school picnic,' conceded Conner. 'OK, I'm not so special. What can I do to help?'

'OK. The Nazis are going to knock off Ike.'

Conner's jaw dropped. 'Don't crap me, Floyd. I don't like being crapped.'

'Conner, I'm as serious as a heart attack.'

'Jesus, I think you are.'

'Check this.' Floyd leaned forward. 'Germany launches a big push in the Ardennes. They dress some of their guys in American uniforms ...'

'I know about that,' said Conner. 'I came across some.'

'OK, they used captured vehicles, jeeps, trucks, even a Sherman tank was reported to be driven by krauts. We think the krauts put somewhere between two and three thousand guys in our uniform.'

'As much as that?'

'It was a wide front. We captured some of these krauts and interrogated them and one or two revealed a plan to knock off Ike. Some said the plan was to drive the truckloads of German POWs under "escort" to Paris as a kind of showpiece and, once in Paris, these guys would storm SHAEF.'

'That's in Versailles.'

'Right, on the southern edge of the city. Other prisoners said that the hit team was a couple of guys in a jeep who could be in Paris within four hours of coming across the line. So they could have been in Paris even before the Germans began their offensive.'

'It's a rumour, Floyd. They wanted us to start shooting at each other instead of shooting them.'

'Maybe, but we figure that if the Nazis wanted to plant a rumour all the prisoners would be telling the same story. In fact, there's too many discrepancies, there's got to be something afoot.'

'I'm not convinced.'

'Fortunately, Conner, you don't have to be convinced, you just have to co-operate. You going to let me continue?'

'Sure, sure.'

'So yesterday there's a panic from above. Our intelligence people have picked up the kraut plan.'

'Oh boy!'

'Listen, will you. It's some confirmation. So then one of our street patrols here in Paris picks up a GI who's seen fighting a civilian. We arrest the GI and bring him in. Once in the cells we discover he has a bad dose of syphilis and I mean a bad dose, so we send him to Casanova Park for treatment. He's there for ten minutes and they discover kraut underclothing.'

'He's a German?' Conner sat up. 'What's he saying?'

'Name, rank and little else. He's called Hoff and is a naval officer.'

'The Navy?'

'Figures. Germany's got its back to the wall, it's taking its sailors and forming them into infantry divisions. Next point: there were two incidents before the offensive began. In the first, two of my guys were gunned down on a stretch of road just north of Paris. The civilian witness said that the guys who did it were GIs driving a jeep. In another incident an officer in charge of a forward patrol up near Skyline Drive reported a jeep with three GIs driving west, just before the German attack.'

'That officer . . .'

'Is yourself, Conner. You filed a report shortly after reaching Bastogne, it was one of a number which were shipped out soon after the town was relieved. We've been sifting through the reports of all possible and confirmed meetings with the enemy in our uniform.' Floyd patted one of the piles of reports which lay on his desk. 'Out of them all – and, Conner, there are hundreds – out of them all, I reckon, that because of the point where they came through the line, and the time they came through on the first day of the offensive and a few hours before my boys were gunned down, the guys you saw were on their way to Paris to nail Ike. We've got one; you know what the other two look like.'

'Hey, just a minute, Floyd, I saw only one clearly, and I wasn't taking any notes at the time.'

'So what do you remember?'

'Would you believe blond hair, blue eyes, square chin, seemed tall as well.'

'Perfect Aryan, just like tens of thousands of GIs.' Floyd relaxed in his chair, and Conner saw it as a gesture of defeat. 'Still, you could take a look at the guy we picked up, you may recognize him, and it could jog your memory about other details.'

'Can't lose anything,' Conner agreed.

''Cept Ike.'

'You're taking this very seriously.'

'We have to, Conner. We've doubled the security on Ike, he can't move without at least two guys go with him. They say he's furious about it. We're stopping every GI in Paris, checking his I/D. Dog-tags aren't enough, we're questioning them on details of home, asking them who won the world series, and where does Li'l Abner live, questions like that.'

'We took to doing that in the field,' Conner said. 'Tell me, does your intelligence stretch to being able to indicate the current state of the 106th?'

'As I recall, Conner, the current state of the 106th is non-existent.' Floyd leaned forward again. 'If I were you, I'd stop considering yourself as being separated from your unit and start to consider yourself as a survivor.'

Conner put his hand to his forehead. 'All those guys. I tell you, Floyd, those krauts that came at us that day, they were top grade, and I mean top. SS troops, King Tigers, it wasn't any of these sailors playing at soldiers. We'd been in the line for four days, straight out of training camp and we were told it was a quiet sector. Chrissake, they went through us like we weren't even there. Do you know what our casualties were?'

'Better than eighty per cent, I hear.'

Conner shook his head.

'You're already looking like being the hardest hit Division of the war.'

'Guess I'll never find out what happened to the rest of my men, hope to hell they got back to the truck. It certainly wasn't there when I came round.'

'You seem to lead a charmed life, Conner. You've come through some tough fighting without a scratch. Not many men can say the same.'

'Yeah, well I'm not about to start pushing my luck.'

'OK. Let's go and see this guy.'

Floyd led Conner from his office, through the open area and then down a flight of stone stairs which wound down three storeys to the cellar of the building. He turned into the corridor at the bottom of the stairs along which, at intervals, doors were set in the wall. 'Most of the guys in here have had too much vino, we let them sleep it off and send them back to their company commander with a report.' Floyd walked purposefully along the corridor, carrying Conner in his wake. 'Anything more serious we ship out to the military prison, but this guy we brought back. He's kind of special.'

A military policeman with a white helmet and highly polished boots and gaiters stood outside one of the doors. He snapped to attention as Floyd and Conner approached.

'Open up,' Floyd ordered.

Inside the cell, Hoff sat on the bunk. He stood with a marked degree of formality as Floyd and Conner entered.

'That him?' asked Floyd, staring at Hoff.

'Could be,' said Conner. 'Could very well be. Perhaps if he could turn his head to one side . . .'

To the surprise of both Floyd and Conner, Hoff obliged, shuffling through ninety degrees to let Conner take in his profile.

'Sort of heavy-set,' said Conner. 'Yes, yes, I think it's him.'

'So where are your friends, Hoff?'

The heavy-set man shrugged his shoulders.

'That's not a particularly Germanic gesture,' Conner observed.

Floyd glanced sideways at Conner.

'Perhaps not,' conceded Hoff.

'Did you spend time in France before the war?'

'No,' replied Hoff. 'If you must know, I was in America for three years. I was a student at Cornell.'

'No kiddin'?' Conner smiled. 'I was at Brown.'

'I heard of that school,' Hoff said. 'It has a good reputation.'

'Cornell's pretty smart,' Conner returned.

Floyd stayed quiet, having graduated from high school and not taken his education any further. He also recognized that Conner was getting more co-operation from the prisoner than he had been able to.

'Where did you study in Germany?'

'In Berlin.'

'Impressive city.'

'You have been in Berlin?' Hoff's eyes lit up.

'Once or twice when we visited Germany.'

'You have relatives in Germany?'

'My mother's German,' said Conner. 'From Holstein.'

'You half German?' Floyd suddenly demanded.

'Yep,' said Conner. 'The other half's Irish. O'Conner was the name my old man grew up with, but he knocked off the "O" when he got married. You get on better in the States with an Anglicized name.'

'Sure do,' Floyd agreed. 'I can't even pronounce my great-grandfather's name. His son changed to Floyd some time back, around the time of the Indian wars, I think.' Then he turned suddenly to Hoff. 'Here to knock off Ike? Right?'

Hoff's jaw dropped a little. He tried to disguise his reaction, but he wasn't quick enough.

'That's right, Hoff,' Conner said. 'We know about it.'

'We were told no details,' said Hoff.

'Just so we understand each other, Hoff,' said Floyd, 'your future is not enviable. You're not a prisoner of war, you're an assassin. And you murdered two of my men.'

'It was a legitimate *ruse de guerre*,' Hoff's cheeks began to shake. 'They were killed by enemy action.'

'Murdered, Hoff,' said Floyd. 'That *ruse de guerre* crap doesn't wash in the field and it won't wash here. But if you play ball with us we could maybe do you a favour. Maybe.'

'So where are your partners?' snapped Conner.

Hoff was silent for a moment, during which he looked at the shabby unshaven Conner as though Conner had betrayed him. Then he said, 'My name is Ernst Hoff . . .'

Back in his office, Floyd said, 'So we're a bit further on.'

'We are?'

'Yes, you've as good as confirmed Hoff as being the second man in the jeep, and that confirms the other as a second assassin. How old would you say he was, the second guy, the blond?'

'Thirties.'

'You'd better stick around, Conner.'

'Sure, I'd like a wash, though. A shave and a sleep if possible.'

'I can fix the first two. Sleep? That's at your own risk. I reserve the right to wake you at any time.'

'OK.'

'Listen, Conner, there's one thing I didn't tell you.' Floyd spoke in a serious manner. 'It's maybe not just an assassination attempt. Intelligence says the guy in charge of this plan is called Skorzeny.'

'Skorzeny . . . it's not a name that . . .'

'He's the guy who lifted Mussolini from under our noses and took him back to Germany.'

'Jesus, you mean they're out to kidnap Ike?'

'That's about it. If they did assassinate him it would be some blow, but he could be replaced, we could go on without him. If the Germans kidnapped him they'd be in a position to start making demands, to say nothing of the information they could extract from him. Ike's been surrounded, he won't be so easy to reach, but the old man's going positive. He wants those bastards hunted down before they can try anything.'

'I suppose he wouldn't leave France for a while?'

Floyd shook his head. 'They say he won't hear of it. He puts up with being followed around during the day, but likes a bit of privacy when he goes back to his apartment each evening. That's a weak point, because we keep a low profile then. But somebody else can worry about that. You and me, Conner, we have to find this blond Nazi; and maybe one other guy, before he or they reach Ike.'

You are running down the street and your handbag is swinging heavily because of the gun you have put in there. You know you shouldn't be running, but you are, you know you are breaking a rule, a golden rule, but you tell yourself that you have to know when to break the rules. You are running in the blackout, reckless, very reckless, you could stumble and fall, fall and break a leg, but there is a bright moon and the moisture on the road is glistening, so you can see a little way. You run on, and your heels are click, click, clicking, echoing in the canyon of deserted, crumbling, bomb-devastated buildings. You glance back over your shoulder, your hair falls in the way so you brush it back, you look hard but you can't see the man, perhaps he was just a shadow, perhaps he wasn't following you. Either way you've put a good distance between you and him, so perhaps you ought to stop, you think perhaps you ought to stop because you can feel panic welling up inside you, growing in the excitement, growing beyond control, but you don't stop, even though your legs feel like jelly, you don't stop because this is so important, this is the biggest of them all. You realized who Skorzeny is, you realize why he must have sent men to Paris, and you tell yourself again that this time it is all right to break the rules because the information must be transmitted, and heels click, click, and echo in front of you and behind you and up the sides of the empty buildings. The thin cold air is drawn into your chest and you rasp and cough for breath and at first you don't recognize the rasping, coughing voice as your own, but it is, it is you. You turn into the side street and stumble on the rubble, scuffing shoes, scratching your flesh, tearing your clothes, but you reach the building, dart through the gaping doorway and you run up the stairs and push open the door of the apartment. You gasp for breath as you stagger in the darkness and locate the transmitter, pull it from its concealed position and switch it on, leaning over it, gasping for air while the valves warm up and the little light glows its soft, comforting red. As soon as you can you send the pre-transmission signal, but instead of the acknowledgement in your headphones you hear a message tapped out in plain English and you want to cry for joy, because you cannot believe what the peep-peep-pip in the headphones is saying. It says: 'This is Benjamin Service. Do not transmit, we know everything, come west, come home.' But you do not cease transmission, you grasp the Morse key and you send, 'Yes, yes, one thousand times yes.' Then you switch off the set and stand and hurry from the apartment. This time you do not bother to replace the transmitter because it's all over, the war is over, you are going west, tomorrow you are going to travel to the arranged place and wait for the Allies, and when they arrive you will travel to England. You fling the door of the flat open and you stop, suddenly, because there is a man standing there. He wears a long leather coat and a hat and you start to laugh. You laugh because you know this man, you have seen him before. His name is Rademacher. You laugh because he is holding a gun, you laugh because for the last two years you and Rademacher have been playing a game, and you have lost.

Chapter Twelve

Petra Oelkers and the man she recognized as the same man who
had looked at her coldly on the platform of the subway station
stood and stared at each other. Her face, once laughing nervously,
was now stone-like; his face still smiled, his gun still pointed at her
chest. Slowly she began to step backwards, waving her left arm in
a search for a handhold while gently teasing open her handbag with
her right fingers. She brushed against a chair, while the man
advanced on her, his hand holding the gun rock-steady. She fell
backwards heavily, she heard the man laugh, but he was now partially obscured from her view. She opened her handbag and her
fingers curled gratifyingly around the butt of her own revolver.
When the man was standing over her she lifted her bag towards
him. For a long time afterwards she thought there had been a brief
look of horror in his eyes, but by then her ears were full of a
deafening roar, a flame was flashing in front of her eyes, and the
man was off the ground, being flung backwards as the bullet
crashed upwards into his chest.

She lay still, listening, recovering. Then she stood shakily and
went over to where the man lay. She had always been taught to
shoot twice at her target, but this man was dead. The bullet had
entered the bottom centre of his ribcage and exited behind his
right shoulder. Even though his eyes were open he was dead.
Very dead. Petra Oelkers looked at her handbag, the end blown
open, documents and money scorched and ruined. Now she had
to flee west, now she had no reason to stay, now she had every
reason to live, and every reason to return to England. Again she
felt excitement and fear ruling her judgement, so she paused,
resting against a chair which had been covered with a sheet,

feeling her pulse slow and her legs recover their strength.

The first obstacle was the second man. The man she had killed, her first in the war, the first in her life, would not be operating alone. There had to be a second man, if not a squad of men. But it was now a full minute since the pistol shot had shattered the silence of the building, the silence that always precedes the first bombs, and still no other man had appeared, no other man had called. Stealthily she took the man's hat and coat and slipped them on in place of her own, pushing her hair up under the brim of the homburg. She took the man's wallet, his Turkish cigarettes, his gold-plated petrol lighter and his clasp knife. Again she paused, feeling the weight of his coat on her shoulders. She glanced at his waist and his feet, so far as she could in the gloom. Eventually, when she did quietly descend the stairs leading to the street door, revolver in hand, she was wearing not only the man's coat and hat, but his trousers, his shoes and also his jacket which, like the coat, had a large hole blown in the back, above the right shoulder-blade.

She stepped into the street. Nothing. Nobody. Just rubble and twisted tramlines, and the fire in the basement was still flickering. She turned towards the Chausseestrasse, picking her way across the rubble in strange shoes which were too large for her, but not impossible to walk in. She reached the Chausseestrasse and, as she stepped into the clearer thoroughfare, the slit headlights of a black Mercedes winked at her. It was an unheard-of breach of blackout regulations which she realized could only have been committed by her intended murderer's accomplice.

In the car Schmitt watched the figure walk towards him and as he watched his mouth cracked into a smile. He stepped out of the car as the figure approached and said, 'You are tottering! So the great Rademacher is squeamish after all. Let me help, here, take my arm.'

Petra Oelkers had heard the expression 'blew his head off', but had never seen it, had never believed it was possible. Perhaps it was the closeness of the range, perhaps it was the way her bullet smashed into his Adam's apple and carried on to chop a section out of his spinal cord. Whatever it was, when the man came to rest in the gutter of the Chausseestrasse his head hung limply to one side, joined to the rest of his body by a few tatters of flesh and splintered bone, and the sound of the single shot echoed from building to building. In the space of sixty minutes she had shot two men.

She got into the car and started the engine, noting with relief that the tank was three-quarters full. She drove away, following the road north, out of the city. The direction of her flight didn't matter; all that mattered was that she get herself and the precious transport that could carry her to Allied lines away from Berlin before the bombs fell. She reckoned she had about thirty minutes. She drove hard and fast, breathing easier and easier as the height of the buildings decreased and the amount of private ground around each building grew greater. She passed fire-fighters standing by sandbagged shelters, Volkssturm outposts, batteries of anti-aircraft guns and searchlights which pointed skywards expectantly. They watched her speed past, but the Mercedes was clearly an official car and she went unchallenged. As soon as the bombs began to fall, as soon as the flashes filled her rearview mirror and the explosions rolled across the landscape like a never-ending thunderclap, she switched off the slit head-lights and let the Mercedes come to a stop. She was at the edge of the city close to a field in which stood hundreds of tents sheltering the homeless Berliners. Petra Oelkers spent the night watching the city, her city, burn – and of all the things she remembered of that night, the clearest recollection was how the bombs set up earth tremors which made the car rock gently on its suspension, even though the fire storm was five miles away.

At 4.0 a.m. when the bombing had ceased, though the city still burned terribly, she started the car and continued to drive north-wards past the town of Oranienburg until dawn, when she drove the car off the road, along a track deep in the forest, and then slept.

The next night she set off on foot, travelling westwards, using the stars to guide her. Always travelling by night, always resting by day, she began to survive as she had been taught to survive at Camp X. For two weeks she survived. For two weeks she set traps for rabbits, which she skinned and ate raw, for two weeks she crept around farmyards, milked goats, stole eggs, surviving but getting weaker each day. After two weeks she was pleased to have covered five miles in one night; after two weeks the soles of her shoes had worn through and had been replaced by rabbit skins; after two weeks she began to hallucinate and see figures, other humans, scores of them, all walking with her, stretching over distances as great as the moon would permit her to see.

Two weeks after leaving the car she entered a barn and slumped on the straw. Suddenly it was daylight, suddenly she was being pulled up and pushed about from one man to another. Outside she heard orders being barked. Nearer to she heard her blouse being torn as somebody slapped her face. She had failed, she had tried and she had failed, but she was too tired to care. Just as she fainted she heard one of the soldiers say, 'Stone the bleedin' crows, Nobby. It's a bleedin' woman.'

Konrad Morke was a frightened man. He felt a hollowness in his stomach, he shook uncontrollably, perspiration ran down his back and oozed from the palms of his hands. He fought to retain control of his bowels. He crouched lower in the corner, shrinking into the shadows, gripping the machine-pistol. Always careless, always clumsy, the maquis had once again given themselves away when six or seven vehicles, with headlights blazing, were seen driving up the narrow road which led only to the villa. Morke and his men had nearly fifteen minutes to prepare their defences.

The Communists had attacked in large numbers and had been met with machine-gun fire. Konrad Morke had accounted for at least five, probably more, as he fired hundreds of rounds at the moving shadows. After the first skirmish the attackers melted into the shadows, carrying off their wounded. There then followed an interminable silence broken only by the wind in the trees, a silence which gnawed at nerve-endings and stretched each second into a minute, each minute into an hour. Eventually Morke had slipped away from his position near the front door and made his way to the basement and to a smaller door which opened into the sunken garden beside the villa, beyond which were the woods where he had buried the bullion under a fallen tree. He listened, straining his ears as his hands began to relax their grip on the cooling barrel of his MP42. He was now not only afraid of the Communists, who were anxious to rid France of the last vestige of Fascism, but also of the newly re-established civilian police force, who could not fail to be alerted by the prolonged exchange of small-arms fire. The nearest gendarmerie was in Tullins, but news travels fast in the Dauphiné. Even now they might be racing towards the villa. Both groups placed him and his men in mortal danger, for the police shared the fervour which had gripped France as each individual anxiously set out to prove he was never a collaborator.

Slowly Morke unlocked the door and pulled it ajar. The only sound he could hear was a klaxon of the type indeed used by the civilian police. Probably there were two, or three. The arrival of the police would force the Communists to call off their attack, but Morke knew it was the end of the villa, the end of his National Socialist outpost. He thought he had perhaps five minutes in which to escape. He glanced behind him at the door of the room which was to have been Eisenhower's cell. Too late now, too late. He knew that somehow he must get word to Klara Heidler in Paris, and beyond that his duty was clear: to escape France, that the Reich might continue.

Morke opened the door a little wider and began to inch out into the chill night air. He ran across the narrow gardens and dived into the shrubbery. Moments later when, to his surprise, bullets had not come crashing around him, he moved forward, crawling and then running towards the woods. Once beyond the tree-line, he threw himself to the ground and heard a shout from a few hundred yards away to his left. There was a scuffling sound, and another, and Morke guessed, as he had expected, that the Communists were fleeing from the police. He moved further up the wooded slope, feeling the thin air grip his chest and wincing each time his foot snapped a frozen twig or caught a mound of frozen leaves. Behind him he heard a shout from inside the villa as one of his men called him; Morke pressed on without looking back. He made his way to where the tree-trunk lay with the root system sprawling in the air. He knelt at the far side of the tree-trunk and moved a large rock to one side. In the hole which had been covered by the rock was the knapsack, wrapped in canvas; Morke took the knapsack from the hole and put his machine-pistol in its place, covered the gun with the canvas and replaced the stone. He slung the knapsack over his shoulders and walked up to the watershed. Looking down the far side, he saw a creamy white mist rising up the valley. He smiled and started down the slope, eventually disappearing into the night and the fog.

The rats were fat on Allied garbage. Jesus, that last one was as big as a dog. Genscher leant back against the wall by a drainpipe and watched a big rat drag an orange into a hole in the foot of the wall on the opposite side of the alley. The incident was just visible in the cracking dawn. The Americans are fighting a luxurious war, Genscher reflected, oranges in December, probably shipped over from California or some place. Christ, they should see what Germans are eating to stay alive; that rat wouldn't last long in Berlin. On the Eastern Front it wouldn't last any time at all.

Past the end of the alley part of the bow of a Liberty ship called the *Robert F. Jackson* was visible, dark grey against the paling grey of the dawn. The *Robert F. Jackson* was sailing on the morning tide, bound for London and then across the Atlantic to New York. Genscher pulled his collar up against the drizzle which blew in off the sea almost vertically, and watched a lone gull sweep over the harbour pool. In the rear pocket of Genscher's trousers was his passport; a blank sheet of headed US Army notepaper deftly appropriated from the cab of the truck in which he had hitched a ride from Paris to Antwerp.

The docks were noisy, the cranes were swinging backwards and forwards, lifting supplies from the holds of ships to the trucks which waited in lines on the dockside. The docks were the only intact port in Allied hands on the European coast and they worked twenty-four hours a day, seven days a week.

Genscher was waiting for an office called 'Dispatch One' to open up, because it appeared that while the docks never stopped operating, the clerical back-up had it made and were working a regular nine to five. Genscher had seen them late in the afternoon of the previous day, the skinny GIs, the elderly GIs, the overweight GIs, the bespectacled GIs, scribbling notes, talking into phones and hammering at typewriters. That's what Genscher needed, a typewriter. He got one at 8.30 a.m.

'Gee, I don't know,' said the little GI with thick spectacles, adding 'sir' as Genscher cooled him with a stare. They stood by the desk nearest the door.

'It's OK, son,' Genscher pressed insistently. 'I'm an American, a correspondent, savvy? A newspaper man.' About him Genscher saw the other office-bound GIs starting their day, opening their desks, taking covers off typewriters. One or two glanced at him in passing, but he didn't seem to be attracting a great deal of attention.

'Still, sir . . .' stammered the GI. 'I come from Portland, Maine, and I think I'd better go and see the officer.'

'OK, son. I'll wait.'

The GI gangled away in a series of uncoordinated movements and Genscher sat down at the typewriter. He noticed a wad of crisp headed notepaper by the side of the machine, but favoured the one in his pocket; it was soiled and creased and would look more authentic. He took it from his pocket and slipped it into the typewriter. He typed:

> To whom it may concern:
> This is to certify that the bearer is William A. Genscher, a bona fide war correspondent. It also verifies that Mr Genscher's personal effects and identification were lost due to enemy action during which Mr Genscher made his services available most courageously to the 82nd Airborne Division.
>
> Lt-Col. A. A. Harvey,
> 82 Infantry Division (Airborne)

He took it from the typewriter and scribbled an illegible

signature above the name. He put the letter in his pocket and waited by the desk for the return of the gangly, bespectacled GI from Portland, Maine.

'Officer says no, sir,' he said upon his return.

'That all?'

'Well no, sir. He said you'd better clear out fast on account of this area being off-limits to civilians.'

'I'm not a civilian. I'm a correspondent,' said Genscher, allowing his voice to rise a few decibels. 'Who does he think he is? I've been under fire. Has he?'

A few clerks looked up at Genscher.

'Sorry, sir, but that's what he said.'

'Well, you tell him he hasn't heard the last of William A. Genscher.' Then he stormed out into the drizzle.

Genscher went back to the quay and climbed the gangplank of the *Robert F. Jackson*. He noticed smoke beginning to rise from the stack. At the top of the gangplank his way was barred by a big man in his fifties with silver sideburns and a chest like a barrel.

'Looking for someone?' menaced the big man.

'This an American ship?'

'Sure is.'

'Hey, it sure feels good to be home,' said Genscher.

'Oh yeah. Who says you're home?'

'Well, I was kind of hoping I could hitch a ride to the States. I'm trying to get back to Stateside.'

'Ain't we all? Who are you?'

'William Genscher. War correspondent.'

'Newspaper man, huh. I thought you guys hitched rides in planes?'

'Sometimes. But I ended up in the docks. You know how it is.'

'Any I/D?'

Genscher took a piece of crumpled soiled paper from his pocket and handed it to the big man. 'Only this,' he said apologetically.

The man read it. 'War hero, huh,' he said and returned the letter to Genscher.

'Hero, me?' Genscher shook his head. 'Me, I'm just a regular American trying to get home.'

'Follow me, buddy,' said the big man. 'We'll see what the skipper says.' But there had developed a noticeable and undisguised gleam in the big man's eyes, and Genscher knew he was only a short step from the Avenue of the Americas and the pretzel stalls.

Klara Heidler took the call at 7.00 a.m. on the morning of December 29. It was dark, rain hammered against the window of her apartment. She groaned, cursed, rolled out of bed and hugged her dressing-gown about her as she crossed the floor to the hall and the ringing telephone. The operator checked her number and then told her that she had a call from Voiron. There was a pause, the line clicked and then a man's voice said, 'This is Jacques speaking. I am sorry to wake you so early, but there is a crisis at the plant in Lyons.'

'I see,' said Klara Heidler.

'Has the consignment been dispatched yet?'

'Not yet. We were going to make delivery later today or tomorrow.'

'Unfortunately we cannot receive it.'

'Will you be able to take delivery at a later date?'

'I think not. Certainly not for some time.'

'I see,' she said again. 'There is no alternative resource?'

'Not at this end.'

'Thank you Jacques. We will do what we can here in Paris.'

'Goodbye.'

Klara Heidler heard Morke replace the phone and some moments later she heard the soft click as the operator disengaged herself from the line. Only then did she hang up.

Later that morning she entered the lock-up in the northern suburb of Paris. Schweitzer was there sitting at the table, shaved, washed, his bunk neatly made up. He stood and snapped to attention as she entered the room.

'There has been a change of plan,' she said fastening her headscarf. 'Be seated.'

Schweitzer sat but held a rigid posture.

'It is no longer possible to kidnap Eisenhower. Konrad Morke telephoned this morning. Something must have happened at the villa. Damn! Damn! One thousand curses. What was to have been a master stroke, a brilliantly conceived plan which would have enabled Germany to force the Allies to sit at the negotiating table, has been lost. Now all we can do is kill him; a cheap assassination.'

'It will be easier,' said Schweitzer.

'It may well be easier, but the rewards are less.'

'When do we act?'

'Tonight.'

Schweitzer stood suddenly and threw out his right arm. 'Heil Hitler!'

'Heil Hitler.'

'Heil Hitler,' said Conner softly, as he swilled the dregs of his coffee around in the bottom of the cup.

'I wouldn't say that too loud or too often if I were you, boy.' Floyd looked coldly at Conner. 'Not in this office.'

'Relax, Floyd. I was just thinking about Hoff.'

'Don't waste your thoughts on him. He's going where all chicken-shit murderers go.'

'Don't be so vindictive, Floyd.'

'Who's vindictive?' Floyd leaned back in his chair. 'I just hate the bastard. He blew away two of my men. What do you want me to do, ask him up for a beer? That and the fact that he's here to assassinate or kidnap the supreme commander of Allied Expeditionary Forces doesn't exactly endear him to me, Conner.'

'Hoff,' said Conner, 'is just a quiet little guy who likes books and who was caught up in something that was too big for him. It's not as though he was a diehard Nazi.'

'He was a quiet little assassin.'

'Still, what would you say if you were him?'

'I'm not.'

'But if you were. If you had just been told you were going to be executed by musketry at dawn tomorrow, what would you say?'

'Christ knows.'

'He said "Heil Hitler". I couldn't believe it, I still can't.'

There was a sharp and determined rap on the door of Floyd's office.

'Enter.' Floyd leaned forward and rested his arms on his desk.

The sergeant opened the door and stepped into the room. Behind him was a man in civilian clothing.

'Excuse me, sir,' said the sergeant. 'This is Inspector Clergue of the Paris Police . . .'

'You mean the Gendarmerie . . .' said Floyd.

'I guess I do, sir.'

'Well, can't you deal with it? It's been a long and a fruitless day spent on an issue that's ten times more important than anything the Frog cops are working on.'

'I think maybe you should hear this, sir,' the sergeant persisted.

'OK.' Floyd smiled at the Inspector. 'How can we help you, sir?'

'Monsieur,' began the Inspector. He was a tall, gaunt figure who seemed to have been savaged by years of German occupation. His eyes had gone past the stage of looking wise and now seemed to be full of despair and futility. He seemed to Floyd to be a man who was tired of life. He held his hat by his side, his fingers were long and thin. 'I regret to call at such an hour . . .'

'OK,' said Floyd. 'You want coffee, Inspector? Sergeant!'

'No. No, please not for me. I have come to ask for your advice and assistance. I am investigating with my men a murder.'

'Oh?'

'A double murder. A man and his wife. They were proprietors of a café in the north of the city.'

'Peacetime comes to Paris,' said Conner.

'OK, Conner, quiet up. How can we help you, sir?'

'Well, monsieur,' said Clergue, 'it seems that on the night of their deaths they were seen serving two American soldiers.'

'Yes?'

'It is peculiar, we thought, that American soldiers should have

238

wandered into such a district, there is nothing there to attract them, and just today we have found that the American paper money that we found on the floor of the café – the till had been emptied, you see, but some of the money had fallen to the floor . . .'

'Yes, yes.'

'Well, today we have found that the dollars were counterfeit.'

'Forged?'

'Yes, monsieur, I understand that to be an alternative expression. They are counterfeits of a particularly fine quality, of surpassing excellence. They are German counterfeits.'

'See, that's why I figured it was important, sir,' said the sergeant eagerly. 'This café is just round the corner from the street where GIs were reported to be fighting. We investigated a few days ago, you remember; the lock-up, the weird old woman . . .'

'Oh my God.' Floyd stood, colour draining from his face. 'That was where they were holed up. We went there, and came away . . . they must have been there . . . one at least . . . Oh my God . . . we had him . . .' Floyd gazed into the middle distance and then collected himself. 'Inspector, would one of your suspects be described as an overweight, dark-haired man?'

'He would.'

'Then we have him in custody on a classified matter. You may interview him, but we cannot release him into your custody.'

'You can't? But . . .'

'I'm sorry. Sergeant!'

'Sir!'

'Ten men armed and ready to leave at once.'

'Yes, sir.' The sergeant doubled back to the open area outside Floyd's office and snatched the telephone from the desk.

'You want to come, Conner?'

'Sure do,' said Conner, standing and reaching for his helmet.

Floyd drove the lead jeep with Conner sitting beside him grasping the grab rail as they turned sharp corners on wet streets. Two other jeeps followed in close company. Five men in each jeep. They turned into the Rue St Josèphe twenty minutes after leaving the Military Police Headquarters. Floyd stopped his jeep outside the door of the lock-up and began hammering on it. Almost immediately he turned to the sergeant and said, 'All right. Bring it down.'

Two MPs began to splinter the door with their rifle butts. In the houses opposite and at either side of the lock-up, gas lights began to burn and people appeared at windows in their night attire. Finally the door gave, the two MPs stepped aside, Floyd, automatic in hand, went over the threshold and up the stairs. Conner was close behind.

'Regular barrack room,' said Conner as he and Floyd surveyed the upstairs room of the lock-up. 'Tubular steel frame bunks, a wooden table, clean, tidy, swept. Would pass inspection any time.'

But Floyd was more interested in the still warm stove and the cigarette butts in the ashtray. 'Whoever was here isn't long gone,' he said.

'Sir!' The sergeant called from the bottom of the stairs.

Floyd and Conner went back down the stairs. The sergeant had pulled away the tarpaulin and revealed the Willys jeep.

'It's got the insignia of the 85th Division, sir,' said the sergeant. 'That's part of the Fifth Army. I got a brother in the Fifth Army. They're in Italy at present. I guess that's where the jeep came from.'

'Guess it is,' said Floyd. 'Guess this is the vehicle Hoff and the others came across the line in. Could this be the jeep you saw, Conner?'

'Certainly could. There was nothing to distinguish it from any other jeep.'

'So what do we have now?' Floyd said, thinking aloud. 'We know that there was a three-man hit squad going after Ike. We assume they split, because the café proprietor was seen serving two GIs, one of whom we now have in custody, the other has probably gone to ground. That leaves one unaccounted for, if we assume that Hoff and the other guy didn't want to go through with the plans.'

'We have to assume the third is going to go through with it,' said

Conner. 'And if he's not long ago left here, then he's probably on his way to Versailles right now, if he's not already there.'

'Sergeant!' Floyd turned to the sergeant with a calmness which Conner thought admirable, and said clearly, 'Call up SHAEF on the radio. Top priority. Assassination attempt believed imminent.'

'Yes, sir.' The sergeant ran out to the jeep.

'You come with me, Conner. The rest of you stay here.'

Four hundred kilometres to the south-east, near the small town of Chamonix, a man stood by his car which had slid into a snowdrift. He was watching the approach of a second car which laboured up the icy mountain road. The man had first noticed the car when it was a small single headlight beam in the distance. He had assumed it to be a motorcycle and had watched it from inside his car. As it drew closer he saw, in the brilliance of the moon on the snow, that it was a motor-car with one defective headlight. He got out of his car and waited for the oncoming vehicle. It was going in the wrong direction for him, but perhaps he could get a lift back towards the border where there was a village with an inn and a telephone. He watched as the oncoming car began to slip on the gradient and noticed the driver doing the sensible thing, keeping the car in high gear to prevent the rear wheels spinning; even so, the vehicle refused the incline. The driver allowed the car to slide back a few feet until it came to rest sideways across the road. The man watched the driver leave the car; he was a short but well built man who was dressed in a leather coat, fur hat, gauntlets, and stout boots. He carried a knapsack on his shoulder. He was not of the area.

'Are you leaving your car?' said the first man as the stranger approached. 'Mine too is stuck and I fear I may be trapped for the night.'

'It is not my car,' replied the stranger. 'I stole it in Voiron. You know Voiron?'

'I do,' replied the man, disarmed and frightened by the stranger's frankness.

'I have no further use for the car. I have left the keys inside, perhaps you could drive it back. Take it as far as you are going and then telephone the Gendarmerie in Voiron, telling them where the owner may recover it.'

'I will, monsieur.' The man was excited by the meeting, intrigued by the stranger.

'I have left an envelope on the front seat,' said the stranger. 'It contains some American dollars. They are for the owner in payment for fuel used and in compensation for the theft of his vehicle. I trust you are an honest man, monsieur?'

'On my honour,' said the man as the stranger walked on without a backward glance.

Konrad Morke was striding into Switzerland with a fortune in his knapsack.

Klara Heidler slowed to a stop beside the wall at the side of the palace grounds. To her left she could make out the sprawl of tents and army vehicles which comprised SHAEF with a staff of fifteen hundred, most of whom slept in the tents or caravans. Schweitzer slipped out of the car and pressed the door which was set in the wall. It opened freely and he stepped into the grounds of the Palace of Versailles. Klara Heidler turned the car around and then switched off the headlights and the engine. It was just a few minutes to midnight on December 29. 1945 was just forty-eight hours away. The rain fell relentlessly.

Schweitzer moved softly and quickly between the low hedge-rows at the bottom of the vast formal gardens of lawns and fountains. In the distance, silhouetted against the night sky, he could make out the palace itself. He had to reach the north wing, second floor. He continued to inch forward, keeping to the side of the gardens, sprinkling aniseed behind him as he went. Schweitzer began to make out other figures walking in the grounds, some solitary, others in pairs, and as his eyes became more accustomed to the gloom, the more figures he saw. He stopped and crouched, his heartbeat was steady but his palms were clammy. He clenched his teeth. They had been alerted.

Somehow the Americans knew of the plan, maybe Hoff or Genscher had been captured and had talked. How they had found out he didn't know; what mattered was that they were expecting him, they knew he was coming; the grounds were crawling with MPs, and he was in among them. Then he realized he could capitalize on the American policy of crowding the grounds with guards. He stood and very calmly began to walk towards the Palace of Versailles, north wing, second floor. He covered two hundred yards before he was challenged. A voice from the darkness said, 'Who's there?'

So Schweitzer said, 'It's me, Schweitzer.' The voice replied, 'OK, Schweitzer.'

Schweitzer walked on, sprinkling a little aniseed every ten or fifteen paces.

Klara Heidler saw the jeep approaching at speed, and she sank sideways below the level of the dashboard as the vehicle swept by. She turned and through the rear window of the car she saw the jeep slide to a halt and a man jump from the vehicle and enter the palace grounds through the door in the wall. The same door that Schweitzer had entered just half an hour previously. She gripped the steering-wheel and allowed her head to fall forward as she heard the man shouting the alarm. She switched the ignition and turned the key. The engine groaned and then exploded into life. It was over. Schweitzer might still succeed but he could not now escape. She drove slowly away, adjusting to her new image: Klara Heidler, schoolmistress. Never, never a collaborator. Why, was not her house raided once, was she not kept in custody by the Gestapo for two days in the cellars of the notorious building on the Avenue Foch? Indeed, was she not arrested in front of her class? A collaborator? No. In fact, in her own small way she was a heroine, having struck her own blow against Fascism. Was it terrible at the Gestapo? It was not pleasant, I would rather not discuss it if you don't mind. She also reflected that there was adequate compensation waiting for her in a Swiss bank. Perhaps her first holiday would be in the

Swiss alps after she had called at a certain bank in Geneva.

Conner approached the rear of the palace, feeling his legs weakening as he ran.

'Who goes there?' The challenge rang out in the dark.

Conner stopped. 'Lieutenant Conner, 106th Infantry Division,' he panted.

'He's got a gun!' a second voice rang out and Conner heard safety-catches being snapped off.

'There's a crisis,' panted Conner. 'Some guy in there about to knock off Ike.'

'Some guy like you maybe. We know about the alert, we're just waiting for a guy in GI's clothing who talks like an American, with a gun.'

'Show yourselves!' shouted Conner. 'That's an order.'

'Who gives the order?'

'Lieutenant Conner. 106th Infantry Division. Move!'

Two men approached from the gloom at either side of the rear gate. They had white helmets and dark uniforms. They both held rifles, pointed at Conner.

'You've got to believe me,' said Conner. 'Captain Floyd of the Military Police is at the front of the palace. I'm to check the rear. Did anybody come this way?'

'Only yourself – sir.'

'Right, we're going inside. Now.'

'We can't allow that, sir. We have to prevent anybody from entering who doesn't have clearance.'

'Listen, there's a man in there, a mad kraut who's going to blow Ike's brains out and you stand there crapping me about clearance . . .'

'We'd better check with the officer,' said one of the MPs.

'You do that,' said Conner, walking forward. He pointed to one MP. 'You go check with your officer.' He pointed to the second. 'You follow me and if you see me doing anything, anything at all which could harm the General, you are ordered to shoot to kill me with that rifle you're carrying. Hear me?'

'Yes, sir.'

Conner ran towards the rear of the palace and to his surprise the MP followed him. As they approached the building they were challenged. Before Conner could reply, the MP behind him shouted, 'MP coming on.'

'Come on and show,' replied the voice.

At the entrance to the rear of the building stood a sergeant of the Military Police and three privates. 'What have you got there, Monroe?' sneered the sergeant.

'Lieutenant Conner, sir.'

'I'm not explaining anything, Sergeant,' said Conner. 'Just follow me. You and your men.'

'Hey, listen . . .'

'Just follow me, Sergeant.' Conner pushed his way between the sergeant and one of the privates and heard Monroe say, 'I think this guy's on the level, Sarge. Vincelti's reporting to the duty officer right now.'

Conner entered a large marble-lined vestibule with a crystal chandelier hanging from the vaulted ceiling. A wide stone staircase wound off to the right-hand side. 'Where's Ike's quarters?'

'Second floor, sir,' replied the sergeant.

Conner ran up the staircase, hearing the MPs pounding behind him. At the first turn of the stair he stopped. An MP lay slumped against the wall, his tunic was scarlet from blood which oozed from a long cut across his throat.

'Any doubts now, Sergeant?' asked Conner.

'Jesus Christ.' The sergeant knelt by the man. 'He's still alive. One of you stay and get some medical aid applied here.'

Conner ran up the stairs. The second-floor corridor extended from the landing. It was long, illuminated by gas lamps which had been turned down low. Oak chests stood at the side of the corridor, paintings and tapestries hung from the walls. A solitary figure in the corridor turned and smiled at Conner. The two men stared at each other, then the figure raised his hand and pointed a gun. But he made no attempt to fire. Jesus, the thought raced through Conner's mind, Jesus, Jesus, he wants me to kill him, he wants me . . . But by then the gun in his own hand had barked and leapt. Twice.

Conner approached the man, who lay still but was alive. He kicked the man's gun out of reach.

'He'll not be long,' said the sergeant of the Military Police, who had run up and now stood beside Conner.

Conner looked at the man, tall, blond, sharp-featured, the same guy who had driven out of the mist and stopped his jeep at his checkpoint. Conner said, 'I could have shot you then and saved us a whole lot of trouble.'

The man started to say something, but he couldn't speak. His chest was a mass of scarlet, he wheezed and gurgled for a minute and then turned grey.

'Which is Ike's room?' Conner turned to the sergeant.

'Next one down, sir.'

'Doesn't seem to have disturbed him. He must be a heavy sleeper.'

'Guess he's been having a few busy days recently.'

'Guess he has,' said Conner.

Epilogue

'England won, rest of Britain second, Empire third, Common-wealth fourth, Yanks fifth, Russia sixth, Germany placed. Japan fell at the last fence, France and Poland failed to qualify.' The man at the next table folded the piece of paper and grinned at Service, awaiting approval. Service gave it in the form of a twitch of the lips which he hoped could be interpreted as a smile. The man with the moustache and greased-down hair evidently did so, for he continued, 'Knew you'd like it. Feller in the pub last night was getting all morose about the war, said to me, "Who won, who really won?" So I said that, straight off the top of my head. I thought it was so good that I wrote it down. Want to hear it again?'

'No, thank you.' Service smeared some of the landlady's homemade marmalade on his slice of toast.

'Had a good war yourself?' pressed the man in the white suit and red tie, who seemed to have a gold ring on each finger.

'Routine,' replied Service, not wishing to encourage conversation. 'Filling in forms, mostly.'

'Ministry man, eh? Well, I suppose somebody had to do it. Me, I was a brown job for a few months, the Herts and Bucks, got a medical discharge, easy if you know how. Walked across the parade ground like I had flat feet, sergeant-major sent me to the MO, who said, "What have you got, flat feet?" "Yes," I said and he gave me a discharge certificate without even giving me the once-over. Then I went out of the camp gates in my civvies like I was marching past the King. Rest of the war I did a bit of this and that, buying and selling, you know. I'm travelling in cosmetics now. Yourself, sir?'

'I'm still with the Ministry,' said Benjamin Service. 'Taking a spot of leave.'

'Jolly good, often think I could do with a rest myself. What brings you to Oxford? Family?'

'Could say that,' replied Service. 'I'm here to look somebody up.'

'Just came in myself, last night. Whole town is full of servicemen, RAF mostly, there's a base close by. Hotels are packed as well. I was lucky to get in here, don't mind a place without a bar for the occasional night. Off today, Swindon bound. That your car outside? The MG?'

'Yes.'

'Nice. The company gave me a Ford. It gets you there, but I could do with a bit of style. You OK for petrol coupons?'

'Yes.'

He drove to the Oelkers' house. It was boarded up, the garden was overgrown, and the path down which Wilhelm Oelkers had wheeled himself five years earlier and shouted in German at the passers-by was cracked and moss-covered. Service opened the gate, it was rotten from years of neglect and a large dry splinter came off in his hand. He stood in front of the house, heavy hearted. The overgrown garden, the boarded-up windows, seemed barriers to his own future.

'There's nobody at home, dear?' Benjamin Service turned. A plump, middle-aged woman leaned on the garden fence. Her hair was in curlers and she wore a baggy, light summer dress. She shielded her eyes against the sun as she spoke. 'You a friend of the family or from the estate agents?'

'Oh, a friend,' Benjamin Service replied.

'Only she said she was putting the house on the market. She didn't want it no more, I expect.'

'She?'

'The girl, Petra.'

Benjamin Service felt his face crack into a smile. 'When was she here?'

'Just a couple of days ago, stayed in the town, sorting things out, solicitors and that. Her parents' estate needed sorting out.

248

I mean, after the old man went, a blessing really seeing how he was, well, Mrs Oelkers didn't last long, her daughter away in Canada and that. I wouldn't have bothered myself, my daughter deserts me and her country, well, I mean, it was her country, wasn't it, then she's not my daughter no more. Her safe and snug in Canada while the bombs were falling in those beaker raids . . .'

'The Baedeker raids,' said Service.

'Yes, them, those old bombs was rainin' down on Oxford and she was safe and snug in Canada, well, I mean.'

'Where did Petra say she was going?'

'Oh, I couldn't say. Not that interested, dearie.'

'Which solicitor did she engage? Do you know that?'

'Well, let me see now. It was a name similar to hers, Oskler, Ossler, yes, that was it. Mr Ossler of Bradbury, Ossler and Knight. In the centre of Oxford. If you take a number – Oh, you've got a car . . . 'Bye, pleasure, I'm sure.'

'I don't know whether I can be of assistance Mr Service,' said Ossler, a fat man who evidently suffered in the heat. 'You see, it would certainly be deemed a breach of confidence. Besides which, I don't know exactly where she was going, though I don't think it was back to London, not immediately. If you'd care to leave a note for her I would be pleased to forward it to her address in London.'

'That would be good of you.'

Ossler tossed a pad across his desk and then skimmed an envelope after it. The effort of doing so seemed to cause him great discomfort.

'I would appreciate it if you could give me some indication of where she was going.' Service took his pen and scribbled on the pad, giving his name and the PO Box number for Bletchley Park.

'Please, Mr Service,' Ossler complained. 'I have made my position clear.'

'Did she say she was going to Dorset? Can you tell me that?' He slipped the note inside the envelope on which he wrote her name and then handed it to Ossler. 'I assure you, Mr Ossler, that my intentions . . .'

Ossler cut him off. 'She did not say she was *not* going to Dorset, Mr Service.'

Benjamin Service smiled. 'Thank you, Mr Ossler.'

It was a pleasant drive from Oxford to Dorset, midweek on a hot, dry summer's day, the first summer of peacetime, with the soldiers standing in clumps at the road junctions. During the war a soldier on leave had only to start walking in the direction he wanted to travel and the first car with room to spare would stop and offer him a lift. Now the brown jobs were reminders of the war at a time when people just wanted to get on with the peace, and so they stood in groups and raised their thumbs hopefully as each car swept by. Eventually Service relented and picked up three boys from the Dorset Regiment outside Andover and took them to Bournemouth. Despite his protestations, they insisted on leaving two hundred cigarettes in the car as payment for the ride.

From Bournemouth he drove to Bishop's Upton, arriving in the early evening. The High Street seemed to be full of cars, mostly black. He parked his own car outside the Green Man just in front of a motor-coach of the most modern design, and went into the lounge bar. It was packed with people with West Country accents, many of them trippers from the coach. It was a group of women who particularly drove him outside to sip his beer; they sat round a table, all talked at once, all laughed at once, and each had a laugh like a machine-gun.

He sat in a wooden chair outside the front bow window of the Green Man. Bishop's Upton had not changed so far as he could see, except in that it had become busier, and petrol fumes rose from the road, filling the nostrils of the beer drinkers who sat at the wooden tables between the pavement and the pub. A lorry growled up the High Street laden with machinery. Service recognized the shape as that of an old army lorry which seemed to have been thinly painted in blue, as it drew level he read on the side of the cab. 'J. Dodd. Haulage Contractor'. In the cab was the man whom he took to be J. Dodd, who had swapped his uniform for overalls, but had retained his beret and looked to Service like someone determined to make his pile in the promised post-war prosperity.

Refreshed by the beer, he booked in at the George Hotel and, after dinner, drove over to see Mrs Johns. He pulled up outside her little cottage and was delighted to see Freddie Johns sawing wood in the front garden, looking healthy, bronzed and muscular, stripped to the waist and wearing army shorts and boots. He grinned as he recognized Benjamin Service.

'Good to see you, Freddie,' Benjamin said as they shook hands.

'And you, Benjamin, and you.'

That's the war, Benjamin reflected with pleasure, one of the good things to have come out of it. It's drawn the British closer together, broken down the class barriers. Without the war he'd have gone on calling me Mr Service, even though we're the same age. 'Mrs Johns in?'

'Yes. But she's tired, she has to rest a lot these days.'

'Can I see her? I won't stay long.'

'Certainly. It'll cheer her up no end. Though she's had a lot of visitors this evening.'

'Good, good. I'm sorry about your brothers, Freddie. And your father.'

'Yes, well.' Freddie wiped his brow. 'They didn't come back and for no good reason that I can think of, but we can only go forward. It's just me and Mum now. They'd want us to carry on. Just go in, Benjamin, she's sitting downstairs.'

Mrs Johns sat, pale and thin and wrapped in a shawl despite the stubborn heat of the day. It took her a moment to recognize him.

'Master Benjamin!'

He bent down and kissed her forehead.

'So many visitors this evening, it's a rare to-do.'

'So Freddie was saying.'

'Yes, he came back, thank God, but there's many that didn't. Why didn't you and Petra come together?'

251

'Petra? She's been here?'

'Yes. She called at your father's house and found the new folk there now that your father's retired to Devon. They told her where I lived and she came to look me up and pay her respects, after all these years. Wasn't it sweet of her?'

'When was she here?'

Mrs Johns pointed a bony twisted finger at the table. 'That's the tea I made for her, you feel that pot.'

He did. It was still warm.

'Where was she going?'

'To the trees. She said she wanted to see the trees of a summer's evening. That's how she remembered them, she said. Funny you didn't see her on the road, she'd hired a pedal cycle from Faulds. She probably didn't know the quick way there and has gone back round the mill race.'

He ran down the lane, paused and collected himself before climbing the stile. She was there, beside the oak, in a yellow summer dress. She turned as she heard someone climb the stile. For a few moments they stood looking at each other, then they walked forward, hesitantly at first but running the last few steps, and fell into each other's arms.

They met at 7.00 p.m. on that June evening of 1945. At 9.00 p.m. they were still strolling round the cricket pitch, hand in hand as the swallows circled and dived overhead, tired with talking but enjoying a harmony, a happiness between them.

'So that's my story,' Benjamin said. 'Can't tell it publicly. We had a grim hush-hush man from the Ministry visit us at Bletchley Park. He said our work was still covered by the Official Secrets Act. Apparently one of the reasons is that the Soviets have stolen Enigma from the Germans, and we've been decoding some interesting Soviet transmissions over the last few weeks.'

'Such a fascinating development, but you knew so much that agents risked their lives to tell you.'

'I know. It upsets me when I think about it, though I suppose if we hadn't sent agents into Europe, the Nazis might have guessed we'd broken their code. The Yanks had the best idea. In their Pacific theatre they made all their transmissions in the tongue of the Navajo Indians. It couldn't be broken because it wasn't a code and it was so obscure the Japs couldn't identify it as a language. Simple and brilliant.'

'I felt useful. Now I just feel used. But at least I survived.'

They were approaching the stile. He noticed goose-pimples on her arms.

'It's chilly,' he said. 'Let's go back to the village. Where are you staying?'

'Nowhere. If I hadn't met you I was going to return the cycle, take the evening train to Bournemouth and go back to London the next day.'

'The George'll let us have a double room, I'm certain.'

She smiled, and slipped her arm through his.

At his car she said, 'Benjamin, in Germany, there was a man. You understand? I didn't love him, but there was a man. I will tell you, I'll explain in time, but I want you to know now.'

'I knew,' he said. 'It doesn't make any difference.'

She kissed him and slid into the front passenger seat. 'I suppose we'll never find out what became of those men who were sent to kill Ike?'

He closed the passenger door gently and wheeled the cycle she had hired to the rear of the car.

'No,' he said to himself, lashing the cycle to the boot lid. 'I don't suppose we ever shall.'

Fontana Paperbacks: Fiction

Fontana is a leading paperback publisher of both non-fiction, popular and academic, and fiction. Below are some recent fiction titles.

- ☐ GLITTER BABY Susan Elizabeth Phillips £2.95
- ☐ EMERALD DECISION Craig Thomas £3.50
- ☐ THE GOLDEN CUP Belva Plain £3.50
- ☐ A THUNDER OF CRUDE Brian Callison £2.95
- ☐ DESERT QUEEN Julia Fitzgerald £3.50
- ☐ THE GREEN FLASH Winston Graham £3.50
- ☐ UNDER CONTRACT Liza Cody £2.95
- ☐ THE LATCHKEY KID Helen Forrester £2.95
- ☐ IN HARM'S WAY Geoffrey Jenkins £2.95
- ☐ THE DOOR TO DECEMBER Leigh Nichols £3.50
- ☐ THE MIRROR OF HER DREAMS Stephen Donaldson £3.95
- ☐ A SONG IN THE MORNING Gerald Seymour £2.95

You can buy Fontana paperbacks at your local bookshop or newsagent. Or you can order them from Fontana Paperbacks, Cash Sales Department, Box 29, Douglas, Isle of Man. Please send a cheque, postal or money order (not currency) worth the purchase price plus 22p per book for postage (maximum postage required is £3.00 for orders within the UK).

NAME (Block letters) _____

ADDRESS _____

_____

_____